CAPTURED
Blood Ties Series

A.K. ROSE
ATLAS ROSE

R✿SE

ONE

Helene

SCREAMS FROM THE DAUGHTERS ECHOED ALL AROUND ME. The shrill sounds turned piercing as the rear doors of the truck were thrown open. Men invaded dressed in camouflage, wearing skull-faced balaclavas to hide their faces. Men who, a second ago, had attacked with savage ferocity, bringing this truck we'd been forced into to a standstill.

"Easy now." One of the soldiers neared a Daughter, who cowered and shrieked, kicking out frantically in a desperate attempt to get away. But he just held up his hands. "We're not going to hurt you, sweetheart. We're here to save you."

Hot, arid air burned against my lips as I sucked in a breath and stared up at the towering mountain of a man standing over me. Piercing rays of sunlight streamed in from the bullet holes that peppered the side of the truck. The sunlight sent bright slashes across his face, catching sparks in those dark, unflinching eyes. Eyes that shifted to the piece of shit next to me

"Bring him." He commanded. "And this one." He turned to me. "Is mine."

Mine.

Mine?

I stared at that outstretched hand, then lifted my focus to the balaclava he wore...

No.

Not just him...

All of them.

"We have to go." The towering mountain urged softly, his outstretched hand waiting.

Coulter's guard lunged, grabbed my arm, and yanked me sideways, shielding him. "Try it and the bitch dies."

I bucked as his hand found my throat, clenching tight.

"That's it." The bastard turned his head, inhaling my scent as those cruel fingers dug deeper. "Try a goddamn thing and I'll fucking kill this ruined cunt right here."

A trapped whimper throbbed in my throat. I waited for the mountain to react with savage ferocity, but he didn't.

Instead, sparks ignited in that dangerous stare. There was barely a shift of his hand, a tiny twitch of movement.

BANG!

The bastard flinched, then dropped his hand and screamed in my ear as he grabbed his foot. *"What the fuck? You SHOT ME!"*

I shoved back from him, grasped the mountain's outstretched hand as he reached for me once more, and shoved to stand.

There was a bullet hole in the guard's boot and blood ran in a tiny rivulet, glistening over the black leather.

"Who the FUCK ARE YOU?" Coulter's red-faced guard roared.

One nod from the man who'd just saved me and his team snapped into action, grabbed the vile piece of shit, and hauled him to his feet.

Ruined cunt. Heat rose to claim my cheeks.

"Wait." I croaked as they dragged him forward.

They all stopped, then looked at their commander. He tilted his head, watching me intently, then motioned me forward.

I could still feel the guard's hand over my mouth and his hard cock pressed against my ass as I stepped forward. His lips were already curled in that vile, fucking amused sneer as I took a step, swept my hand behind me, and unleashed.

Slap.

His head snapped to the side. Fire lashed my palm, but it was worth it. It was so fucking worth it. "I hope you die screaming," I croaked, then turned away.

"Just like your lovers," He spat.

Watch this.

His words invaded and the memory along with it. Riven, Kane, and Thomas falling to their knees on the loading dock back at The Order.

3

Bang!

I flinched as that sound echoed in my head.

"I have to get out of here." I cried as I stumbled forward. Men crowded around me, the men trying to save us. But they weren't the men I wanted.

Get to them...GET TO THEM NOW!

I shoved that bastard guard from The Order aside, and barged into the others as I fought to get free of the truck.

The sun was blinding as I lunged.

My bare feet hit the searing asphalt. My knees buckled instantly, sending me crashing to the ground. Agony drove all the way through my ankles and into my knees as I pushed upwards. But I didn't care about that anymore. All I saw was the waiting four-wheel drive with the engine running and the doors open wide.

Get to them...

PLEASE, JUST LET ME GET TO THEM.

I limped and ran, veering around the front of the vehicle as fast as my legs would carry me, and lunged for the open driver's door.

"No, you don't." A soldier came out of nowhere, grabbing me around the waist, lifting my feet from the ground.

"Let me GO!" I screamed as I kicked and bucked. *"I HAVE TO GET TO THEM! I HAVE TO GET TO THEMMMM!"*

"Easy now. *Easy!*" he growled, right before I drove my elbow backwards.

4

He moved, dodging my blow easily.

"THEY'RE GOING TO BE KILLED! DO YOU HEAR ME? THEY'RE GOING TO BE—"

But his arms were a cage, immobilizing me. My body sagged, the fight overwhelming. Still, I threw my head backwards in one last desperate attempt.

His hold slipped, leaving me to crash to the scalding road. Hot asphalt seared my thighs. I howled and shoved backwards until I hit the tire of the four-wheel drive.

Thud.

Thud.

Thud.

Heavy steps slowed, and a shadow descended. Tears burned. My throat was thick with rage and desperation.

"These men you scream for. They mean that much to you?"

I lifted my head. Those tears slipped, trailing slowly as I met the mountain's stare. Did he know who I fought for? I wasn't sure. "Yes," I croaked.

He stared for a long time, then gave a slow nod. The sound of an oncoming truck lifted his stare from me. I wiped my tears, then pushed to stand. Pain burned across the balls of my feet, leaving me to limp to the front of the four-wheel drive, lifting my head as a truck hurtled toward us at breakneck speed.

The faint crackle of a two-way fought the sound of the engine. My rescuer lifted his hand, pressing the button on his vest connected to an earpiece.

"Will do." He responded. "You know where to take them."

Take who?

I opened my mouth to ask as the truck hit the brakes, screeching the tires. Dust billowed, kicking up as the camouflaged transport pulled up hard.

"Get them all loaded inside." He commanded the others, then glanced my way, jerking his head toward the four-wheel drive. "You're with me."

He didn't wait for me to argue, just strode around the front and climbed in behind the wheel. The engine roared as the gears were engaged. I had no choice but to limp and lunge for the door as the vehicle rolled forward.

"We need to go back!" I yanked the passenger's door open and climbed in.

I barely had the door closed before I was thrown back against the seat. My heart pounded as he spun the wheel hard and hit the accelerator. Through my window the other Daughters were loaded into the back of their truck.

"Where are you taking them?" I yanked on my seatbelt, snapping it into place as the bellows of the soldiers faded outside.

He handled the wheel like he was born with adrenaline in his veins, not once answering my goddamn questions. I gripped the seatbelt as the remaining soldiers climbed into the truck. It lurched forward and turned around onto the shoulder of the road to follow us.

Minutes, that's all it had taken, minutes to snatch us from our way to Hell. The only question now was, where were we going?

Only, as I watched behind us, I saw The Order's truck following us, as well. I jerked my focus to my silent abductor. "What's going on?" He said nothing and every second that stretched out between made me even more desperate. *"I said, what the fuck is going on?"*

He slowly shifted that unfathomable stare my way. Yet, all I saw was the balaclava...the skull and the dirt as I inhaled the heady scent of the sweat. He shifted gears, watching me as he pushed the four-wheel drive harder. Trees rose in the distance. The trees I was desperate to see. Still, I said nothing as we hurtled toward them.

The fence line appeared through the crowded trees. Sunlight glinted off the steel, shining as we drew closer. I waited for the vehicle to slow, for the gears to be shifted and the brakes to be tapped. But none of that happened.

I swiveled hard in my seat, watching the entrance fly past. *"Stop!"* I jerked my gaze back to him. *"I SAID STOP! YOU NEED TO TAKE ME BACK THERE! YOU NEED TO—"*

"No."

No?

His answer was cold and callous, leaving me desperate. I turned and clawed the door handle.

Thunk.

The locks engaged. With a savage scream, I lunged and grappled for the wheel. His head snapped my way, that glare stopping me cold. *Do it*...the look warned. *I dare you.* A flicker of fear rose.

7

"You don't understand!" I screamed through clenched teeth as tears filled my eyes. *"They're going to kill them all!"*

Those dark eyes turned back to the road. I knew then...I knew *all too well.* He understood, maybe better than I realized. My throat thickened. Still, I forced out the hiss. "Who the fuck are you?"

He never answered, just turned the wheel when we came to the intersection. Only we were going in the opposite way to the city. I jerked my gaze to the side mirror, watching the truck turn the opposite way.

"Where the fuck are you taking me?"

Silence.

Empty. Cruel. Silence.

My mind was racing, trying to find a way out of here. But even if I could escape this bastard, I'd never make it back there in time. My shoulders sank, curling in.

Grief filled me as I pulled my burning feet upwards. I wrapped my arms around my knees, just like I did around the agony.

I am your blade now, Daughter. Riven's voice echoed as I stared out of the side window. *I am the honed edge you crave, the prick of the needle you long for...and the drug you can never escape.*

My hands trembled, tightening into fists as those words invaded. I did need him—I closed my eyes as tears slipped free —now more than ever.

Their faces rose.

The Principal.

The Teacher...

And the Priest.

That suffocating emptiness wrapped tighter around me as we turned down a road I'd never been to before. I didn't care where I was, didn't care if it was The Order or a whole new hell. Not anymore.

Gears of the four-wheel drive downshifted. I slowly opened my eyes. Some part of me knew I was barely hanging on. Broken nails were slipping, digging into the edge of my sanity. The cavern of darkness waited.

Broken.

The words whispered.

Like you always were.

He slowed as he twisted into a narrow driveway and the vehicle climbed hard. The tires skidded, then caught, throwing me against the seat as above us a hidden gate rolled open, leaving us to drive through.

Suddenly, we were driving into what looked like a compound built into the side of the mountain. A dark, stony house on one side, another rose higher in front of us, bridging the gap between one rock face and the other.

Dark glass glinted against the black stony walls that blended into the cliff face.

My rescuer who was now my captor turned the wheel, pulling up in a driveway big enough for us to turn around and drive right out of here. He yanked on the handbrake and killed the engine. I waited for the barking commands to come, or for him to force me from the car.

But he didn't.

Instead, he opened the door and climbed out, closing the door with a *thud* behind me and walked off, leaving me behind. My eyes darted instantly to the ignition, finding it empty. He dropped his hand, the keys jangling from his fingers.

Bastard!

There was something about him. Quiet, hard...and full of answers I needed. I had no choice but to open the door and follow.

He pretended I didn't exist, walking toward the house carved into the side of the mountain. I closed the door behind me, shifting on painful feet and glanced over my shoulder to the steel gate closing behind us.

Asphalt gave way to cooler stones, giving me a little reprieve from the burn as I numbly staggered after him.

Then he was gone, stepping into the shadows under the towering mountain house, leaving the door open for me to follow.

The fight for survival pushed in and stopped me at the doorway.

"Where are you?" I called.

Silence answered.

A chill coursed along the back of my neck as I stepped in. I left the doors open behind me as I went further. Cool tiles made me hiss even harder with relief. I curled my toes, my feet stinging as I made my way deeper inside. The rush of water came from deeper inside. I followed the sound toward the rear of the house, finding him in an expansive and expensive looking kitchen.

He placed a glass of water on the counter and hauled what looked like a medical kit up next to it.

"You want to tell me what the hell is going on?" I growled as I came closer.

Clunk. The clasps snapped open before he plucked a sleeve of pills free, stared at the printed foil backing, then pressed two out next to the glass.

What the fuck was this guy's problem?

My lip curled, anger carving through my grief as he turned, grabbed me around the waist, and lifted me to the counter before I realized he'd even moved.

I bucked at the last moment, punching the tree-trunks he called arms to get away.

I may as well have been a goddamn fly.

My pathetic blows glanced off his muscles as he turned, grabbed the glass and the pills, and handed them to me. "Drink, and take them."

"No fucking way." I slammed the glass down hard enough to spill the water. *"Not until you tell me what the hell is going on!"*

He glanced at the tiny puddle and grabbed cotton swabs and cream from the pack. His rough hands were gentle as he grabbed my ankle and lifted my foot.

Too gentle for a callous bastard.

That unnerved me.

"You have blisters," he murmured quietly, opening the cotton swabs and squeezing the cream onto one before smoothing it over the stinging ball of my foot. "This will help."

Relief hit instantly. I gripped the edge of the counter and moaned, shuddering as pain moved through me then slowly eased.

"I have sneakers and a change of clothes in the room upstairs for you." He eyed the sweats and red shirt I was wearing.

His brow creased as he stared at my clothing. I saw the thoughts ticking behind those guarded eyes. He wanted to ask why I wore this instead of the red lace lingerie we'd been forced to parade around in. The same lingerie the other Daughters wore when they were forced into the truck.

But he didn't push, just smoothed the cream over the sting of each foot and picked up the pills once more. For that I was thankful.

Get her to the table.

My pulse sped at the memory. My breath was seized in my lungs, burning, searing. I closed my eyes and tried to hang on as what they'd done to me last night rose.

"I won't hurt you," he said carefully.

Silence.

Unmerciful, crippling silence.

I slowly opened my eyes.

"Oh yeah?" I snarled, meeting that stare. "I've heard those words before."

There was a pinch at the corner of his eye, then a slow nod. He stepped away, handing me the cream. "Twice a day, the burn should be almost gone within a week. I'll show you to your room."

My room?

What. The. Fuck.

Just like before, he snapped the med kit closed and walked away.

The fuck he does.

"Wait a damn minute!" I shoved off the counter and hit the floor. Agony tore through my feet, making me stop and cling to the counter until the wave passed. "*I said, wait!*"

His heavy steps faded. I grabbed the cream and raced to catch up, climbing the black timber stairs to the first floor. The place was cool...and sleek and reeked of money. Who the fuck was this guy?

I followed him to a room, hovering at the doorway before I saw the piles of clothes, boots, and sneakers on the bed. I took a step and turned to him. "So, what, now I'm your prisoner?"

He froze, then turned and gave me his undivided attention.

"No, Helene." His voice deepened to a growl. "You're no one's prisoner, not anymore."

"Then what are you doing?" I glanced at the clothes that looked hand-picked, then back to him. "*Why. Am. I. Here?*"

"I'm protecting you."

But it wasn't the gruesome skull-faced balaclava I saw, or his intimidating as fuck size. It was him...the one called *Hunter*. Fractured memories pushed in, flickers of moments in that hell I'd endured.

It was Riven's voice I heard, coming through loud and clear.

Hunter will know what to do.

Hunter.

Hunter.

Hunter.

This Hunter?

"From who?" I whispered, my pulse booming as all the pieces fell into place.

Those dark eyes bored into mine as he took a step closer to stop in front of me. He searched my gaze. "Riven, Kane, and Thomas," he answered. "My brothers."

TWO

Riven

THE COLD BITE OF THE GUN MUZZLE PRESSED AGAINST MY head. "I'm sorry," I whispered, staring at the billowing dust the truck Helene was in left behind. *"I'm sorry."*

I'd killed us all...

Every.

Single.

One.

Of.

Us.

Crack!

I jumped, staring straight ahead, waiting for my turn to come.

Crack!

Crack...

CRACK!

"Get *down!*" Coulter's gunman roared.

Everything moved in slow motion. Soldiers came from the trees...dressed in camouflage, wearing a familiar balaclava of terror to cover their faces. One I'd seen many times before.

Hunter was here.

I turned my head, ducking as Coulter's men rushed forward behind us, firing back as they grabbed Coulter and dragged him back to safety.

"Riven?" Kane murmured, kneeling with his hands cuffed behind his back, staring as the soldiers invaded.

"*Riven?*" One of them barked. "*Riven Cruz?*"

"That's me," I answered as he hauled himself up onto the loading dock and his men followed. He looked at his team and nodded, motioning with two fingers to the door leading into the building. Then he turned his attention toward us. "Kane and..." He stared at Thomas. "The Priest."

"Get us out of here!" Thomas barked, thrashing as he tried to free his hands.

The soldier motioned one of his men forward.

Snip.

Snip.

Plastic ties were cut from him, then Kane, and finally me. I shoved forward, rising to my feet. I was scurrying forward, scrambling down to the ground in an instant.

"*Wait!*" the soldier called.

"Get me out of here!" I roared. "I have to get to her. I have to get to—"

"There's no need." He stopped me cold.

I slowly turned around, finding his hard stare.

"He already has her."

He has her. He has her. The world seemed to tilt. Jealousy raged to the surface, searing hot and molten. I met his stare. "Take us..." My words were a croak. "Take us to her, now."

Crack!

A shot ripped through the trees where I stood. Only I didn't flinch, nor did I duck for cover. Kane and Thomas lunged, jumped down from the loading dock, and raced toward me.

"Head through those trees," the soldier barked, stabbing his finger through the forest. "We'll be right behind you."

He pressed his hand against his earpiece and spoke. "We have them, yeah. Yeah, I'll bring them now."

I knew who he spoke to. The only one who'd descend like a ghost to save all our asses. Our brother, Hunter Cruz. I shifted my gaze to Walker's body lying motionless on the filthy concrete.

I wanted to stay and hunt the bastard who'd killed him through the hallways of this fucking prison. More than that, I wanted to carry Coulter's head back to Helene and drop it at her feet. One monster would be down, two more to go.

But I didn't do any of that. I turned as my brothers tore away from me, plunging between the thick brush and towering pines and I followed, leaving him behind.

She was all I cared about now. Get to her, then find the bastard who'd done this.

I wanted them all to die screaming.

I swung my arms, slamming aside low-lying branches, and raced after them. Thomas still limped, and Kane did his best. But it was pure rage and adrenaline that had me catching up, then overtaking them.

Sunlight glinted off glass in the distance. I leaped over fallen trees, picking up pace as I headed for the vehicles. A soldier lifted his rifle, stepping out into the open as we neared.

"Easy," I gasped, sucking in hard breaths as I held up my hands. "Riven, Kane and Thomas. We were told you could get us out of here."

He gave a nod toward the four-wheel drive. "Get in. We leave with the others."

Anger flared, making me bite down on my words. I didn't give a shit about the men who'd saved us. I only cared about finding her.

A crash came through the trees behind us.

Crack!

The shot flew past me. I spun, finding Coulter's men slashing through the trees after us.

"Get the fuck down!" The soldier roared, swinging his gun and firing back.

Boom!

BOOM!

18

Something slammed into me, spinning me around like a top. I stumbled, lunging for the safety of the vehicle as more gunshots followed.

Boom.

Boom.

BOOM!

Hunter's man went down hard. Blood spurted from his mouth as he crumbled. I ducked, scurried toward him, and lunged as Coulter's men rushed from the trees. One of them bellowed as he rushed forward. The brutal *thud* of colliding bodies was sickening.

I snatched the gun from the dying soldier's grasp. One look into his panicked eyes and I knew there was no hope of saving him, only in saving ourselves.

My finger was around the trigger as I lifted, aiming for Coulter's other men, who flanked us through the trees.

"Try it." I aimed the gun at the bastard's head as a grunt sounded from the fighting men.

Only it was Hunter's man who rose, the front of his shirt sodden with blood. He sucked in a hard breath, looking down at Coulter's dying man.

"Let's go." The soldier motioned to the vehicles.

He didn't need to tell us twice. I stumbled forward, only Kane wasn't as fast, sitting on the ground behind the black Jeep. I moved forward, carrying the gun as I stood over him. "Kane?"

He lifted his head. There was blood on his white shirt on the side.

Fresh blood.

"Jesus," I muttered as I knelt beside him, yanking his shirt from his waistband.

"Oww, *shit,*" he winced and snarled.

Fresh blood ran as I pressed harder. "We need to get him to a doctor."

"I have something better," Hunter's man muttered. "We have a medic on our team. Come on." He stepped close, then bent down, grabbed my brother's arm, and swung it around his shoulders as he helped him to stand. "Let's get you out of here."

The faint crack of gunfire drifted through the trees as I hurried around to open the back door. Kane gave a grunt, then a moan as the soldier loaded him into the back seat.

"I'll sit with him," Thomas muttered, leaving me to nod and climb into the passenger seat.

Car doors thudded. A second later the engine howled to life. I barely made it inside, yanking the door closed after me as we were reversing, slamming into a bush, and lunged forward. The Jeep bounced hard as we skidded over ruts and surged ahead.

Hunter's man jerked his gaze to the rear-view mirror and pressed the microphone on his shirt. "I see you, everyone make it out?"

I glanced over my shoulder as more men came from the trees, clambered into the other vehicle, and pulled the four-wheel drive around.

"Thank fuck you got here," I muttered, glancing at the driver. "Are you taking us to Hunter?"

He never answered, just divided his attention between the car behind us and the track that took us further away from The Order.

Good.

I wanted to be as far away from that place as I could.

"Kane, how are you doing?"

"About as well as expected..." he muttered. "After being shot."

He looked pale, beaded sweat across his brow made him look even more sickly. I just gave a nod, met Thomas's careful stare, and turned back. It took us twenty minutes to get out of that forest and back onto asphalt. Twenty minutes I didn't want to waste.

"Is she okay?" I asked, glancing at the soldier. "Helene and the others."

He didn't answer, just pushed the Jeep harder, pulling away from the vehicle behind us. I settled back. My breaths were hard as I focused on getting to her. The moment I had her in my arms, she was never leaving my side.

Not for Hale.

Not for *anyone*.

That thought was all that kept me from falling apart. I gripped the soldier's rifle as we hurtled to wherever my brother hid nowadays.

Hunter didn't like me.

Not really.

Not like a younger brother should.

But it didn't matter—I turned and stared out the window—I respected *him*, and that was all that mattered. Still, the anger he harbored for me still stuck on me like hot tar. He'd never exactly said the words out loud. But he didn't agree with the way I'd searched for our sister. He wanted to burn The Order's nests one by one, then hunt down the ants scurrying for safety.

Me...

I wanted to control them...the main one, at least. I wanted to find every tunnel and every crevice, then I wanted to find our sister before striking the match.

Only, it hadn't turned out that way, had it?

I winced as we turned toward the city. No, it hadn't turned out that way at all.

The engine gunned and the sparkling city rose in the distance. But before we came too close, we veered off, heading to a commercial suburb on the outskirts.

The more we turned, the more desperate I became. My hand gripped the rifle, the other clenched tight around the door, ready to lunge the moment we stopped. The four-wheel drive slowed. Hunter's man reached up, hitting a button high on the visor and, in the distance, an eight-foot tall fence with a solid gate that rolled open.

I saw the back of The Order's truck before I saw anything else. The thing was parked and the rear door was open. I saw bullet holes on the sides and winced as we pulled to the side and parked.

This place was some kind of compound. A large building loomed on one side with a parking lot where the truck was parked on the other. I was already yanking the handle and climbing out as we stopped.

I stared at the place as I opened the back door. "Let's get you inside," I muttered to Kane.

But I wasn't really thinking about him, not if I was honest.

Thomas climbed out and came around to help me with Kane.

But it was the truck that called me, the black interior hiding the truth of what had really happened.

"Riven," Thomas grunted.

I jerked my focus back, moving around Thomas to climb along the back seat and help Kane. He moaned, clutching his side as I gently pushed him out. Hunter's man grabbed him as the second four-wheel drive pulled into the compound and the gate rolled shut behind them.

Car doors opened and closed.

"You good?" one of them asked me, striding toward us.

"My brother's been shot," I answered, staring at the truck once more.

But the soldier grabbed my arm, turning me around. "Looks like he's not the only one."

Surprised, I looked down.

Bright red blood soaked through the sleeve of my shirt.

"Fuck." Thomas lunged, grabbing my arm. His eyes were wide as they met mine. "Why the hell didn't you tell us?"

Why?

Because I hadn't known.

I shook my head and took a step, leaving them behind. "Just get Kane inside. I'll get myself looked at after I find her."

Fate whispered in my ear as I strode past the truck and headed for the compound. Voices drifted out, deep baritones that tried to be as soft as they could.

I opened the door and stepped through, finding myself in a room full of mercenaries...and Daughters.

"You don't have to do that," one massive male urged as a Daughter sank to her knees in front of him.

He bent, gently grabbed her thin arms, and pulled her upright. "Look at me," he commanded gently. "And hear my voice. *You don't have to do that...not anymore.*"

She just looked at him blankly.

And that alone made his lips curl. He jerked that savage glare my way. In fact, they all did.

Hate radiated around the room the moment I stepped in. Lucky for me, I was used to it.

"My brother?" I muttered.

The beast of a male never answered, just turned back to the Daughter. "Come on, let's get you something to wear."

She just scowled. "Wear?"

"Yeah, cub. Wear."

He led her away from us and deeper into the compound. I headed for the next soldier, who was handing out bottles of water to the other Daughters.

"I was told Helene is here?" I forced, scanning the faces in the crowded room before swinging back to him. "Where is she?"

"I dunno." He stepped away, giving me his back. "You'll have to ask your brother."

Twitch.

"And *where is he?*"

The soldier swung back as Hunter's man half carried Kane inside behind us. "Not here."

I stepped forward as that menacing rage grew bolder. "What the fuck do you mean, *not here?*"

"Hunter isn't here." The soldier who'd saved our asses answered, walling Kane into the room and deeper into the building. "And neither is Helene."

That burning strangle-hold on my heart clenched tighter. "Then tell me where the fuck he is." I held out my hand. "And give me your goddamn keys."

"Can't," he grunted.

I followed him. "Can't or *won't?*"

He stopped, turned his head, and looked at me over his shoulder. "Is there a difference?"

Twitch.

"Why?" I smashed the word through clenched teeth.

"Because, *Principal,*" he snarled, and that same hate flickered behind his eyes. "Your brother doesn't trust you...and frankly, neither do we."

Doesn't *fucking trust me?*

DOESN'T. TRUST. ME?

Motherfucker.

He had her.

He had her right where he'd wanted her all along.

Alone with him.

THREE

Helene
___

GET HER TO THE TABLE.

I kicked, driving out my feet, *and screamed.* "No! *NOOO!*"

Hands gripped me, pushing me down. Down into the darkness. Down into the foul water that forced its way inside. Black lake water rushed over my face, flooding my mouth as I howled and fought. I coughed and choked, surfacing and spluttering to stay alive. Still, they held me against that table, their grips around my ankles too strong as they forced my legs apart and drove me back under.

Midnight.

Deep.

Endless.

Depths.

Consumed me.

I opened my mouth, screaming in muted sounds of nothing and stared up through the murky blur.

Fight.

Fight them.

GET THE FUCK OFF ME!

I yanked my eyes open and shoved upright in the bed, breaking free of the water...and the nightmare. My pulse boomed inside my ears, the sound deafening as slowly the room I was in sharpened. But it was the fire that lashed my throat that hurt. I swallowed the sting and tasted blood. Darkness. That's all there was...until the faint murky outline of light at the edge of the room drew my focus.

Soft bedding pressed under me. I tried to remember where I was and stared at that faint murky light that hugged the edges of the doorway.

"You were screaming."

I flinched, freezing at the soft, deep murmur.

In an instant I realized why the soft glow spilled around the edges. *Because he took up the entire space.*

"S-ssorry," I croaked, my throat on fire.

He took a couple of steps closer, moving into the room, and stopped at the edge of the bed. His careful movements still made my breath catch.

"There's water." He turned his head, glancing at the nightstand beside me, then he turned and slowly headed for the doorway.

He left me...just like that.

I glanced at the water, my throat scorching, and grasped the bottle. It was just a dream...just a dream. But the moment I broke the seal and swallowed the water, that same terrified feeling came rushing back. I swallowed, coughed, and spluttered, swiping the dribble off my chin, and moved.

The sheets were cast aside as I kicked. I scurried from the bed, wincing as my feet hit the floor. Pain lashed across the soles of my feet. But this pain I could deal with...not the one that waited for me the moment I closed my eyes.

The faint thud of his steps reached me. I limped toward the doorway and out onto the landing. Darkness waited down there...but darkness was everywhere, wasn't it? I felt that more keenly now than I ever had. My fingers trembled as I gripped the banister and eased down one stair at a time.

A sharp, bitter scent of coffee wafted to me as I made it down the last stair. I followed the scent to the kitchen I'd found before. The mountain waited, pouring two cups before he placed the glass carafe back under the coffee machine.

He pushed the creamer my way, grabbed his black, and lifted it to his lips.

"Thanks," I murmured as I winced again.

Those predatory eyes were fixed on me as I searched the kitchen and yanked out the cutlery drawer. But he didn't watch me like he wanted to attack. No, he made no move to come near me at all and that quiet, controlled presence seemed to ease the panic inside me.

I poured and stirred, then rinsed the spoon under the tap and placed it on the sink edge. He grabbed his coffee and headed back around the counter, walking slowly enough that it was a command on its own...*follow.*

So I did.

We headed through the house, stopping as he unlocked the front door and left it open for me. The night waited. I had no idea what time it was...late or early, either way, I shivered, gripped my coffee, and followed him to the other building.

It felt safe here. The mountain hiding us; the gate keeping us safe. Hunter moved silently, opening the door to the separate building, leaving me to follow. My steps stuttered at the entrance. Lights clicked on inside, showing the way.

I bet it was more for my sake than his.

The man moved like a ghost.

A deadly.

Vengeful.

Ghost.

I stepped inside, leaving the door open, and scanned what looked like a massive armory. Guns, vests, knives, and grenades lined the wall on one side, two-ways and satellite tracking units on the other. Everything in there was precise, gleaming, and *very expensive.*

His heavy steps thudded up a set of stairs. I looked up, then followed, tracking his movement as he headed further toward the front of the building. But the moment I stepped onto the landing, I realized this was no normal building.

It was a command center.

My feet made no sound on the tiled floor as I approached and stared at the bank of monitors.

"What the fuck?" I whispered, coming closer.

He moved like I didn't exist, placed his coffee on the curved desk in front of him and pulled out a chair, taking a seat in front of the displays. I stared at the screens, finding satellite views of houses that looked faintly familiar.

London's.

Riven's.

Mine.

I froze, then glanced his way as he punched in details to a computer then sat back, grabbing his coffee, taking a sip, watching the screen fill with information.

"You were spying on me?"

He looked my way, those unflinching eyes behind the mask having no trouble finding me.

Of course he watched me.

It wasn't just houses, though. He had a whole screen divided by external cameras aimed at The Order. But next to that...was a camera showing the interior hall. I froze. My heart was hammering as heat rushed to my cheeks.

He could see everything.

A sting came across my hand. "Owww." I jerked my gaze down to the trembling cup spilling hot coffee over my thumb. I sucked in a hard breath as he slowly glanced my way. I carefully placed the cup down on the counter and sucked the scalding liquid from my hand.

Then *froze.*

Beside the monitor divided by four interior cameras was one screen...showing one recording alone. I recognized the inside of Kane's office instantly.

Pause.

The word was written across the top of the screen. I clenched my trembling hand, then looked his way, meeting that steely gaze fixed on mine. I couldn't stop myself. *I had to know.*

So I reached out and pressed *play.*

I was on the screen, staring right at the camera. Kane stood at my back, his hand wrapped around my throat. He spoke to me, words that didn't come through the speakers...but I knew what they'd been.

This is what you wanted, wasn't it, Helene? For your sisters. You remember your sisters, don't you?

The floor seemed to drop out from under me as I watched him sliding the red strap of my bodysuit down my shoulders. Heat found me, filling me with embarrassment.

On the screen, The Teacher dropped his hand from my throat and cupped my breast.

My body tightened.

Thighs clenched taut.

Behind me, the mountain rose.

"You watched this?" I whispered.

Red lace rubbed my nipples on the screen.

Say it, Kane demanded on the screen, his lips moving. *Say what you'll do to protect them.*

Those empty eyes stared back at me. I was so far gone, so drugged out, *controlled.*

Anything, I answered on the screen.

I knew what would follow.

And so did my body.

Revulsion recoiled in my head, but my body wasn't listening. Heat rushed, pulsing between my thighs. Even now I wanted him. I wanted him so much I couldn't breathe. I closed my eyes as the memory took on a life of its own.

Would you let my brothers fuck you? We could take turns all night and day. Fill your pussy until you overflow. Stretch that tight cunt—

I yanked open my eyes and spun around, slamming into the rock-hard chest of Hunter Cruz.

I stared up at him, to those unflinching eyes.

"You. Watched. Me?"

He said nothing.

My pulse raced, my breaths panting until it was like I couldn't breathe.

No air...

There was no air.

The screens around me blurred as the room spun. *I was going to faint.*

I forced myself to move instead, taking a step closer until I stood in his shadow.

There was no disgust in those eyes. No revulsion or anything. He may as well be carved from steel. *Was he? Was he carved from steel?* I reached out, my hands trembling with the panicked racing of my heart, and wrapped them around his hard forearm.

He was warm.

Warm and hard.

Corded muscles flexed under my grasp as I clenched tighter. Part of me wanted to be cruel, to hurt him. To *feel something.* So I poked him, pushing hard into his mammoth chest. The man must be at least six-foot four. I was guessing probably close to 300 pounds of pure...raw...*power.*

The desperate need to kneel in front of him was overwhelming. I wanted to slide these clothes from my body. I wanted to be used...to be ruined. *To be owned.* I wound my hands around his wrist instead, clenching tight until my arms trembled with the strain.

I wanted to hate him and fuck him all at the same time.

The way he looked at me was unnerving.

Empty.

Raw.

Fuck him.

Fuck him now?

I dropped his wrist and reeled back instead, then unleashed, slapping his chest as hard as I could. *SLAP!* The sting across my palm was instant. Still, he never moved. Nor did he hate. My throat thickened as I pressed my hand against the hard swell, smoothing, touching. *Christ, he felt so good.*

I was falling apart, unraveling at the seams.

Shattering on the inside.

"Can you...can you please hold me?"

He never moved, not at first. Nor did he stop me as I pressed my body against his. He smelled of sweat and survival. Both hit me hard. My nipples tightened as I rubbed my face against his chest and took what I wanted.

No...

What I needed.

I licked my lips and lifted my gaze to those dark eyes hidden behind the mask. The ones which had held me transfixed from the moment he'd rescued me. Instinct drove me to reach for his face. Only, he moved then, like a viper, to grasp my wrist. One small shake of his head stopped me.

My chest boomed with every brutal thud of my heart.

He searched my eyes.

I pushed harder, inching my fingers up to that gruesome skull and brushed his hard cheek. He didn't push me away...just held me.

Something passed between us.

Something born out of desperation and the need to survive.

"Please," I whispered. "I need to see you."

I inched my fingers to the edge of his balaclava, slowly tugging it up the hollowed throat and along the dark stubble. There was no shake of his head this time. He held my wrist as I peeled the mask over his chin and his mouth up to his nose.

That's where he stopped me.

I stared at his mouth as he tilted his head down to mine.

That hard, beautiful mouth.

Part of me still howled and screamed after what those bastards had done to me. But I locked that part away. Compartmentalized, as Dr. Kane Cruz would say. I leaned into that as I rose, feeling the burn across the balls of my feet, and kissed him.

His mouth moved and his hard lips were warm against mine.

He is their brother.

It was that thought that spurred me on, opening my mouth wider until the mountain moved. He grasped me around the waist and lifted, carrying me to the counter, and eased me down.

The more I kissed him, the more desperate I became.

I gripped his arms as he slid his hands around me. My legs parted around his waist as my ass slid on the counter. That *squeal* resurrected the terror instantly. I froze, and it took barely a second for him to realize something was wrong.

He broke the kiss as those dark eyes searched mine.

Somehow he knew.

"Who," he whispered in that deep, gravelly tone. "Do I need to kill?"

FOUR

Riven

_____

"Hold still."

I shifted, wincing. "I told you I was fine," I forced through clenched teeth to the medic.

The asshole who'd poked and prodded my arm just straightened. "Oh yeah? And how many years of medical training brought you to that conclusion?"

My lip curled and anger burned as I stared into that smug stare before he gave a nod and resumed. Bolts of agony tore through my shoulder where the bullet had barely grazed me...only my brother hadn't been so lucky. I glanced across to where Kane lay in a drugged sleep, his side patched after they'd fished the bullet out of his body.

The only saving grace was nothing major was hit. He'd survive with one nice scar.

Just like Helene's.

Where the fuck was she?

The asshole pinched and snipped the stitches, then turned away.

I didn't want to be here.

Not with the Daughters...or Hunter's men.

I needed to find her, then Hale, right before I hunted down Coulter and Julius Harmon.

This sitting around and waiting? This was a waste of fucking time. "We should be out there, finding Hale."

The medic turned back to me with a betadine swab. "You say something?"

I glanced his way, then shook my head.

The asshole who didn't like me looked over at me, his elbow resting on his knee as he stabbed a fork into an open can of something that looked disgusting. I looked away as the medic swabbed my arm, then taped a dressing in place.

"Okay, that should—" he started.

But I was already moving, sliding off the seat, leaving the medic and his years of medical training behind. Heads turned my way. The group of three Daughters stiffened as I neared. All three watched me intently, one even licked her lips.

My gut clenched as I looked away. I strode through the five soldiers sitting around the expansive room and headed along the hallway. Bedroom doors were closed. The other remaining Daughters were asleep.

"Riven?"

I turned at my name, finding Thomas standing behind me. He glanced at the door at the end of the hallway and turned back to me. "Going somewhere?"

I clenched my jaw and leaned close. "Have you heard from him?"

He scowled. "Hunter?"

"*Yes, Hunter.*" I snapped. "Who the fuck else?"

He flinched at my tone.

"I'm sorry." I dragged my fingers through my hair. "I'm just worked up, that's all. Every second we're here feels wasted."

"And so is going out there without a plan," he warned.

I winced. But it wasn't Hale's face I saw in my head. It was hers. Her empty goddamn stare after what those bastards had done to her. My gut tightened until it felt rock hard. I was going to need a goddamn medic alright, one I needed to heal me from the fucking ulcer I was making.

"To answer your question, no. No, I haven't heard from Hunter."

I jerked my gaze to his. I had no idea where he was...or what he was doing with Helene. For all I knew, he could have her chained like a goddamn animal. Or locked away...yeah, he'd have her locked away. Maybe he was even torturing her? Finding out the information he wanted.

Agony ripped across my chest as the image rose. I had to get out of here, I had to—

I turned around and headed for the doorway. One push and the cool night air flooded through me. I sucked in the air, leaving the door to close behind me. Movement came at my side as one of the soldiers stepped near, carrying his rifle and glancing my way.

He didn't speak, just glared at me, then kept patrolling the grounds. I shifted my gaze to the truck from The Order, the one which had tried to take her from me. I headed for the open rear door and stared into the darkness. Moonlight spilled through the doorway, illuminating a few feet. I gripped the side and climbed in.

She'd been in here.

I knew it.

Black blotches on the floor glistened slightly in the silver glow of the moon.

Blood.

That's what that was...

The guard they'd taken prisoner.

If there was anyone who knew what had happened to her, it'd be him.

I climbed out and scanned the rest of the compound. He was here; I knew it...the only question was, *where?* My boots crunched against the ground as I made my way across the main compound.

"Riven," Thomas called from the corner of the building. "Where are you going?"

"Not now Thomas."

I headed further into the compound, past the enormous garage packed with trucks, four-wheel drives, and even motorbikes.

Still, my brother followed me as I slipped through an open garage door and around the vehicles.

"What the fuck are you doing?" Thomas hissed.

I ignored him and headed for a doorway leading out of there. They were keeping the guard alive. That's all I'd found out. But the moment I'd started asking questions, they'd clammed up. Fuck them. I'd find out on my own.

I turned the handle and pushed through, stepping into some kind of hallway that led to another warehouse.

"You're going to get us kicked out."

I tried my best to ignore my brother and kept walking, stopping at a closed closet door and opening it. Darkness, nothing else. The scent of sweat and sex was overpowering. I closed it and kept walking to the far end and pushed through into the separate building.

It wasn't as big as the main one. But this one was equipped as an armory. Guns, knives, and every other kind of weapon lay across the table and crowded the walls. A half-filled coffee cup sat beside a broken-down Glock. Someone was busy cleaning while guarding. I glanced around...*guarding what?*

"Riven," Thomas hissed as I left the coffee and the gun behind and moved deeper into the building.

There was a closed, solid door to my left. A padlock dangled, locked. *Fuck.*

I spun, and slammed into my brother.

"Think about what you're doing here," he snarled.

"I am." That was all I was doing, thinking...*envisioning him and her.*

I strode back to the armory, grabbed a set of bolt cutters from the wall, and made my way back. My arm trembled with the strain. The stitches the medic had been so fucking careful with tore. Blinding agony tore across my shoulder as the cutters carved through the steel with a *snap*.

CLANG.

The cutters and the lock hit the floor. I was already opening the door and pushing in. Shadows shifted inside.

"What's the fuck do you want?" came a snarl from within.

I hit the light switch.

The asshole crouched in the corner threw up his arm, shielding his eyes.

It was him.

I stared at that uniform I fucking loathed and stepped closer. He was cuffed by separate ties on each hand, designed to restrict movement, but not cut off the circulation. That meant they planned on keeping him here for a while.

"Principal?" he croaked.

I stepped closer until I stood over him. "Don't call me that."

"Why?" he spat. "It is your title, isn't it?" He glanced behind me. "You're supposed to be dead."

"And yet, here I am," I answered, staring at the mess of his face. They'd worked him over. Nothing too bad...until I saw the way he held his foot and the neat bullet hole in the top of his boot.

Maybe they'd worked him over more than I realized. "Where is she?"

"Who?"

I crouched down. "You know who."

The smile was fast and sickening. "The cunt we held down and fucked?"

Rage roared through me.

He gave a shrug.

I lunged, grabbed his foot, and squeezed. His screams were chilling, deafening, bouncing off the walls of the room as I twisted.

"I will *not* ask twice," I snarled.

"WHAT THE FUCK IS GOING ON HERE?" came the roar from behind us.

I jerked my gaze over my shoulder to the soldier in the doorway. He strode in, but Thomas spun to step between us.

"Wait!" he ordered, holding out his hands. "Wait a fucking minute."

My brother gave me the precious seconds few I needed. I twisted the piece of shit's foot until I heard the shattered bones crunch and crack. *"Where the fuck is she?"*

"I DON'T KNOOWW!" he howled. *"HE TOOK HER. SHE WAS ALL HE WANTED...SHE WAS ALLLL HEEEE WANNNTEDDDD!"*

I was yanked backwards and hauled to my feet, then thrown sideways. There wasn't just one of Hunter's men in here anymore. There were two...the asshole with the hard-on for the Daughter came closer, stabbing his finger in the center of my chest, driving me backwards with his sheer size.

"I'll only say this once," he snarled, those dangerous eyes glinting with promise. "Inside those goddamn walls, you might be someone, but out here...you're no one. In fact...you're someone I'd like to put in a room of my own...you feel me?"

The cold rage inside me turned into a flicker of fear.

I was the enemy here.

The only thing that stopped that big bastard from making good on his promise was my brother. "You want me gone? Then take me to Hunter, now."

FIVE

Helene
___

"Say their names, Helene," Hunter murmured. "Say their names and they're as good as dead."

Goosebumps raced along the nape of my neck. It was almost as though he wanted me to force his hand...as though he expected me to say someone he knew.

Not just knew.

Was bound to by blood.

Heat rushed to my cheeks. That was it. I searched those dark eyes, then shifted my focus to his hard lips. "You think Riven did this?"

"Didn't he?" He stepped closer and lifted his hand. His callused fingers gently brushed the throbbing ache at the edge of my cheek. "Say his name and I'll kill him, brother or not...no man that hurts a woman like that deserves to live."

I'm afraid you won't be making your date, Helene Montgomery...tonight, or any other night for that matter.

That *savage* Riven had come to life. That bestial male that had drugged and tied me up on his sofa. He'd raped me then, he'd fucked me until he was the one I craved. I closed my eyes, every cell in my body humming with the thought of his hands on me.

"You watched the corridors," I said carefully, then opened my eyes. "So you know what happened."

He scowled, then glanced at the screen. "I searched, but there was nothing."

He'd searched?

So he *did* think it was Riven.

I lowered my gaze to the darkening bruises around my wrists and tried to hide them behind my back. "It wasn't him. He wouldn't—"

"You want to explain my own brother to me? I know what he's capable of. I know what they're all capable of."

Get her to the table.

I swallowed as those words surfaced again. "It was Coulter," I whispered.

"What?"

I lifted my head, anger blasting to the surface. This felt like that moment in the cafeteria all over again, the one where I'd been forced to own what had happened to me. My voice shook now, just as it had shaken then. "It was Coulter and his men. They'd tried to get me twice that night. Once I escaped, the last time I..." my voice slowed and sounded distorted in my ears. "I didn't."

"Coulter?" That scowl deepened. "The bastard who took over The Order?"

"Yes."

He gently pulled my hands from behind my back. "They did this?" He softly touched the bruises their hands had left behind. "And the ones around your ankles?"

Get her to the table.

They'd done a lot more than that.

But I wasn't going to think about that, let alone say it.

My throat thickened as tears threatened to fill my eyes. *Don't let them win. Don't you dare.* That dark, endless lake from my nightmare lingered in the back of my mind, the depths drawing me under. But I refused to go. Instead, I forced that horror down, pushing it all the way under until I couldn't see it...nor could I feel it.

My tone was stronger this time. Stronger and colder. "Coulter and his men are the ones you want. Not Riven. He and Kane... they..."

Owned.

They owned me.

"They owned me." The word slipped free.

"What did you say?" Those words were a rumble in his chest.

Throb.

"I said, they saved me."

He scowled and shook his head. "That wasn't what you said."

A hunger rose, one that was so strong it pushed the memories of that night deeper into those murky depths. I knew what that lake was now. It was what I wanted to be, quiet, calm, unfathomable.

My knees buckled. I slowly dropped to the floor in front of this man who *felt* like them. Cold. Brutal. *Merciless. Power. The kind that controlled.*

"What the fuck are you doing?"

"Obeying," I whispered and reached for the buckle of his khakis. "I'm obeying you."

They were blood-splattered.

Filthy.

Stained with sweat.

Each draw of my breath was choking, like a rag shoved down the back of my throat.

"Get up," the mountain commanded. "Get up *now.*"

He didn't move, just stared at me with a look that was part rage and all *desire.* The skull was all I saw, the glaring white skull.

"Please," I whispered as I unbuttoned his pants and tugged down his zipper. Christ, he was hard as a fucking rock. "I'm hurting."

He moved then, reached down, grasped my shoulders, and lifted me.

You want to be owned. To be used. You're just a thing for me. A tight cunt I splay wide. You're trouble...trouble I need out of my system.

"This isn't you." The mountain searched my stare. "This is the drugs they fed you. The conditioning they used to control you."

"Isn't it?" I hissed as a flicker of anger rose. "You watched me on that screen."

He stilled, not answering me.

So he wanted to play that game?

I turned, my gaze moving instantly to the monitor where Kane and I played out in silence. His fingers were deep in my pussy, my back was arched, my eyes frantic and wide with a desperate look of hunger. I had his arm in my grip, my knuckles white under the force. The sight of that was mesmerizing. "Tell me again that that isn't me."

Silence.

I swung around. *"Tell me again THAT ISN'T ME?"*

He said nothing as I sucked in hard breaths. I was so done with fighting this need. So *done* with pretending I was nothing. just the daughter who obeyed her father. The *sister* who suffered, all because of our fucked-up family. The *woman* no one saw... or remembered.

Only, I wasn't invisible now.

Not to Riven or Kane...or Thomas.

I stepped closer, my heart pounding. "Do you see me?" Those words were a harsh whisper. "Do *you* see *me?*"

"You fucking need *them?*" He growled, those dark eyes suddenly coming to life in a chilling way. He lunged, crossing the space between us with blinding second. Jesus, he was fast... and as he grasped my throat in his massive hand, my heart slammed against my chest. "Is this what you're trying to tell me? You want me to grab you by the throat and fuck you like they did? Is that how you want to be treated? You want to be *used?*"

Panic filled me.

I didn't know this man.

But he somehow knew me.

He'd watched me, searched for me.

He'd come for me.

Yet those eyes...those eyes demanded an answer now.

"Yes," I hissed, feeling the pressure of his thumb against my throat. "Yes, I want to be held down and fucked, and I also want to be the one using. I want—" *Get her to the table.* "I want to be the one in control."

My stomach dropped.

Revulsion burned.

The mountain dropped his hand. One slow nod and he took a step backwards. Shame burned in my cheeks as he turned around and started walking.

But he didn't leave. No, he headed for a sofa that sat along the wall, one designed to be pulled out to sleep.

"You want to use someone, Helene?" he growled and those words rolled like thunder through the room. "Then use me."

He turned around to face me and sat. Those massive hands dropped beside him as his knees splayed wide. Shadows caressed his face, casting darkness across his mask. That skull stared back at me...daring me to move forward.

Fear pinned me to the floor where I stood.

What?

I wanted to whisper, but I knew what he'd said and also what he'd meant.

He sat there...*waiting.*

My cheeks burned as I stared at him.

I'd wanted to be seen...well, now *he* saw me.

I took a step, then another, stopping in front of him. The man never moved as I reached for my shirt and dragged it over my head. But his eyes...they gave him away, shining as I dropped the garment. Cold air licked my nipples, puckering them.

There was a tightening of his throat, trying to hide the swallow. But I saw. I affected him in ways I didn't understand. Riven's face pushed into my mind. For a second there was a flicker of guilt, until I shoved it away. This wasn't about loyalty...this was about survival.

Get her to the table.

Those words haunted me, driving me to act. "You think I'm broken?" I whispered. "But I'm not. I'm here, aren't I? I'm alive."

He said nothing, just watched me as I neared and climbed on top of him.

A tiny scowl came, creasing the skin between his brows before it was gone.

"Say something." I gripped the sofa on each side of him. "Do something."

Those hard, exposed lips moved. "What would you like me to do?"

"Touch me," I demanded as I rolled my hips, grinding myself against him. "Force me, hurt me. Do whatever you want with me."

Stars ignited in those hard eyes. He reached up and brushed my cheek with the back of a curled finger. His knuckle came away glistening with tears I hadn't known I'd shed. His fingers unfurled as he cupped his massive hand against my cheek.

Of all the things he could do, he chose to do...*that?*

My body trembled, quaking and shuddering. I tried to hold on, clenching my jaw as I rolled my hips, forcing myself to rub. Until that dam inside me broke, and I crumpled.

I slumped against him, dropping my head against his shoulder. Choked sobs tore free as I dropped my hands, gripping his shirt. "I hate you," I whispered. "I hate you for not forcing me. I hate you for...I just hate."

"Hate me," he murmured. "Hate me all you want. I won't force myself on you, Helene. I'm not my...I'm not my brother."

I lifted my head and through the blur of tears, I saw him.

A ghost, waiting.

I shifted my focus to his lips, to that hard mouth and his guarded eyes. I tasted the salt of my tears as I lowered my head and kissed him. His mouth moved, parting, inviting me.

My hands trembled as I cupped his face and that mask.

I deepened the kiss, taking more as his hands circled my back.

But he never dragged me deeper, just let me cling to him.

Like he was my life raft in that black, endless lake.

When he broke, the kiss he gripped the back of my neck, holding my gaze to his. "I see you, Helene," he murmured huskily. "Maybe better than you see yourself right now."

Tears still streamed down my face.

I felt ugly at that moment, ugly, choked, and raw. Rawer than I'd ever allowed myself to be in my entire life. He pulled me close and those big arms wrapped around me. "Give me everything, Helene. Give me...everything."

My chest caved as I wept and my shoulders curled in. I barely even noticed as he gathered me up in his arms and moved, rocking forward with his massive body and rose from the sofa.

I clung to him as he walked, his big body still rocking me as we went down the stairs and back out into the night.

"My shirt," I moaned.

"Leave it," he answered. "You can wear mine."

I closed my eyes, letting the ghost of a man take care of me in the kind of way my father never had. He strode back through the door of the main house, stopping only long enough to close the door behind us and engage the locks.

Silence.

That's all there was with him.

Somehow, it was all I needed.

He climbed the stairs, his arms wrapped firmly around me, hugging me against him. I didn't even look where we were headed, only cared about how he felt, and right then, that was *safe*. Yes, this man...this *ghost* was the safest thing I'd felt in a long time.

He turned, and gently lowered us on top of the bed. I dropped my leg from his side, curled against him, and shifted the other leg.

"Don't," he murmured, his voice a low growl in the dark. "Don't leave."

I didn't, shifting it back as I caged myself around him.

He lay like that, boots still on, his arms wrapped around me. The warmth of his body and the steady rise of his chest were constant, lulling me. There was no pull of the depths this time, no nightmare waiting to pull me down.

Just calmness.

My eyelids fluttered, then closed as sleep staked its claim.

SIX

Helene

BEEP.

The sound dragged me to the surface. I opened my eyes, finding dim light floating all around me. *Where...where the hell was I?*

The faint sound of rushing water followed, like someone else was in the shower. Warmth wrapped around me and soft cotton brushed my bare skin. I looked around, finding the opposite side of the bed empty. The covers were moved aside, but the pillow was indented as though someone had lain here.

Hunter...

Oh, shit.

Memories of last night surfaced.

Me, standing in front of the man who'd rescued me, wearing nothing but cut-off sweats and rage. I closed my eyes. So...so much rage.

You want to use someone, Helene? Then use me.

A moan ripped free. "Jesus." *Don't tell me I—*

Beep.

I raised my head and looked toward the sound. The moment I pushed upwards, everything came rushing back to me, the way he'd held me, the way he'd comforted and carried me like a damn child to his bed. I ached in some places, like I'd slept on a damn tree trunk. He must've laid there all night with his arms around me.

I'd never had that before.

A man...do that for me.

I swallowed, pushing the longing away.

Beep.

That sound snagged my focus once more. I glanced to the doorway, listened to the shower still running, and pushed aside my bedding. A cell sat on the dresser, the screen lighting up with message after message.

A pang tore across my chest as I glanced toward the doorway again, then snuck over and picked it up.

David: It's all across the fucking news. We need to make a plan for this asap.

All across the news? I clicked on the message and scowled when it opened immediately. Did the guy not know about passcodes? I stilled and thought about it, remembering how goddamn big he was. I mean, you'd have to be suicidal to steal from him, right?

I glanced at the cell again...

Right.

The sound of the shower finally shut off. A squeal of a shower door followed, making me yank the cell behind my back and hurry back to the bed. Heavy footsteps neared as I clambered back into the bed and yanked up the comforter, turning to curl onto my side and slammed my eyes closed.

Seconds, that's all it had taken. Seconds before he neared the bed and stopped beside me. I was sure he was naked. If he wasn't, he had to be close to it.

My breath turned heavy. I was sure he'd sense I was awake, but more than that, I was sure he knew I had the one thing he didn't want me to have...a connection with the outside world.

I clenched the device in my hand and prayed to God the thing didn't beep again.

His heavy breaths were loud, before he finally moved away from beside the bed. I clenched my eyes tighter, *please...please leave.*

Those steps moved to the closet, causing the floorboards to creak before a soft *thud* came. I envisioned a towel hitting the floor as he dressed. Before I could start sweating buckets under the covers, he made his way out of the bedroom and slowly down the stairs.

I waited for as long as I dared. "Thank fuck," I whispered as I ease the cell back out and stared at the screen.

Multiple people found dead at The Order following Haelstrom Hale's death.

"Death, my ass," I whispered, scrolling through headline after headline all saying the same thing.

There'd been a massacre at The Order...*again.*

Cold washed through me.

Only, they'd never reported on the other murders ...why would they? They'd been only Daughters, after all.

They'll all think I'm dead.

My stomach clenched, but I thought about that for a moment. No Order. No Hale. No bloodshed. Just disappear, just like that. Viv and Ryth's faces rose, full of anger and desperation, making me wince. Could I do that? Just drop out and leave them to fight the battle on their own?

Could I see them on the news being loaded into body bags and know I could've done something to protect them? My pulse boomed and a savage, agonizing ache filled my chest as I looked away from the cell.

No.

I couldn't.

Not now.

Not ever.

They were more than faded images I'd pinned to my wall.

They were my sisters...they were my blood.

My fingers shook as I turned back and punched in Vivienne's cell number. It rang and rang and rang. I waited, hope fading, but then it was answered.

"Yes?"

"Viv. It's me."

"Hell, is that you?"

Hell? The corner of my lips twitched with the nickname. "It's me."

"Thank fuck you're alive," she moaned. "It's all over the news."

"I saw," I said.

"What the fuck happened?"

I closed my eyes. What happened? *What happened?* I tried to put it into words but I couldn't. What could I say? *I'm sorry, Viv, but I've kind of fallen in love with the men who tormented and brainwashed you and Ryth. No, more than that...I've fucked them. I've fucked them so many times and I still want to fuck them.*

How fucked up was that?

"So so much." My words were husky.

But there was no answer, not for a second.

"Viv?"

"It's London," the deep snarl came through. "Where the fuck are you?"

I wrenched my eyes open. Cold plunged all the way down through me. I tried to speak, but I couldn't. Had the bastard been waiting just to ambush me?

"I'm sorry." I caught her murmur in the background.

My cheeks burned hotter the longer I sat there...but I couldn't speak.

Instead, I stared into those dark, unflinching eyes as the mountain stood in front of me. I hadn't even heard him enter.

Not. One. Damn. Sound. I should have—I lifted my gaze—especially for a man his size.

He knew, didn't he? He'd known I'd call and he wanted to know who.

He never looked away, just searched my eyes with a dangerous, manic stare as London's growl filled my ears.

"Tell me right now and we're coming to get you. We're done with this. Do you hear me, Helene? *We're done.* Tell me where you are and you're coming home."

The mountain flicked his focus from one of my eyes to the other. Then he slowly lifted his hand.

My stomach dropped. It was more than being ambushed by my sister's lover. It was guilt at being caught by the man who'd risked his life to save me.

His fingers were open, waiting, instantly returning me to the back of that truck. The one where he demanded my trust...now it was my turn to trust his. I reached out and handed the cell to him.

"Helene?" London's deep bark echoed again. *"I will fucking destroy them if they have you prisoner, do you hear me? Tell me where you are and me and the Sons—"*

"Deep Valley Road. Six-point-nine clicks from the turn off to High Valley Mountain. We'll be waiting."

He spoke quietly, distinctly...then hung up the call.

I couldn't move.

"I've made you breakfast," he said carefully. "But you might want to shower before your family gets here."

With that, he just turned around and walked silently out of the room.

I unleashed a moan as I caught the stairs creaking under his weight and kicked off the blankets. Of course he knew...he was a ghost, wasn't he?

I pushed out of the bed and headed for the bathroom, trying to mentally prepare for the onslaught that was my family. Thank God Riven and the others weren't here.

The thought of London, the Sons, and my sister being in the same place as the men they loathed made me tremble with dread. It would be all-out fucking war. Even with just Hunter, it was bound to get bloody.

I stepped into the bathroom and closed the door.

Steam still lingered in the air. The mirror was still cloudy. One swipe of my hand and I stared at the deep purple bruising on the side of my mouth, and on my neck...a remnant of that bastard in the back of the truck.

There was no hiding what had happened.

I shifted my gaze to the unhinged, panicked look in my eye.

Not from Vivienne.

She'd know instantly.

"Fuck," I whispered. "This is going to be bad."

SEVEN

Riven

I STEPPED CLOSER. "DID YOU HEAR ME? *I SAID, TAKE ME—*"

"I heard you," the big, bearded motherfucker cut me off.

Coulter's guard rolled around on the floor, gripping his foot and still screaming like a banshee. I ignored him, fixing my focus on the only person who could get me what I wanted.

Helene.

Thomas stepped forward, his eyes panicked and desperate as he looked from me to Hunter's man. Kane was there, pale and drawn. Still, he forced himself from that bed for one reason and one reason alone...*Helene.*

"Well?"

"No," the gruff bastard answered.

"*No?*" Rage burned through me as I tore my arm out of the soldier's grip and spun, making my way out of the room where he held Coulter's man prisoner. "Then I'll call every fucking news station I can. Let's see how quiet my *brother* wants to be then."

I snatched a long steel crowbar as I passed the bench in the workshop, heading for the open warehouse door until what felt like steel shackles wrapped around my arm and yanked me backwards...hard.

Only, I'd known it was coming.

I swung the bar, driving it across the big bastard's throat as he slammed into the wall. "You don't seem to be listening," I snarled, bearing down on the bar. "So I'll make myself clear. *I want Helene King.* Anyone who stands in my way is *not* my ally."

Dark eyes glinted as he fixed on mine.

I'd kill him...and anyone else who stood in my way. I swallowed, feeling a flinch at the thought of that.

"You want to see her?" he choked, leaning into the damn bar. "Then...*let...me...go.*"

I inhaled and fixed my gaze on him. *Do the right fucking thing here.*

"I'll take you to your brother...in the morning. First, we sleep."

My lips curled. But Thomas was there, driving his hand against my chest. "Easy," he urged. *"Easy."*

I slapped Thomas's hand away, desperate to heave myself at the motherfucker once more.

"You want to see her?" Thomas warned. *"I want to see her too.* But there's only one way it's happening." He shot a glance over his shoulder. "And that's through him."

He was right.

I knew it.

Still, I didn't like being at the mercy of another...especially one of my brother's henchmen. "Fine," I snarled, stepping away. "You want to wait till morning, then we will."

Cold moved through me. Cold and a numbness I'd never felt before.

I felt it now...and had done ever since she was taken away in that truck.

I turned, dropped the crowbar in my grasp. It hit the concrete floor with a *CLANG*. I didn't stop, not even to see if my brother followed. I just walked out of the warehouse, glancing at the truck as I passed. A nagging feeling wore at me. Something about this felt...*off*.

Why keep the truck?

Or the guard, for that matter?

They'd killed the others.

Hell, the shootout at The Order was probably all over the news by now.

I glanced up at the stars sparkling overhead and felt a heavy pain in the center of my chest. Was she scared? Was Hunter at least being fucking civil to her? Or did he have her in some goddamn cell of his own?

Christ. I rubbed my knuckles against the ache.

I couldn't deal with this...this *not knowing*.

Was she hurt?

Was she bleeding?

She sure as hell wasn't okay in her head. I'd know because...

I'd done that.

I winced and strode toward the main building, right through the open door. Heads snapped my way, widened eyes fixed on me from the few Daughters who were still awake. I never even looked at them, just headed straight for the kitchen.

Coffee...

I needed coffee.

And to think.

I'd find us a way out of this if it was the last thing I did.

I grabbed a mug and poured the black, thick-looking brew into the damn thing. The moment I did, all I could hear was the *crack* of a gunshot. Then in my mind I replayed the moment Walker had fallen with a *thud* to the filthy concrete beside me.

He'd been loyal.

He'd been so goddamn loyal. I braced my hands on the edge of the counter and rocked forward. *Get away from me, Mel. Why the hell are you always around me. Can't you see I want to be on my own?*

A boy's voice echoed in my head, replaying the words which haunted me.

No.

I shook my head.

This wasn't happening.

Not now.

I'll find a way out of this. I'll—

"It's not your fault."

I slowly lifted my head as the icy bite of rage returned. "What the fuck did you say to me?"

Thomas stood in the entrance to the kitchen, watching me. "I said…"

I crossed the floor, grabbed him by the shirt, and yanked him forward. "Say one more goddamn thing and it'll be the last time you speak. Do you understand?"

His shirt was twisted in my grasp, but he never fought me. He knew that was pointless.

"You don't say that to me, got it?" I shoved him away, my pulse roaring in my ears as I repeated. "You don't say that. Not to me…ever."

I pushed him aside and stormed out, leaving behind the coffee I'd just poured. I needed to get away, away from him and those fucking words. They were *not* what I needed, now or ever. He could save his shrink talk for his goddamn patients.

Get away from me, Mel. JUST GET AWAY!

The thud of my boots was like fists against my chest as I strode through the building, searching for a place to hide. Dull lights flickered, calling me. I stopped at the small communications room, glancing along the bank of monitors to the three computers alight.

The big bastard watching the cameras lifted his head and glared at me.

"Let him through." The guttural command came from behind me.

I glanced over my shoulder to the bearded asshole in charge, the one who'd mere minutes ago had a steel bar across his throat. He hated me, that I knew. Still, he glanced at the merc behind the monitors. "I'm trusting you here, Cruz. Don't make me regret it."

He lingered for a heartbeat then turned and walked away, leaving me behind.

Why the fuck would he do that?

I winced, hating that heavy feeling in the back of my throat. The mercenary behind the monitor turned back to what he'd been doing, leaving me to walk in behind him. There were dozens of private chat rooms open on a screen in front of him.

Taste of Paradise.

Harvey's perfect pies.

The Auction House.

Those names I knew, chat rooms for sick bastards like Hale. Men who bought, sold, and traded women like a commodity. But there were some names I didn't recognize.

The Machine.

The Night Shift.

House Rules.

Those chat rooms were buzzing. I scowled and leaned closer.

Mr. Bright: Mine are awol. Devices not responding. I have a search and find team out but so far, nothing.

"What's that about?" I nodded to the screen.

The asshole turned slowly, meeting my stare, not answering. "He said you can stay here, not that I answer to you."

A twitch came at the corner of my eye.

Harvey Osborn: Mine too. Someone is commanding the Sons. We need to find out who.

The Sons?

A pang tore across my chest. I glanced from the screen to the chatty bastard in front of me. "You're tracking Sons?"

He turned away. Typing out a response.

Mr. Davis: Mine haven't responded for over twelve hours. Does anyone have any information on who they might've been talking to, or where they've been meeting? Any information would be appreciated.

Heat filled my cheeks as I slowly sat down, mesmerized by the flow of information that was coming from comment after comment. The Sons were never spoken about, not even from Hale. They felt like a hidden secret, from the orphanages to the training camps they were forced to endure.

I'd asked about them, but I never pushed.

Because they weren't the target. No, Hale's black ops site was.

"How many are out there?" I asked softly.

He glanced my way. "Sons or buyers?"

Buyers? I winced at the term. My voice turned husky. "Sons."

He gave a shrug and answered, leaning forward to pull up a file on the screen beside him. "Who knows, a lot of them didn't survive."

I stared at the image that appeared. The place wasn't a training camp, it was a concentration camp. Emaciated young boys stood dressed in baggy soldier's clothes staring back at me with unhinged looks. Two stood out from the rest, one small and skinny with piercing blue eyes, the other slightly bigger, his dark eyes glinting with rage. His lips were curled, his fists clenched. He stood slightly in front of his brother, protecting him.

I know them.

The words rose.

"The main orphanage," the merc beside me murmured. "Sure glad the bitch who ran that fucking place is dead now."

I jerked my gaze to him.

He stared at the image on the screen. "That woman sure as hell didn't deserve to live."

A shiver raced through my chest. I turned back to the chatter, drawn into the information that came. The more that did, the more the merc beside me took notice. He punched in information, pulling up maps and making data points. Typing furiously as I watched.

Until it hit me.

I winced, scowled, and looked away.

"He's supposed to find our goddamn sister. Not boys we don't know."

"Hunter is right about you...you're a goddamn moron."

I flinched and swung my gaze back. "What the fuck did you just say to me?"

"Look." He stopped typing and turned to me. "These...Sons are programmed killers. Ones more brutal and dangerous than *anything* we've ever seen. Now they're suddenly missing just when Hale stages his death. Why do you think that is? And more importantly...where do you think they are?"

My chest tightened as fear plunged deep. "He has them. He has them all."

"Bingo, Einstein." He turned back to the chatter and started typing, asking more questions, pretending to be just like them.

Like we had.

That sickening, festering feeling grew inside me. This whole thing was even viler than I knew...and I knew plenty. Hours passed by as I watched the screen. Chat after chat, names and information of all those killers on the loose.

Someone was behind it all.

If not Hale, then who?

The merc beside me yawned and stretched, then slowly rose. "It's six a.m. Don't you have somewhere to be?"

Six a.m?

I glanced at the time on the screen, sure enough...six oh two. But as I rose, something tugged me. A knowing of some kind. This was all connected...our sister, Hale, and the Sons. I reached down, grabbed a pen, and scribbled my number on a scrap of paper next to his desk.

"This is my cell. Will you keep me informed if you find anything?"

"If Hunter wants me to, sure."

"Riven," I answered. "My name's Riven."

"Riven," he repeated slowly, his brows pinching as though he wasn't expecting any of this.

Turns out, neither was I.

I gave a nod and left him behind, slowly making my way out of the comms room and back through the building. Hunter's men looked up at me as they sat, watching the group of Daughters huddled asleep on the floor in the corner.

I looked at them.

Their eyes closed.

Faces serene.

Jesus, this fucking thing was a goddamn mess.

I looked away to find Thomas as he stepped out of the kitchen, his eyes red and bloodshot and fixed on me. My throat thickened with all the things I wanted to say. Sorry, just wasn't enough. I knew that. Still, I had no way to start. Maybe one day I would.

I glanced at the brightening sky.

Just not today.

EIGHT

Riven

___

IT WAS LATE BY THE TIME WE HEADED OUT. LATER THAN I wanted it to be at least. I sat in the passenger seat, staring straight ahead as the bearded bastard drove slower than a fucking eighty-year-old beside me. My thoughts were divided, half savage about the idea of seeing her and half stuck on the image of that training camp they'd inflicted on the Sons.

They weren't Sons though, were they? They were weapons. Men bred and designed to hunt and destroy.

But what they really were bred for was the Daughters.

Another *'shipment of Assets is missing'*? My own voice invaded.

I still remembered the way Hale had shaken his head, even though the truck carrying fifteen Daughters hadn't been heard of for the last ten days.

Not missing, Hale had answered. *There is nowhere they can hide that the Sons wouldn't find them.*

Nowhere they can hide...or be hidden, he meant.

The Sons somehow felt the Daughters, that I knew. How? Now that was another worry altogether. I didn't know if it was altered DNA. I sure wouldn't put it past Hale and those slimy eels he swam with. They could've very well infected those women he'd used for breeding. Those...like my sister.

Get away from me, Mel! Why are you always around me? Can't you see I want to be left alone?

I looked out the window at the endless pine forest as the screams of an eleven-year-old resounded in my head. It was my fault she'd gone missing, my fault she'd been snatched right under our noses. My fault Melody had walked off, sulking, to play at the park down the street from us...alone.

Just like it was my fault Helene was alone.

My fault.

My fault.

My...goddamn...fault.

That ache throbbed in the back of my skull as I stared at the trees. The moment the four-wheel drive started to climb, my pulse flipped and stuttered. A tightness lashed across my chest. I winced and rubbed the ache, desperate to keep my shit together.

"Riven?" Thomas murmured.

I swallowed hard and kept looking straight ahead. "I'm fine."

I wasn't fine. None of this was fine.

Because I couldn't fucking breathe.

I stabbed the button, winding down the window to suck in the cool, pine scent. All it did was trigger me more.

Bang!

The sound echoed, replaying the moment Walker had hit the ground beside me. Blood was neon red against the white of his skull, neon and gruesome and sickening. That cinch tightened around my chest again. *Jesus fucking Christ.*

"*Riven,*" Thomas's snarl behind me was urgent.

I turned my head and the outside world bled to gray until the vehicle turned toward the overcrowded trees along the side of the road. Tires crunched, then slipped into the ruts as the gray Explorer rose. Through the overhanging branches, a camouflaged steel gate slid back.

"I'll be damned," Thomas murmured from the backseat.

My grip tightened around the armrest as we surged forward, leaving the mountain road behind. But this wasn't another private road into nowhere...it was a compound. A massive Hummer sat parked in front of a building which looked to be some command center. I stared at the huge, multi-story house that sat nestled between two towering rock faces of the mountain. Sunlight glinted off the windows, making me catch my breath.

That sure as hell was no prison.

I was already yanking the door handle before the Explorer rolled to a stop. Shadows spilled out of the doorway to the mansion. Shadows that moved. My brother strode forward, dressed in khakis and a scowl, the same one he always wore. But I didn't care about him. He wasn't who I'd come here to see.

My breath caught at the sight of her. It took all my strength not to slam my boots against the ground and lunge toward her. Car doors closed with a thud behind me. But I was already searching her face as I strode toward her.

"Riven," she called my name, sounding unhinged and desperate.

I'm here. I wanted to call out. *It's okay, I'm right here.*

Until Hunter's massive hand hit the middle of my chest, stopping me cold.

"Uh-uh," he murmured and slowly turned his head to meet my gaze.

I flung his hand off, then stepped around the bastard.

But he just stepped back in my way.

"What the fuck do you think you're doing?" I snarled.

"Protecting her."

Rage seethed under the surface. "You want to say that again, *brother?*"

He held my stare, those unflinching brown eyes that looked so much like our sister's. "I said, *protecting her.*"

I looked past him, to the one I wanted, and lowered my voice. "You don't want to stand in my way right now."

He had no idea what he was dealing with. The things we'd done. The terror we'd endured. "It's okay, Trouble." I focused on her, searching the bruises on her face and the marks on her neck. "My brother and I are about to discuss this *privately.*"

But she shook her head, her eyes wide as she murmured. "You can't be here, Riven."

I froze. "What?"

She stepped around Hunter, grabbed my arm, and drove me backwards. "You can't *be here*. You have to go...all of you. You have to go *now!*"

I stumbled backwards, stunned.

Agony roared to the surface once more, dragging with it all the hate and the loathing, until I snapped out of it and yanked my arm from hers. "What the fuck is going on here?"

The faint sound of engines came somewhere behind us.

Helene whipped her gaze to the Explorer.

No...not the Explorer.

The growling engines that signaled someone else was arriving.

The sound of those engines grew louder, coming closer and closer to the compound.

The sun glinted off shimmering chrome, bouncing back to blind me. "Someone want to explain what the fuck is going on?"

Shadows and the brilliance. That's all I saw as another car pulled in hard beside the Explorer, kicking up dust as it came to a skidding stop.

Car doors were thrown open. I waited for the *slams*...but they never came. Instead...the slow, heavy thud of someone's boots staggering followed.

"Helene?" A woman cried out.

I stiffened, knowing that voice.

The one I heard in my goddamn nightmares.

"Wildcat...*wait!*"

I slowly turned, to find London St. James striding after a *very pregnant* Vivienne King, looking *very* pissed off. He took one look at me and lifted his hand to point a gun at my head. But it didn't matter, because he'd brought the entire fucking squad with him.

"Helene!" Came another female cry as Carven and Colt came behind London, both glaring at me.

The *Sons.*

The sight of them hit me hard. Colt's lips were curled in a snarl as his murderous brother, Carven, palmed a blade as he headed straight for me, ready to hurl it through the air and end me where I stood.

"Ryth!" Nick Banks roared as a slip of a woman rushed after Vivienne, both women heading for their sister. "For fuck's sake, *baby, WAIT!"*

His two pain in the ass brothers were hot on his trail. Caleb was right behind him, but it was Tobias Banks who slowed, a chilling fucking smirk aimed at me that made me regret a lot of my life's choices...

Including meeting him.

"Great," I muttered, taking a defensive step backwards as they all came for me. "This is just fucking great."

Helene jerked her gaze to mine, her arms wrapped around both her sisters as all six fucking males raced forward. I stumbled backwards, swinging a fist a second before my shirt was grabbed and the cold bite of a gun muzzle was pressed against the side of my head.

"Say goodbye you fucking bastard," London growled.

"Easy!" Helene yelled. I barely heard her through all the heavy fucking breathing in my ear.

"London..." she roared. "Nick...Christ's sake, *Tobias...I said STOP! STOOPPPP!*"

They did. I shoved and bucked, desperate to get out of their grasps.

"Don't hurt him." Helene headed my way, putting herself between us. Didn't she know these men were fucking ruthless?

"Don't." I surged forward and grabbed her around the waist. "Don't do this, you could get hurt."

I held her as she grabbed hold of my arm. As dangerous as that was...as *precarious* as it was with my life teetering on the edge of extinction, touching her was my *everything*. I turned my head to her, pushing all their hate and rage at me to the back of my mind as she slowly looked at me.

"Don't hurt him," she said slowly and loudly, searching my stare. "Because he's with me."

"What...the...fuck?"

I think London said it. It could've been Nick. I didn't know, nor did I care.

All I cared about was her.

I took a step closer to her. A flash of steel caught the sunlight. *Thunk.* Barely a flicker. That's all it was...*a glint,* and I lowered my gaze to stare down at the knife embedded in the ground right at the edge of my boot.

My throat turned arid at the sight as I lifted my gaze. Piercing blue eyes met mine. I'd never been a fearful man, not even when I'd looked death in the face. But *the Sons,* they chilled me in a way no one else had. My throat throbbed and ached, but I forced myself to focus on her.

I lifted my hand, hating how my fingers trembled as I brushed the hair from the side of her face. "I thought I'd lost you, Trouble," I murmured.

"The fuck you are!" Came a woman's scream.

It all happened in slow motion. Still, we were helpless to stop it as Vivienne launched herself at her sister, grabbing her arm and yanking her out of my hold.

"WHAT THE FUCK ARE YOU DOING?" she roared.

London was wide-eyed but unmoving.

Both Carven and Colt grabbed at me again. I shoved and swung, kicking myself for not having a weapon. Not that one would've saved me...just maybe slowed them down, or probably pissed them off even more.

One of the two.

"Viv, *stop!*" Helene grabbed her as Colt wrapped the tree-trunk he had for an arm around my throat from behind me.

And London St. James moved closer.

I thrashed in the bastard's arms as both my brothers twitched, helpless to do a damn thing other than watch.

"I think it's time you explain yourself," London demanded. "Before your blood is spilled all over this nice driveway."

"It's *not what you think!*" I choked out.

"Oh yeah?" Shadows spilled across his face as London stepped closer. "I *think* it's *exactly* what I think."

He didn't turn his head.

Didn't look at Helene, nor did he look at anyone else. Just lifted that gun and took aim. "There is nothing you can say that will spare this monster's life...his or his brothers'."

Once again, I was here.

Looking death in its righteous face.

The last time, I'd felt empty. Hollow. *Alone.*

I wasn't alone now.

No...now I had her.

I gave the bastard a slow nod.

Ready.

I'm ready.

"Last words?" St. James murmured, those dark eyes glinting as they fixed on mine.

"I love him."

I stiffened, then slowly turned my head...

As did everyone.

Helene just stood there, her spine straight, her beautiful face a mess of cuts and bruises as she stared at London and everyone and repeated the words I'd take to my goddamn grave. *"I. Love. Him."*

NINE

Helene
___

"*Noooo.*" Vivienne unleashed a wounded sound, taking a slow, wobbly step toward me. "You did *not* just say what I thought you said."

Anger. Heartache.

I saw it all in the faces of my family.

Every. Single. One. Of. Them.

The family I'd so desperately wanted.

And suffered to protect.

Now looked at me with revulsion.

"What the fuck did *you* just say?" London swung that glare my way.

I wanted to cringe at the bite of his tone. Even hearing the words myself sounded so fucking absurd. No, not absurd. There wasn't a word for this betrayal. Not at the hands of the same men who'd tortured and brainwashed both my sisters.

There was no amount of explaining how something so fucked up like this could happen.

But it had happened.

The harder I stared at the horror written all over their faces, the more of them I really saw, like the way London reflexively moved toward Vivienne and the way Nick, Caleb, and Tobias all looked to Ryth to gauge her emotions. It made me feel that desperate longing even more.

They loved my sisters.

To the death and beyond.

And I knew that in some careful way, they felt some loyalty for me too. But it wasn't love, was it? It wasn't the facing off with those who hate you the most kind of love. Or falling to your knees with a gun pressed against your head kind of love.

The kind that killed to protect.

And to avenge.

I had that love. I felt it...and saw it. I looked at Riven. That cold, demented stare was fixed on me, begging for me not to turn my back on him...or us, *all of us.* A flicker of desire surged through all the guilt and the heartache as I faced down London St. James, the Banks boys, and finally, my sisters. My very pissed off sisters.

"I said, I love him."

Vivienne reeled back on her heels. She looked like she was about to collapse on the spot. But Ryth...Ryth just looked at me with that haunted, fragile stare. I knew that maybe right this moment I was ruining it all.

"Please," I whispered, leaving Riven behind as I stepped toward her. "Please hear us out. Once you understand why this has happened you can—"

She turned her head away.

Just like that.

One swivel and she gave me her back.

Agony roared through me. A montage of all the fucking things I'd done for them punched me in the chest. All the men I'd killed to protect them. The lies I'd told. The life I'd stopped living the moment our father told me the cruel goddamn world we'd been born into.

A world of women who were sold and men who were tortured. None of that had hit me. None of that had made any sense to me until that day when I was nine and dad showed me two images. Two little girls, a few years younger than me. One with unruly long hair and a wild gleam in her eye even then, and another of a smaller girl, shyly hiding behind her mother as her father took the snapshot.

Our father.

The same one who'd told me that was why he left me all the time. To return to them. To protect them...and try to find a way into the nest that was The Order. He did leave me. He walked out and I sat there alone. A guard would drop in now and then, a housekeeper would restock the food and cook meals.

But they never spoke to me.

They never cared.

I was utterly, and cruelly, alone.

"I never once asked for anything." The words left my lips. "Not in all the years I fought for you. I never asked for anything, only for you to know who I was and who our father was. I bled for you. I *spilled* blood *for you.* I never wanted anything in return. But I'm asking now. No...I'm *demanding.* Hear us out. Try to put yourself in my shoes. Try to see things from my—"

"No" she said. That faint word was barely a whisper. "I won't. Not *ever.*"

She took a step, walking away from me.

That hurt me most of all.

How someone I loved could just cut me off like that without ever knowing...

"They raped me."

She stopped cold.

"There were too many of them. I fought. I fought so hard. But they were stronger than me...so they took what they wanted. And the *only* ones who came for me were Riven and Kane...and Thomas."

She slowly turned. Tears shimmered in her eyes.

I took a step, my stomach so heavy it felt like a boulder inside. "And before you say something like I shouldn't have been there in the first place, I want you to look at me, and at Vivienne, and I want you to ask yourself what would you do to save me? How far would you go? What would you do?" I gave a soft jerk of my head toward our sister. "Go on. If her future was at stake, if there was even a slim chance that you could find a way to stop all of this fucking hell once and for all. I want you to tell me you wouldn't have put yourself in harm's way."

She stared at Vivienne with those tears shimmering in her eyes.

But she couldn't say it. One look at Vivienne and I knew she couldn't say it either.

"You would protect her, wouldn't you?" I asked. "You'd do whatever you could."

"Yes" she said softly.

"And me?" My heart hammered. "Would you do the same for me."

"*Yes,*" she hissed, wrenching a savage glare my way. "Yes, I would do the same."

I risked another step. "Would you hurt someone? Would you hurt many someones? Would you lie and cheat? Would you lose yourself and become a...a monster?"

She flinched, those blue-green eyes darkening. A tremor rose inside me. She knew what I was about to say. She knew. Still, she answered. "I don't know."

Vivienne looked her way.

"Would you, Viv? Would you become a monster?"

I didn't even have to ask. I knew she would. Because she *had* become a monster. Colt stepped toward her protectively, drawing her focus.

"Yes," my sister answered. "Yes, I'd become a monster for those I loved."

"So would they," I murmured, and looked at Riven. "The most savage, ruthless and soulless bastards that ever existed."

"You're seriously not trying to blame love for the things these men did, are you?" London snarled.

I stilled, hating this. But I looked at Riven, then Kane and Thomas...and lastly Hunter. This secret wasn't mine to expose. Not after all they'd done to protect it.

"Tell them," Riven croaked.

Kane gave a slow nod, same as Thomas.

"Do it," The Priest looked away as he spoke.

"Hunter?" I asked, looking at the towering man hidden behind the mask, who'd barely made a sound. He met my stare, searching my eyes. One slow nod. That's all it took for me to turn back to my family, who still stared from face to face.

"Hale has their sister," I said carefully.

I barely knew their secret and yet here I was, taking a rusted hatchet to a festering wound.

"He *what*?" London jerked his glare at Riven.

But Riven's skin was pale, and his lips had gone ashen.

"Her name is Melody." Kane stepped forward. "She was taken from the park where we all played as children when she was six years old. The police were called, then her name and her face were splashed all across the news, but they never found her. Not one person came forward saying they had seen anything that day. It was just...silence. It destroyed our parents. Our father ended up packing his bags and leaving in the middle of the night. We were alone with our mother, who slowly sank into depression and even though she had the three of us left to love her, she ended up taking her own life three years later. We were shipped around from one foster family to another, until finally we were old enough to track each other down. Only then did we discover the truth. There *was* information about that day. A number of witnesses had come forward, each describing three men wearing black suits who came and took her from the swings, pushing her into a car they had nearby, and drove away. One of those witnesses even took down the license plate. But all that was swept under the rug. All because of some twisted cult, one that would eventually change under the vile rule of one man and become—"

"The Order," London whispered.

Kane gave a slow nod.

"Holy shit."

"Yes," Kane murmured, his voice breaking. "Holy shit. It took us years to find her. When we did, we were gutted. She'd been brainwashed and tortured. We were older then, so we tried to infiltrate and get her out of there. But the night we planned to invade and get her, the compound mysteriously burned down. She wasn't dead. That we knew. We picked apart those ashes, searching every inch of that place. But they were all gone. Every single one of them. There were whispers that they were taken by a man called Haelstrom Hale. A man closed off from the rest of the world. A man who made his own world. One so corrupt and vile that it rips out everything that's good inside you and corrupts it."

"You did all this to find her?" Vivienne wrenched a glare toward Riven. *"YOU did to US what they did to your sister?"*

His eyes widened, there was a sickening look of desperation. One that physically hurt me to see. I swallowed hard.

"I don't want you to forgive me," he murmured, his tone biting. "You could never give it to me and I will not ask for it. Not from any of you."

It was me he looked at.

"All I ask is that you put aside any hate you have for me and give me a chance. Just one chance. Please..." his throat thickened until the words were a rasp. "I'm begging you."

"Jesus fucking Christ," London spat and looked away.

There was disgust in London's stare underneath the pity.

"We all want the same things."

I flinched and jerked my gaze to Hunter as he spoke. Somehow, the rest of my family listened. The gruff voice was used to commands, but I could see he tempered that now.

"We are here for one reason and one reason alone. We want to destroy The Order and every man or woman involved. We also want to do it by protecting each other. We can do that...*if* we work together."

"You want us to work *with* you?" Tobias stepped closer, moving like a damn street fighter.

But Hunter never flinched as T came up and stopped in front of him. Tobias was shorter, by a lot. But experience told me he was hotheaded and dangerous.

"Yes." Hunter met his stare and answered carefully.

"And why the fuck should we trust a man who won't even show his face?"

"Because I know of a way to get to them," he answered, and slowly lifted his gaze. "Which is more than any of you have put together."

The mountain had pricked London's attention.

"But we only have a limited time. I have a plan. It might just work. If nothing else, it'll get us in the door."

"In the door *where?*" London demanded.

But Hunter didn't answer. "Before I tell you anything I have to have your word. *All* of you."

"Fuck that," Carven muttered. "I say we take the information for ourselves and we hunt them down."

Riven flinched as he looked at the son. He opened his mouth to say something...but in the end, he closed it again.

"You want us to trust you," London started. "And yet you give us nothing?"

"Basically...yes."

London shook his head. "We don't even know you. Why the fuck would you expect us to put our lives in your hands?"

Hunter just turned his focus to me. "Because this is our last opportunity. After this, the black ops site disappears and takes Hale with it. If it was just his death I cared about, I wouldn't be standing here asking you this. But it's not. There are new players in town. Men like Julius Harmon and his foul fucking commander Coulter."

I stiffened at the name. My knees trembled so hard I could barely keep it together.

Riven's gaze whipped my way.

But he wasn't the only one. Kane surged forward, then Thomas followed.

"It's okay." Riven gripped my chin and turned my focus to him. "Look at me. I will kill that man before he is anywhere near you, do you hear me? You're safe now. You're safe."

There were no hugs, no gestures of comfort.

Only the promise to wipe that man from the face of the earth.

That's all I needed.

"You good?"

I gave a slow nod, then slowly became aware they all stared at us.

"Harmon and his men are in charge of splintering The Order," Hunter continued. "They'll divide and go underground, maybe we're already too late to stop that from happening, I don't know. But I do know this. They want their last shipment of Daughters...and they want it bad."

"Last shipment?" Carven snarled. "You want us to *deliver* them to those fucking bastards?"

"Yes," Hunter answered. "That's exactly what I'm saying."

"How?" London was the one who asked the question that shone in everyone's eyes.

"Simple." Hunter strode forward, heading for the Hummer he'd brought me in.

He rounded the back, yanked open the door, and returned instantly, his arms full of khaki green.

The uniforms hit the ground with a *thud*, skull masks bouncing as they settled on top.

"We use the guard we kept alive. Make him give up the location and we give them what they want...a truck full of women...*and us.*"

London and the others stared at the pile. It was Tobias that strode forward, picked up a gruesome mask and dropped it. "Why us? You have a whole team, right? You had to have to pull any of this off. So why invite us here? Why not do it yourself and be done?"

"Because this doesn't belong to them. This belongs to *us*. Our blood is what ties us to this. Our family. Our souls. You will *never* sleep a full night's rest again. You'll always be looking over your shoulder, wondering not *if* but *when* they're coming to take what's yours once more. You want that? You want a life without knowing?"

"London," Vivienne hissed.

Her hands were around her belly and her eyes shimmered with tears.

He moved instantly, grabbing her around her waist as the Sons watched with ruthless desperation.

"Tell me what to do," London answered, staring at her, then turned to Hunter. "And I'll do it. Whatever it takes, this ends... and it ends now."

TEN

Helene
_____

IT ENDS NOW.

Those words hung heavy in the air, weighed down by the desperation we all felt to finish this once and for all. But still, my family never looked at me...no, they never looked at *us*.

Riven shifted against me. The warmth of his body brushed against my arm as Tobias lifted a mask in the air and stared at the gruesome white skull.

"We have the truck," Hunter continued, his gaze fixed on that mask. Somehow, I knew he was aware of every move of Riven against me. He scowled as he spoke. "And we have the Daughters. All those men care about is their *'assets'*. We rock up with them in the back and they'll throw open the gates and let us through."

"With a truck full of bullet holes?" Riven muttered beside me.

Hunter never even glanced at his brother, but I heard the bite. "Which is being repaired as we speak. All it needs to do is get us through those gates."

"Seems risky," Caleb declared, glancing at London.

But London's dark eyes glinted. I knew that look...I'd seen it before. That ruthless hunger. That mindless rage. "It'll work." He said and slowly looked at Viv. "They want the Daughters, so the last thing they'll be looking at is the truck."

"And how are we supposed to account for the fact that they've been missing for the last...what, twenty-four hours?" Carven snarled.

"All taken care of." Hunter met the Son's stare. "We've mirrored their tracking signal, moving them around to a point where just two hours ago, they dropped out completely. When the guard we have calls, they'll be so frantic to get them into the compound, they won't care."

"And this compound is where Hale is?" London asked.

But it was Riven who answered. "No. This is where Julius Harmon and his men are located."

London turned on him, scowling. "So where the fuck is Hale?"

Silence filled the space.

No one knew.

"Do we even know for sure if the bastard is still alive?" Nick scanned every face.

There was silence for a second.

"I've had text messages, but that's it," Riven answered. I knew even revealing that was hard for him. Riven wasn't one to share information...or anything else.

"So no *real* proof of life?" London stared at Riven.

The Principal gave a shake of his head.

"Jesus," Caleb muttered. "This is a goddamn twisted ball of knots."

"Which we're unraveling one strand at a time," Nick finished.

"If you know of another way," Hunter said, "I'm all ears."

That was the problem. They didn't. No one did.

No one had a goddamn idea when it came to Hale or his festering pit of vipers. The only man who did wasn't here. A pang of pain tore through my chest. No, it seemed like my father had far more important things to take care of.

That icy nagging feeling wore at the pit of my stomach.

"So when does this go down?" London asked.

"Tomorrow, midnight. That should give them enough time to tear the city apart looking for them when we drive calmly through their gates."

I could see it now. The truck full of Daughters and us pulling into an empty compound after every mercenary in the state had been hired to find us.

"We'll be ready," Vivienne answered.

London's gaze snapped her way, as did Colt and Carven's.

"No," London shook his head. "No goddamn way. You're sitting this one out, Wildcat."

"Sure I am." She gave him a soft smile and reached up to ruffle his hair before she wrapped her arms around him. Those dark brown eyes cut my way. Under that soft, agreeable tone was a look of pure rage. My sister wasn't about to sit back and just let this all happen, pregnant or not. She was going to see this through...one way or another.

"*Both* of you are," Nick glared at Ryth.

My sisters looked at each other.

"Sure, Nick," Ryth answered. "Whatever you say, honey."

Nick just scowled as Riven shifted to the side and looked my way.

"Open your mouth, Riven, and I will tear your tongue out," I muttered.

He stayed quiet. Smart man.

Only, as my sisters' lovers crowded around them, I felt a sense of...emptiness. How could I feel complete when the one person I'd loved my entire life wasn't here?

"Did Dad say anything?" I asked.

I caught the wince from Ryth. She was the youngest and more connected to our father than Viv was. So, if anyone knew anything, it was her.

"He...uh. He said he had other things to take care of." Ryth murmured.

"Things that are more important than me, I'm guessing," I responded, swallowing the agony which filled my chest.

My father's absence shouldn't have hurt as much as it did. After all...I should be used to it. But the truth was, it cut all the way to my heart.

"I'm sure there is a—" Kane started, until I shot a glare his way.

"Save it," I answered. "I've heard it all before."

I turned around and started walking, leaving them to stare after me. The faint sound of their voices came, someone even called my name. But I couldn't speak around the lump in my throat. Tears blurred the gray Explorer in front of me, until soft footsteps sounded.

A shadow fell, covering my path. I felt him before I saw him, towering, silent.

"You don't have to worry about me," I rasped.

Still, the mountain said nothing, just stood there beside me, staring at the same glint on the Explorer's grill as I did. Tears spilled, running down my cheeks. We stood there while the others talked amongst themselves until I swiped my tears away. "Fucking family, huh?"

I glanced his way.

He was waiting, seizing my stare as he gave a slow nod. "Fucking family."

I turned back to the others, watching as they gathered themselves. Viv gripped Ryth in a massive hug that had her molding her body around Viv's belly. Both turned to me as I neared.

"I'm sorry." Ryth's voice shook. "I didn't want to tell you."

"It's fine." I wrapped one arm around her and the other around Viv. Whatever our father failed at, he did one thing right and that was bringing all three of us together.

"Then we have our plan." London reached out and grasped Caleb's hand in his grip before turning to Nick and Tobias. "Call me if anything changes."

He spoke to them as though they were the ones planning it all, never once directing the conversation to Riven or Hunter.

Nick just glanced our way.

"Sure," Hunter muttered. "If anything changes, you'll be the first to know."

They left then. My stomach clenched as I watched them climb into their cars and drive away. I waved to my sisters until they were gone and we were alone. *Fuck...we were alone.*

I turned around, to find Kane and Thomas both peeking at Riven and watching Hunter carefully as he gathered the masks and the camouflage uniforms from the ground and strode toward the main house.

"Riven," Kane called. "You ready to go?"

The hairs on the back of my neck rose as Riven stared after Hunter, then muttered something savage under his breath and followed him.

"Fuck," Thomas muttered. "That can't be good."

No...

No, it can't be.

We all took off, chasing after the other two. By the time we yanked open the front door and raced inside, Riven's snarl echoed through the house.

"What fucking game are you playing here?"

I winced at the danger in his tone. We tore past the entryway and through the living room before we found them. Hunter had stopped, his arms still laden with the mess of masks and uniforms. But he didn't answer, just stepped around Riven when he stepped in his way.

Neither of them was moving or allowing the other to pass.

"You don't want to do this, Riven," Hunter warned.

"Oh yeah?" The hint of insanity in Riven's tone sent a shiver along my spine. "I think I do, brother. I think I do *very fucking much.*"

We all gathered around them. Hunter looked our way, but not Riven. His focus was on the mountain in front of him. Hunter turned and tossed the pile of uniforms to the floor in the corner of the room. "You want to do this, then let's fucking do this."

Riven let out a bark of laughter. One that quickly turned into a snarl as Hunter glanced my way.

"You fucking look at her like you want something, brother," Riven warned. "Been watching too many live feeds, I see."

A jolt tore through me. All I'd seen was the image of me and Kane on the screen in the comms room. He had been watching me, that I knew, but now what? He *wanted me?*

"So let me help you out here." Riven took a step closer to his brother.

"Riven," Kane warned. "No."

But The Principal paid him no mind. Instead, he stared the mountain in the eyes. "You wouldn't know what to do with a woman like that."

"And what's that," Hunter lowered his head. "*Beat her?*"

There was a twitch in the corner of Riven's eye.

"Or maybe handcuff her to my sofa so I can rape her," Hunter continued, glaring at him through the mask. "How about that, brother? Is that what a woman like Helene deserves?"

Riven's cheeks burned bright red. "No," he murmured, then glanced my way. "But it's what she likes."

The low snarl that rumbled from Hunter sent goosebumps along my arms.

Everyone turned toward me. But Riven was the one to move first as he crossed the room, flanking my side to stop at my back. "Isn't that right, Trouble?"

Hunter scowled, looking at me. He wanted me to be outraged, to slap Riven hard across the cheek as he gripped my throat, his commanding growl hitting me right between the thighs. "Tell him." His grip tightened. "Tell him how wet you were strapped to my sofa, how you came so fucking hard over and over again. How you..." he turned his gaze to mine. "Like to be controlled."

"Riven, careful," Kane warned.

"You drugged her, programmed her." Hunter clenched his fists. "She doesn't love you, she can't."

Riven's focus was fixed on me. "Oh yeah." He lifted his hand from my throat and brushed his thumb across my lips. "Why don't you tell me why?"

"Because she deserves better...better than you."

Riven just smirked. "Now that I can't argue with. So are you going to tell him, Trouble?"

"Tell him what?" My words were a raspy whisper.

He leaned down. "How fucking wet you are just thinking about me pinning your hands against the wall and licking that beautiful cunt until you buck and scream."

"Programming," Hunter snarled.

Kane shook his head. "It doesn't work like that."

Hunter glared at him as Kane crossed the room to me. "The subject has to be susceptible to the triggers. The other Daughters had already been tested before we started." He fixed his stare on me. "All except for Ryth, Vivienne, and Helene."

He reached up and brushed the strand of hair from my cheek. The mention of my sisters only triggered that panic inside.

"We didn't know about Helene until she entered our lives. But she is the perfect candidate. The way her breath catches and her pulse races at the mere mention of the words like being owned or degraded. The way she is already predisposed to the adrenaline rush release brings." He reached out, brushed his thumb along the silver scar line on the inside of my arm, and searched my eyes. "She likes it."

"No," Hunter growled.

"I could tell you all the ways in which a woman likes to be dominated. Release, trust, the deep-seated need to be nothing more than a vessel for pleasure, removing all the guilt and the shame associated with sex. I could go on for hours." He moved closer, so close his body brushed mine, forcing my gaze up to his. "But talking is so fucking boring. It's so much better to show you." He searched my eyes. "If you want that, precious?"

Get her to the table...

The faint words tried to invade.

But they didn't claw their way in.

I wouldn't let them.

Not with us.

They didn't belong with what we had.

"What you experienced was traumatic," Kane urged. "They took your power, your control. This is your chance to reclaim it back. Our hands on your body, our lips on yours. You're safe with us. We won't do anything you don't want here. This, this is all you."

"Blood will come." Riven urged, his dark eyes glinting with revenge. "Mark my words. We will make them pay for what they did to you. But this...this is your chance to reclaim your control. Whatever you want, Trouble...all you have to do is say the words."

"I, ah..." I started, my pulse beating a thousand miles an hour. Sparks ignited in my head. Flickers of memories. Riven... Kane...us, and under that, The Order. The way they'd lined us up and the words they'd said...

You are nothing more than a vessel.

I closed my eyes. "I want..."

"*No,*" Hunter snarled.

I wrenched my eyes open, watching him cross the room toward me.

He was a ghost filled with vengeance as he grasped Kane's shoulder and shoved him aside. Kane stumbled, wrenching a glare at the mountain in front of me. But all I saw was those dark eyes behind the gruesome mask as he snarled. "If she needs anything, she takes it from me."

ELEVEN

Helene

HE LOOKED AT ME AS THOUGH I NEEDED SAVING. WIDE, panicked dark eyes pinned me to the spot. The pupils were big enough to take in every twitch of my body and every catch of breath. He was scared, so fucking scared. If I didn't know better, I'd say Hunter was two goddamn seconds away from bolting and never coming back.

I repulsed him.

I swallowed hard.

The need to feel that rush.

I repulsed him.

"Helene," Kane urged.

I licked arid lips. "It's okay," I murmured.

My pulse thrummed, the sound was all I heard as I lowered my gaze to those rough fingers clenched by his side.

Get her to the table.

I pushed the words aside. "I need you to touch me," I started. "Your hand around my throat, your thumb against my pulse. I want you to feel me as much as I feel you. I want to know your..." *your power.*

A surge of excitement tore through me.

"You don't have to hurt her," Kane urged. "It's all about control and her knowing she has it all."

Hunter slowly lifted his hand. The fabric mask sucked tight against those hard lips with his sudden draw of breath. I was caught by the action, aching for his hands as well as his mouth. His chest rose and fell hard. I'd never seen someone so terrified about sex.

His big hand rested against my collarbone, his thumb limp.

"Higher," I commanded, grasping his hand in mine.

He weighed a ton as I curled his hand around my throat. There was a wince before he froze.

"There's no shame if you can't do this." Kane glanced at his brother. "No shame at all. We all have our own boundaries."

That spurred him on. In an instant, his big palm gripped the front of my throat. Callused fingers arched to press against the vein in my neck as though killing was his natural state of being.

That was it...

He was scared he was going to kill me.

Hunter towered above me, his powerful body trembling with just this tiny act of dominance. He was a murderous machine, Capable of taking a life with chilling precision without a thought. I'd seen it the moment he'd stepped into the back of that truck, just as I saw it now. I bet he'd never even flinched when he took a life...I bet he'd never given it a second thought. But this...this fucking terrified him...

I grasped the bottom edge of his mask and tugged it upwards.

"Easy," I whispered, my breaths rapid. "I just want to kiss you."

The edge slipped, driving against his cheek until the mask moved over his eyes. Those lips...that's what I wanted. Those hard, brutish lips. I bet he'd never even kissed a woman, not like this...not where it *meant* something.

I licked my own and moved closer.

He bent down, giving me what I wanted.

"Do you feel my pulse racing?" I whispered.

He swallowed hard. "Yes."

His voice was husky when he spoke, raw and strained.

I kissed him once more, taking it slower as I licked the corners of his mouth.

"This is all you need to do if that's all you want," I murmured against his mouth. "Do you want that?"

He gave a slow nod.

"Taste me," I whispered.

He opened his mouth, his fingers trembling against my throat. Kane was there, moving against me, his strong touch knowing instantly what to do.

"It's just us," Kane murmured against my ear. "You're the one in control here."

I closed my eyes as he grasped the front of my shirt and yanked it roughly upward.

"You're our fucking wet dream, you know that?" Kane palmed my breast, his fingers kneading my nipple until it puckered and turned hard. "We don't have to hide or pretend. We have you all to ourselves."

I tried to concentrate on his words and force the urgency to the surface. But it stayed out of reach. I squeezed my eyes shut tighter and fixed on the feel of Kane's fingers and the hard, forced breaths from Hunter.

But only one man rose inside my head.

One man with his hard, bitter smile.

I opened my eyes and turned my head, finding Riven watching us.

"Use them, Trouble," he murmured. "Take whatever you need."

What I needed was him and he knew that. But this wasn't like what we'd had before. This wasn't him being in control and me being swept away in his turbulent, savage hunger.

Everything about us was changed now.

Get her to the table.

I shook my head, trying my best to cast the words aside once and for all and broke away from Hunter. "Stop...*stop.* This isn't working."

Kane's hand stopped. Hunter dropped his hand instantly, tugging his mask back into place.

"What is it?" Kane asked.

I shook my head as a pang of pain filled my throat. Tears threatened to come. Maybe this was it. Maybe this was...*over?*

"Who are you?"

I flinched at the snarl and lifted my head. The room blurred, trembling with tears. Still, he sharpened...

"Well?" Riven urged as he stepped closer. "Answer me."

There was that authoritative tone. Dark. Callous and *unforgiving.*

"Helene King," I whispered, forcing the words free.

"Wrong."

He stepped closer, never once glancing at the others.

"Try again. *Who. Are. You?"*

"Helene—"

"WRONG!"

I jumped at the roar. Hunter unleashed a low snarl, but then stepped aside, watching Riven as he came closer. Kane moved from behind me, making way for his eldest brother. Just like they always had.

Those steel gray eyes glinted. Hard breaths made his chest rise. I knew this man. I *knew* him. The tender brush of his fingers. I lowered my gaze to his mouth. Those lips. I knew those lips. Still...he was an enigma, tender one minute...dangerous the next.

Just like now.

Now he was *very* dangerous.

He stopped in front of me. But there was a flicker of something behind that callous stare. A need that hadn't been there before...before us.

"Who *are you?*" he asked.

Just a nobody. A nobody who likes to come all over my fucking couch...

His snarl surfaced.

"Nobody." The word was a whisper.

His lips curled, that spark in his stare igniting.

The moment I said it, the world and every ugly thing that had happened to me just...*fell away.*

"Again," he demanded. "Who are you?"

"Nobody," I whispered, but my voice was stronger.

I was nobody at that moment. No Daughter. No sister. I was nothing more than what he wanted me to be.

"And tell me this, *nobody*. Why the fuck are you still dressed?"

He surged forward, grasping me around the throat. His strong hand was not as big as Hunter's but still...it felt more real than anything I'd ever felt before. He clenched tight, tight enough to cut off my airway, then eased his hold.

I bucked for a second, fighting to draw in a gulp of air. Everything narrowed to the careful grip around my throat. The strength in his fingers. The power behind that stare.

"And that, brother, is how you gain her attention. Isn't that right, *nobody?*"

My head was slowly nodding before I even knew it.

He lowered his gaze to my shirt. "This...will not do."

He dropped his hand from around my throat, grasped the neckline, and wrenched, tearing it down the middle.

"You wear another man's clothes. Is that it, nobody?"

And we were back there in an instant. In his apartment in the city with me at his mercy once more. I jerked forward as he tore the ruined remnants of the shirt Hunter gave me free and tossed it to the floor.

"Khakis." He looked disgusted. "Really?"

Hunter clenched his fists. "Careful," he growled.

The reaction only seemed to incite Riven more. He reached down, yanked the button, and tore the zipper open. "Don't you know a body like this needs to be looked at? It needs to be inspected, admired, licked...and fucked."

He dropped to his knees before I knew it, tugging the pants until they crumpled to the floor at my feet. "Lift, nobody."

I complied instantly.

"You think just because we have feelings for you that *this* changes?" He lifted his head, that stare boring into mine.

"No," I whispered as he tugged one boot free and then tapped my leg for the other.

"Damn right," he answered. The boots were gone, my pants along with them, leaving me in...nothing.

Riven slowly lifted his gaze, taking in every inch of my body, and bit his lip. "Fuck me, Trouble." I flinched at the feel of his hands on my thighs. "This body is too fucking perfect not to be shuddering as you come."

His firm grip massaged my muscles as he moved upwards. "Legs. Wider."

I looked down, unable to do anything but obey.

In the corner of my eye, Hunter shook his head. "You're going to just force her like that?"

"See for yourself, brother." Riven drove his hands upwards, his thumbs digging in until he splayed my pussy wide. "There's no amount of force that can do that."

I bit my lip as his finger slid along my crease.

"So. Fucking. *Wet.*"

My lids fluttered closed as I gave in to the feel of him. "I need to come," I whispered, the words alien. "Please, Riven. Make me come."

A dark, sinister sound rumbled in the back of his throat as the warm blast of his breath hit my thighs. "I thought you'd never fucking ask."

The harsh brush of his beard scraped my mound. But it was his tongue that stole my attention. Warm, wet, sliding into my crease to slip over my clit.

"Tell me how bad you want to come, nobody?"

"*So fucking bad.*"

"You belong to us," Kane urged. "No programming, no demanding. Nothing but your every desire taken care of. Look at him. Look how you have my brother on his knees."

I slowly opened my eyes. Those dark gray eyes hit me instantly as Riven opened his mouth wider and dipped. I unleashed a moan, my hand dropping to the back of his head.

"Wider," he commanded.

I shifted my stance, opening for him.

"Tell me now, brother, that this is anything but a beautiful fucking cunt that needs to be eaten," Riven growled as he dipped lower.

"Oh, *God,*" I moaned, my fingers clenching as I fisted his hair.

Hunter moved, so fixed by the sight of his brother between my legs that he came closer. Only this time, he needed no instruction. His big hand gripped my throat, those rough fingers hard against my skin.

"You...like this?" he asked.

"Yes," I moaned, holding his stare behind the mask. "Yes, I like it. Kiss me...*please, kiss me.*"

He reached up with his other hand and tugged the mask up over his mouth. Fingers pushed inside me as Hunter leaned down, kissing me.

"That's the way, Trouble," Riven urged. "Let us take every tear and every moan. Give it to us and know you are protected."

Agony drove through my chest. The tears that threatened to fall now rose with a vengeance. This was more than sex.

This was...

A claiming.

It was the same words Riven had told me as he fucked me within an inch of my life. It was the truth...*it was the truth.* Riven thrust his fingers in deeper, making me grasp the back of Hunter's neck and drag him closer. I moaned into his mouth and thrust my hips.

"That's it," Kane urged, his voice throaty. "Give yourself to us."

I lifted my leg and Riven was there, sliding it over his shoulder and cupping my ass. He pulled me harder against him until his rough stubble rubbed me in all the right places.

They were all I could feel.

The strength of Hunter's grip.

His hard lips as I moaned into his mouth.

The roughness of Riven's chin.

And Kane...as he pushed against my back.

"Come, baby," he murmured against my ear. "Come all over our brother's face."

I bucked with the words, slamming my hips against Riven's mouth, and bit down on Hunter's lip, drawing blood.

The salty, metallic tang hit my tongue. Hunter moaned, clenching his grip around my throat harder until the booming thud of my pulse was all I could hear.

In a blinding white flash of light inside my head, I came...*hard.*

Get her to the—

I pushed those words away. They didn't belong here...they didn't belong with us.

Instead, I moaned, forcing the guttural sound into Hunter's mouth and clung to him. Shudders tore free, making my knees quake and give way. But they were there to catch me.

"I got you," Kane urged.

My hold slipped from the back of Hunter's neck as I slowly dropped to the floor. My bare ass hit the floor, my legs splayed around Riven. His mouth glistened with desire, as did those eyes.

"Now that's what I call a re-introduction." He swiped the back of his hand along his mouth. "You want to be fucked, Trouble?"

My senses were out of commission. My thoughts were mindless, leaving me to nod.

That slow smile was back again as Riven reached down and unbuckled his trousers. "That's my perfect fucking slut."

My core clenched with the words and my heels slid against the floor as I opened my legs.

"And just...like...that," he smirked, reached down to grasp his cock, and aimed it between my legs. "She is ours."

I rose on my elbows, watching him.

This was nothing like what had happened to me.

This was...

Us.

Riven dropped his head, concentration pinching his brow as the smooth head of his cock pushed in. "Oh fuck, I missed this. *Never fucking leave me again.*" He lifted his head. "Got it."

Thick, hard, the vein was already pulsing as he pushed all the way inside.

"You're never fucking leaving my sight, not for a goddamn minute." He grunted as he thrust all the way in. "You get that, Trouble? *You're mine.*"

I lifted my gaze to Kane as Riven thrust inside me. His hand dropped to the bulge in the front of his trousers and behind him, so did The Priest's.

"I'm yours," I whispered.

"Damn straight you are." Riven gripped my hips and yanked me hard against him, pushing in hard.

It wasn't enough. "Harder," I moaned. "Fuck me like you goddamn mean it."

With a roar, Riven lunged and grasped my throat. His eyes were incensed as he slammed home over and over and once again. "You feel me now?"

Oh, Goddd....

My body clenched, gripping him tightly. For a moment, that savage look wavered, giving into panic.

"Fuck...*me*," he moaned and thrust once more before he stilled.

Warmth filled me.

His warmth.

He sucked in hard breaths and eased out. "You make me come like a fucking teenager, Trouble. I can't fucking last with you."

My chest heaved with a heavy breath as reality hit home. *Hunter.* I glanced his way, finding him staring at the mess his brother had left behind.

"Hunter," I whispered.

"You...let my brothers...do that?" he asked, his voice barely a whisper.

"Yes." Heat filled my cheeks.

"And me?" he murmured. "You'd let me...do that?"

I pushed upwards. There was fresh blood on his lower lip. A remnant of my bite. "Yes."

"Then roll over," he commanded. "I want to...I want to touch you."

I caught my breath, never once looking away. My knees still trembled as I rolled over and watched them over my shoulder.

He tugged at his belt, then the button and zipper on his khakis, pushing them down.

"What, you can't stand her filled with my cum?" Riven growled as he pushed to stand.

"No," Hunter answered.

"So you'll fuck her out of spite?"

"Every *motherfucking time*," Hunter snarled and lowered his body to the floor behind me.

I wanted to turn around, to say that isn't what we had, until the feel of his rough fingers sliding along my entrance stopped me.

"But more than that, I fucking want her," he finished. "More than I've ever wanted anything in my goddamn life. Including strangling you, *brother*."

I turned to the other side, watching Riven as Hunter slid his fingers along my sodden crease.

"Gonna fuck the feeling of him right out of you," Hunter snarled and lowered his head. The mask was tugged upwards so those hard lips brushed the small of my back.

"Do you see me?" I whispered the same words I'd screamed in a fit of rage last night. "Do you see me now?"

"Yes." He lowered his body, that tongue sliding over my ass until he gently bit the soft, plump flesh. "I taste you too."

He rose, and when he did, his cock drove inside me. I arched my back with the invasion as he kept pushing, and pushing and *pushing*.

"Oh my *fucking God*," I moaned.

My pussy stretched wider and wider. I breathed hard, trying to take all of him. But he was *huge*.

"You wanted me," Hunter murmured. "So now you have me."

I rocked forward, then back, easing him in deeper.

His heavy hand landed on the small of my back. "Easy now." He slowed at the entrance. "That's the girl. Look how fucking well you're taking it. Goddamn, I'm proud of you."

I unleashed a whimper and pushed back harder.

"Take it...Jesus *Christ*, take ittt..."

I slid my knees wider and lowered my head to the floor.

"Fuck me," Kane moaned.

But Riven said nothing as his brother pushed all the way inside.

Slow, careful thrusts had me whimpering. No wonder he hadn't wanted to force himself on me...he'd have torn me apart.

"That's so good, my little fighter. Christ, that's what you are...*a fighter*. Go on, Fighter...take every damn inch of me."

I whimpered, rocking back and forth until he stretched and rubbed and *God, it felt so good.*

A moan rumbled from the mountain.

Something cracked and crumbled inside me, making me arch my back as he thrust harder.

"Jesus...*fuck!*" he grunted.

I felt everything, as the head of his cock flooded me with the warmth of him.

"I told you," Riven muttered. "You are just as much of a sucker as the rest of us...*only bigger.*"

TWELVE

Riven

I WATCHED MY BROTHER LOWER HIS HEAD AS HE SUCKED IN hard breaths. His hand was spread wide across the small of her back, then moved possessively over her ass. A twitch came at the sight, pulsing at the corner of my goddamn eye. I clenched my jaw as he withdrew his massive cock and turned that hateful fucking stare to me.

Jesus...what the fuck happened to you?

"Hold onto me." He reached out, taking hold of her hand, never once taking his eyes from mine. "I told you I'd give you anything you needed."

Twitch.

Motherfucker.

My lips curled as I took a step forward.

"Riven." Kane stepped in between us. "Maybe we need to look at making a plan for tomorrow?"

I jerked my focus to him. He was always there, always stepping in between us. I caught the smirk from Hunter in the corner of my eye. But it was Helene I focused on as she grasped his hand and slowly rose. Bruises, scars...and under that, a look of worry.

"Brother," Kane murmured so quietly I could barely hear him.

But I did.

My lips curled as I stepped closer and brushed the hair from her face. "You wash up, Trouble, and I'll make you some delicious vegan pancakes, how does that sound?"

"Vegan?" Hunter muttered and jerked a confused stare to her.

Now it was my turn to smirk. "Yes, brother." I shot him a glare. "Looks like you don't know *everything*."

"Jesus." Kane shook his head.

"Boys," Helene snapped.

I jerked my stare to her, as did the others.

"Is this how it's going to be?" she asked each of us.

Hunter said nothing. Kane glared at me. It was Thomas that strode forward. "I guess that's a yes," he muttered and left.

I watched him as he limped out of the living room, heading to the front door. Helene watched him go. He didn't like her, not in the ways we did. Maybe somehow he still blamed her for what had happened to him.

But we do terrible things for the people we love.

The only thing to do now was to live with the consequences.

I gave her a smile, ruffling her hair. "He'll come around."

"Will he?" she asked, staring after him.

"I'll find you more clothes," Hunter offered. "Hopefully, this time they won't get ripped."

"If they smell like you, it'll be a given," I growled.

"Honestly." Helene shook her head, bent, and snatched her clothes from the floor before heading for the stairs. "I'll find my own damn clothes...*and I'll cook my own pancakes, as well!*"

I winced at her pissed off tone, watching her leave.

"Nice one, asshole," Hunter muttered and turned, yanking up the zipper of his pants.

"Wait a minute here...*I'm the asshole?*" He left without answering. I clenched my jaw. "Don't say it..." I warned, watching Kane's lips part. "Don't say a goddamn thing."

I snatched my shirt from the floor and punched my hands through the sleeves. My brother hated me. My...fucking woman was pissed off with the both of us at this moment. Why the fuck did I come back?

The faint rush of water sounded somewhere upstairs. For her... that's why I'd come back. *For her.*

I yanked up my zipper and turned around, scanning the ugly goddamn mansion. "Where the fuck is the kitchen in this goddamn place?"

"Just take it easy, yeah?" Kane urged.

"Sure." I strode away. "Easy, that's my middle name."

He muttered something else but I couldn't hear him. I was too busy making my way through the place to find the kitchen at the back. Surprisingly, it was impressive. Miele ovens and cooktops in a sleek black finish. But it was the counter that made me stop and stare. It was a thick slab of stone. One obviously taken when they'd carved into the mountain to make way for the house.

I reached out and ran my finger along the sleek surface polished to a gleam. Envy rose. The bastard had the balls to hide and watch everything from up here in his little oasis and still blame us for what went down?

No.

Not us.

Just me.

"Yeah, well, fuck you," I murmured and turned around, pulling open cupboards, until I found the pantry. Mentally, I made a list of what she needed in my head. It felt good, *purposeful.* I needed her and more than just to touch and fuck. I needed her to occupy my mind.

Within a few moments, I'd pulled out the basic ingredients, finding pasta sauce, instant lasagne, and vegetables in a fully stocked refrigerator.

The bastard ate well, that was for sure.

Steak.

Chicken.

Lean cuts of lamb.

I couldn't help but grin.

All the things she hated.

I cut vegetables and splashed olive oil into one pan while I placed the sauce and broken lasagne into another pan. By the time I heard the soft padding of steps, I was searing zucchinis and vibrant red peppers.

"Damn, that smells so good," she muttered.

"Pity none of this is for you," I answered right before she slid her arms around my waist and hugged me from behind.

"Yes," she murmured. "That *is* a pity. You *know* how well I reward those who cook for me."

She had me turning in an instant. "No, I'm sure I don't know."

Her smile was pure fucking perfection and it hit me how far removed I was now from the man I'd been. I would murder for that smile. I'd even share with the ones who distrusted me the most. That was no mean feat.

I curled a damp strand of hair around her ear. "Are you okay?"

It was a loaded question.

Did I mean from us, from Hunter, from the men who'd attacked her at The Order? Or all the above? That spark of happiness in her eyes dulled for a second. She glanced at the stove then answered. "Give me a gun in my hand and about five minutes alone with the bastards who did that to me and I will be."

My jaw clenched. I wanted to be the one who made them pay. I ached for it. *Dreamed about it.* But she was the one who needed it the most. She needed...closure. I'd be the one who gave it to her.

I switched off the stove, grabbed the single plate off the counter, and heaped the sautéed vegetables onto the side before I spooned the thickened lasagne and sauce on top. "Don't even ask me what this is called. All rules are out the window where you're concerned."

She was right behind me when I turned around, her hand cupping my cheek. Desire flared in her stare, a hunger that stole my breath. My pulse boomed as I leaned down and kissed her.

Her hand went around my neck, pulling me against her. I almost dropped the damn plate as she kissed me. I let out a moan, almost falling into her as she broke away. There was a mischievous grin on her lips as she took the plate from my hand and plucked the fork from the other. I couldn't do a damn thing but stare as she gave me a flirty wink and stabbed a slice of carrot and slipped it into her mouth.

Goddamn woman.

She had me.

She had me so goddamn bad.

"This...this is good," she said, chewing at the same time, and I thought it was the most goddamn adorable thing I'd ever seen.

"Any of that left?" Kane asked as he strode into the kitchen.

"Yes."

"*No.*"

I scowled at her. She lifted the plate to my brother and handed him the fork.

"Didn't cook for him," I muttered under my breath and busied myself cleaning the kitchen.

"Hunter asked if we wanted to go over the finer details of tomorrow night." Kane asked.

Purpose.

That's what I needed.

I hurried to wipe down the counters and loaded the pans into the dishwasher. "About time." I lifted my gaze.

"Hey." Kane drew my focus. "We need to work together here. We're all on the same side, right?" He gave a small jerk of his head toward Helene as she stabbed zucchini and lasagne, scooping it into her mouth.

"You're right." I nodded, stepping around the edge of the counter. "We are all on the same side. Come on, Trouble. Bring your food and let's see what our brother has planned."

Her brow rose in suspicion, but we all walked out of the house and headed for the command center. The crackle of the two-way greeted us as we stepped through the door. Helene carried the plate of food and made her way up the stairs in front of her. Kane stared at her ass until I glared his way.

The man was tormented, that was easy to see.

"After you, brother," I muttered and waved him forward.

He licked his lips and followed her. For a second, I felt a flare of concern for our new toy. She had no idea what she was in for. But my attention soon shifted to the room above as I followed them. The place was the perfect command center, fitted out with banks of monitors, some showing the CCTV view of the property we were on. But others were trained on different locations, The Order being one of them.

I stared at that camera as Hunter started to speak. "My men will have the truck ready. The plan is we hide amongst the Daughters. They're expecting guards, so when their scanners pick up our heat they won't be taken by surprise. Someone will need to ride up front. We want a tight leash on the bastard driving. The moment we're in, someone needs to put a bullet through his head."

Where is she? my own words rose in my head.

Who? The bastard had smirked. *The cunt we held down and fucked?*

"Me," I offered instantly, my focus sharpening. "That will be me."

Hunter met my stare, then gave a slow nod. "Then you're up front."

That was all I cared about. I listened to the rest of the plan, but all I really heard was the sound of his screams in my head. Helene had stopped eating. Her skin was suddenly pale as she fixed her attention on me.

I met that stare. *I told you before, Trouble...they'll all die by the time this is through.*

Hunter's plan was discussed. Kane asked a few questions. But really, it was all straight forward. We'd get in there and kill everyone in sight, taking Harmon captive until he got us to Hale.

This was the end.

The end of it all.

And I couldn't fucking wait.

"We're expecting a quiet compound when we enter." Hunter brought up his cell, flicking through call after call for mercenaries needed for an urgent search and rescue. I knew instantly who'd sent them, only there was no rescue involved. All they wanted was the Daughters, and once they had them they wouldn't care about anything else.

"We good?" Hunter asked Kane.

"Yes." Kane gave a slow nod and glanced my way. "You okay with this?"

"I'll be better when it's all over," I answered. "And they're all dead."

I TRIED to pass the day away from the others, my mind all wrapped up around Coulter and the fact I wasn't the one in control. I didn't trust anyone when it came to The Order or Helene, for that matter...*especially Helene.*

The place was a goddamn fortress. I made my way around the compound, stopping at the house for a while. I could hear Kane and Thomas talking, making plans as they ate. But the thought of food made my stomach churn. Instead, my mind was caught on the other compound. More importantly, the chat rooms about the Sons. My pulse sped with the memory of St. James' hunters, Carven and Colt. There was a ruthlessness about them, a chilling mechanical hunger behind their eyes.

I knew men who killed with no remorse. But this wasn't that. This was...*mind control.*

I needed to know more.

Thud.

Thud.

THUD!

I neared the command building and caught the sound of fists driving into something soft. Heavy grunting followed as I stepped into the doorway. You would've thought the bastard would be all worn out after fucking the woman I loved, but nope...here he was tearing a heavy punching bag apart with his bare fucking hands. Only now he didn't have on that gruesome fucking mask. Sweat shone against his massive bare back. Tattoos covered his skin. Looking at him, it was hard to see the scrawny kid who'd once looked up to me.

He stopped, sensing me behind him, and slowly turned, his bare knuckles bright red from the impacts. No words were exchanged as those cold gray eyes met mine. The hard planes of his cheeks did nothing to hide the true sight of his face.

Hard lips curled in a sneer. It didn't take a fucking genius to know who he envisioned when he drove his fists into that bag... *me.*

I turned away and made my way up the stairs to where the computers waited, connected to his team. It wasn't until I sat down, found the list of his team members online, and started to email the one I needed that the brutal *thuds* of his blows came once more.

Thud.

Thud.

Thud...

I winced and started typing, unable to shift that nagging thought in my head. *This is Riven, is there any more information on the Sons?*

Then I waited...

THIRTEEN

Helene

RIVEN WAS ACTING STRANGE...STRANGER THAN NORMAL. He didn't look at me as we gathered our things and made for the four-wheel drives waiting for us in the driveway. In fact, he didn't look at anyone, just kept his head down and tried to look busy. I hauled my bag into the back of the Explorer driven by one of Hunter's masked soldiers and turned around.

"Helene," Hunter called as I strode past to where Riven and the others grabbed the rest of their gear and headed toward us.

"Hey." I fixed my stare on Riven.

He grasped a Glock, placing it into the holster at his side and clutched the hideous skull mask in his other hand. But he never fixed those steel gray eyes on mine, leaving me to grasp his chin and force the connection. "What's going on with you?"

Something was bugging him.

Something big.

Bigger than all...this.

"It's nothing." He pulled his chin out of my grasp. "Promise. I just want this over."

That nagging feeling in the pit of my stomach said there was more to this. More than he was saying.

"That's not it," I said. "And I know it. I can't make you talk if you don't want to. But don't you pull away from me, Riven. Not now when I need you the most."

He flinched at the words as I turned around and headed back to the waiting four-wheel drive.

"Everything okay?" Hunter asked as I neared.

"About as okay as it's ever going to get, I think," I answered and hauled myself inside the vehicle's back seat.

The door closed with a *thud* behind me. I looked out the window to Riven as he lifted his gaze and a flicker of fear moved through me at the connection as the Explorer's engine came to life with a growl. He was scared...no, more than scared...he was terrified.

The Explorer pulled out just as Riven and the others headed for the other four-wheel drive. I tore my gaze away as we drove out of the compound and through the towering fence. It felt like a lifetime since Hunter had dragged me kicking and screaming through these gates and into a place closed off from the rest of the world.

It had felt empty, until Riven, Kane and Thomas had come.

Now, it felt like a lie.

Hunter said nothing as he drove, then turned hard onto the asphalt and headed back down the winding mountain road once more. Part of me wanted to stay there, to hide away from the world forever, the world where The Order had consumed my life. But that was just a fantasy. Sooner or later the rot would creep in. It always did.

I looked out the window, not looking at Hunter behind the wheel or his man in the passenger seat in front of me as we headed back toward the city.

My main bag was in the back of the Explorer, but a small pile of clothes sat next to me. Lingerie in fact...bright red, of course. I glanced at the lace on the seat beside me and fought the revulsion that followed. One more time, that's all, just once, then I never had to wear that fucking thing ever again.

I turned away, focusing on the trees as they turned to the clear landscape. The city rose in the distance. We were early, hours early. A rough sleep alone last night and bitter black coffee did little to help my mood. Actually, it did little for all of us. Long stretches of silence were met with snarls. We avoided each other this morning. It seemed like a good idea at the time. But looking back now, I wished I'd been more present. Riven was holding onto something...something that now wore at me.

I turned my attention back to the unfamiliar city streets as we headed to the more industrial part of the city. Hunter gazed into the rear-view mirror and those dark eyes met mine. There was a sense of familiarity about them. *They were like Riven's.*

That's why he'd looked so familiar. Hunter scowled and looked away, turning the four-wheel drive into the driveway of a massive compound surrounded by a towering ten-foot-high fence. Barely a second passed and the massive steel gate rolled open, leaving me staring at the military compound as we entered.

The Explorer pulled up hard, coming to a stop in a cloud of dust. A man came striding out of an open door in the closest building. He was massive, almost as big as Hunter, with warm brown eyes that swept through the Explorer, stopping on me. He had a scruffy beard, one that made him look even more imposing.

Hunter killed the engine and climbed out. I followed, grabbing the red lace lingerie as I went.

"Kyrell," Hunter called as he climbed out. He glanced toward the building. "Any problems?"

"Not since that asshole Principal left," the soldier muttered.

Hunter gave a scowl and shook his head toward the man.

"What?" the mercenary questioned.

"Don't mind me," I reassured Hunter. "He is an asshole."

I closed the door and turned around, coming to a stop in an instant as one of the Daughters stepped out of the doorway after the guard. She was dressed in khakis four sizes too big. The pants were cinched around her small waist, and she was nearly swallowed by a pale t-shirt that hung from her narrow shoulders.

I knew her...she was the one who'd been dragged back by the guard at The Order. The one Kane had made an example of by forcing her to her knees and making her spread herself apart. Her cheeks burned as she met my gaze before she looked away.

"Are all the Daughters here?" I turned to Hunter. "The ones you rescued with me?"

He gave a nod.

I hadn't expected them...here. Maybe in some safehouse somewhere. But the moment more of Hunter's men stepped out into the compound, their hard gazes finding me, I realized this was probably as safe a place as any. The deep snarl of an engine had me turning my head to watch the other four-wheel drive nose into the compound behind us.

"Is everything ready for tonight?" Hunter's voice reached me as I watched Riven in the passenger seat as they pulled up next to us.

"About as ready as we'll ever be. The truck is ready to inspect, then there's just the issue of the guard."

I flinched, then turned to him. "The guard?"

"Yes." Hunter glanced my way. "The one from the truck."

My pulse sped at the words. Of course it was. I licked my lips and tried to swallow. I could face that sonofabitch, I knew I could. Still, the thought made my throat tighten.

Car doors closed with *thuds,* making me jolt and jerk my gaze toward the others as Riven rounded the front of the vehicle and headed our way. One look in my direction and he scowled.

"What is it?" He neared, then dropped the duffel bag Hunter had given each of them at his feet.

I started to shake my head, but it was Hunter who answered for me. "The guard in the workshop," he muttered.

Riven met his gaze, then slowly nodded.

"The truck is ready. The Daughters will be, as well. Helene?" Hunter turned to me. "You going to be able to handle this?"

I hated the question. I'd never been the kind of person who backed down from anything. I was a fighter, a hunter. *I* was the one my father sent in when shit had to get done, but now...now after—*get her to the table*—now after everything that had happened, I was...*weak.*

"We'll be with you every step of the way, Trouble. They won't get anywhere near you. All you have to do is get us inside and we'll take care of the rest, okay?"

I met those gray eyes. Eyes that looked so much like his brother's and nodded. "Yeah, I can handle this."

"That's my little fighter," Hunter murmured, those hard lips curling into a chilling smile.

We turned around and headed inside to where the other Daughters and soldiers waited. They went over the plan, once, twice. I zoned out after the fourth time, and watched Riven quietly slip away. I waited for a second, then followed.

I found him sitting beside one of Hunter's men, staring at a screen of what looked like chat rooms.

"What's that?" I asked from the doorway.

Riven winced, then slowly turned his head, and I knew in an *instant* this was what he'd been hiding. My senses sharpened and I turned back to the screen. "Riven?"

"It's a chat room," he answered carefully.

I shot him a glance. "Right. A chat room about what?"

"The Sons," the mercenary beside him answered. "It's about The Sons."

"The Sons?" I asked, taking a step closer. "As in Colt and Carven?"

"Them and others," Riven answered. "We've been trying to track their location down."

"You've been trying to track them down." I couldn't stop from repeating myself. "And did you?"

"We're not sure," the merc answered. "But if we haven't, we're damn close."

"And how did you do that?" I tried to look at the screen, catch sight of the names. But Riven rose and stepped to the side, blocking my view. "Riven." I glared at him. "You're in the way."

"Not now, Trouble." He grabbed my shoulders and forced me to turn around. "They're busy."

"No, they're *not*." I tried to turn around but he was there, driving me out of the room and away from whatever was written in that chat.

I shrugged him off, turning around to hiss. "What the fuck is going on with you?"

"One crisis at a time, Trouble," he muttered in a tone that told me there was no fighting this.

I stopped struggling and instead held his stare. There was a pleading in his eyes, one I'd never seen before. "Fine," I snapped as I yanked my arm out of his viselike hold. "For now, but don't think I'll leave this forever. I want to know what's going on with you and that room."

"Okay," he gave in. "Deal, but after we've done this tonight. I need your head in the game." His voice softened as he brushed his curled fingers along my cheek.

There was no stray hair for him to dislodge, he just liked to touch me. But as always, that desperation turned into something more carnal. He drew in a breath and licked his lips. "We have time, Trouble."

I gave a smile. "Sure, let's just fuck in front of everyone, shall we?"

He scowled, lifting his gaze. It was as though he'd forgotten we had an audience, or maybe it was that he was used to just not caring.

"When this is all over..." he warned, turning that wicked stare my way.

When this is all over...

What then?

I wasn't sure. But the one thing I did know was that Riven, Kane, and Thomas would be in my world one way or another.

"They're going to talk to the guard," Kane said from behind Riven.

That drew both our attention. Riven swiveled around in an instant and started walking. "Not without me, they aren't."

I followed him, hurrying to catch up as he headed out of the building and toward what looked like a massive workshop. Hunter and his men waited at a huge open door. One glance at his brother and the towering mountain turned and stepped deeper into the dimness.

Goosebumps raced along my arms as they stopped outside a locked door at the end of the space. I waited, listening to the *clunk* of a lock disengaging before the door was pushed inwards. Low snarls came from the darkness, spitting threats and promises of revenge.

I followed them, lingering in the doorway until finally the lights came on with a *click*. I winced at the sudden glare as light flooded the room. In the corner a handcuffed man kicked one leg against the floor, trying his best to ward them off as they came toward him.

Riven was frozen, staring down at him. But one glance and I knew it wasn't out of fear. He wanted blood...he wanted *this* man's blood.

I swallowed and turned my attention to the bastard who, just yesterday, had had me by the throat, whispering in my ear all the filthy, terrifying things he was going to do to me. Fear ripped like an icy wave through me. For a second, I was the only one in there. The only one facing that...*scumbag*. I opened my mouth to speak just as Hunter neared him and slowly dropped to one knee.

His tone was so calm as he started talking. "This is what's going to happen. In a few hours, we're going to take you from this room and take you to a room where you're going to call your contact. You're going to tell them you were attacked and run off the road. You're going to explain that the team is okay, as well as the assets, then you're going to tell them you're bringing them in."

"And why the *fuck* would I do that?" the idiot sneered, his lips curling.

There was a manic gleam in his eyes, one that went with the sickening sweat sheen across his brow. There was blood on his shirt and blood crusted in his nostrils. It didn't take a genius to know what had happened. The only question was who had done it?

My attacker jerked when his gaze caught Riven. I knew then, knew it was The Principal. Riven stepped closer, making the guard on the floor flinch and jerk a panicked stare toward him. "Get him the *fuck* away from me."

So, it was him.

I could only imagine what had happened between them.

There will be blood, Trouble. That I promise.

My pulse sped as those words resounded.

"You don't need to worry about him," Hunter murmured, and turned around. The merc with the beard handed him a set of tools wrapped in black canvas. He carefully opened them. "And this is why you're going to do exactly what I said. Because if you don't..."

One swipe of his big hand and he unrolled the set. Sharpened steel glinted on a vicious-looking pair of pliers. Those were made for torture.

"Because if you don't, it won't be my brother you'll need to be worried about. It'll be *her.*"

Hunter turned to glance over his shoulder, and that steely stare found me. A surge of adrenaline slammed into me. Hard breaths shook me as I turned back to that bastard whose lips started to curl.

"Her?" he smirked.

I forced myself to step forward, even though it was the last thing I wanted to do. "Yes," I murmured, lowering my gaze to the instruments waiting for me. I moved fast, kneeling to snatch the pliers from their sheath and hold them in front of his face. I searched those sickening eyes, trying to find the monster who'd terrified me so much. All I saw was a weak, pathetic male who liked to terrify others. Now it was time for him to get a little of his own medicine.

"Me," I whispered, watching his eyes. "I'm going to enjoy exacting my revenge. I think I'll start with your tongue, so I don't have to listen to you beg."

He gave a chuff, smiling...for a second, until that smile died away.

"You won't..." he started.

"She will," Riven answered as he moved closer. "And we'll fucking help her."

"So, you will go into that room and you will make the call. Because if you don't, Helene and my brother here are going to rip you apart, inch...by...inch."

The asshole turned gray, his panicky gaze shifting from the pliers in my hand to Riven...then finally to Hunter, and he nodded. "Okay. Okay, just whatever you do, don't let them hurt me."

"You have my word." Hunter smiled and clapped his heavy hand on the bastard's shoulder. "They won't harm a hair on your head."

FOURTEEN

Hunter

"COMMANDER."

I jerked my gaze to Kyrell.

"Have you heard a word I've said?"

I scowled, fighting the urge to look her way.

"Yeah." I pushed off the truck. "I heard you."

The exterior was fine, the bullet holes patched and painted. I strode along the outside, checking for anything out of the ordinary for the twentieth time. That was the only thing I felt slipping away...*time*. The last thing I wanted to be doing right now was worrying about all the ways tonight could go to hell.

Beep.

I glanced at my cell.

St. James: We'll be there in 30.

I winced and pocketed it. "Get the Daughters ready. St. James and the others will be here in thirty."

"Where will you be?" he asked as I walked away.

"Around."

I headed for the command center, ignoring the curious stares of my men and the other Daughters we'd rescued from the truck. Disgust rose, the bitter tang rancid on the back of my tongue. I swallowed it down and tried not to meet the Daughters' confused, desperate stares. If I was any kind of man, I'd set them free, let them run and take their chances out there.

But deep down, I knew they'd never be free. Not really. Not while men like Harmon and Hale existed.

"Commander." One of my men stepped out of the comms room.

"Not now," I murmured and kept walking, turning from the living room to the long hallway and the closed bedroom doors.

They were here...somewhere. I slowed, glancing at a closed door and listened. Sobs came from behind the door, faint, muffled sobs. I winced and forced myself to keep walking, heading to where the deep rumble of my brother's voice could be heard.

A turn of the handle and I stepped inside. He held her as she stood there naked. Anger burned for a second before I glanced at the bed. One of the red lace bodysuits they were forced to wear lay on the edge, glaring, neon.

"Everything okay?"

Riven glared at me as he held her tighter. "Fine." The word was acid.

I strode closer, bending to snatch the lingerie from the bed. "You'll never have to wear anything like this again."

She turned to me, her skin pale, eyes shining with the tears she refused to shed. Christ, she was strong. Riven took a step backwards, then turned. "I'll be outside. Help her into the suit, brother."

He started walking, oblivious to the agony that cut across her face. My fingers clenched around his arm. "What the fuck are you doing?"

"What I have to do," he said carefully, his voice like rolling thunder as his eyes met mine. "Now I need you to do the one fucking thing I asked, *brother*...and take care of her."

He wrenched his arm from my grasp and strode from the room without any hesitation. The moment the door closed with a *thud,* I turned to her with a raised brow.

"He thinks if you fuck me, you'll protect me."

"What?" I shook my head, rage burning inside me. "That motherfucker."

She stepped closer, meeting my stare as she took the lace lingerie from my hand.

I stared at her. She gripped the lace. "Do you hate him for it?"

"Yes." I clenched my jaw. "Your body isn't to be bargained for, not by a man, at least."

There was that dark need rising to the surface again. She took the garment and stepped into it, sliding it up over her body before tugging it into place. "Women do it all the time. A fancy dinner or a holiday to Greece. You think women don't fuck to get what they want?"

Her voice was harder, strained, like she was barely keeping it together. "I know they do," I answered. "But that doesn't mean he has to do it for you."

She stilled, sliding the strap into place and lifted her gaze to me. "Maybe when this is over and done, we might all strike a bargain ourselves?"

I stilled. Did she mean...

"You want my body. I want yours." She flicked some elastic into place and lifted her gaze. "And your brothers'...if they're willing."

I hadn't thought about that. She couldn't want all of us, could she? I was starting to understand that I knew nothing when it came to the needs of a woman. Especially not this one.

"If that's what you want," I agreed.

Her eyes widened and her brows inched upwards. There was a tight curl at the corner of her lips before she moved, grabbed the bottom of my balaclava and tugged it upwards. I grasped her hand, hard at first then eased my hold, remembering who it was I held.

Memories of her flickered in my head. Images of her on the monitor in front of me.

Images with my brother.

Her legs wide. His fingers buried between them.

Fuck, she sent my damn heart racing.

I curled my spine, yielding to her.

"Maybe then you'll let me see the man behind the mask?" she whispered against my lips.

I turned her hand and pressed my lips to the inside of her wrist and inhaled the scent of her. "Maybe."

Beep.

My cell ruined the moment. She exhaled and turned her head. Still, I couldn't stop myself from leaning into her and kissing her lips. "I'll be right behind you tonight," I murmured. "No one is going to get past me, little fighter."

She gave a ghost of a smile. The one she used to hide her worry. Still, I saw it. Just like I saw everything. I straightened, tugged my mask back in place and strode to the closet, yanking one of the guy's shirts from inside.

I tugged the shirt over her shoulders. "They don't get to look at you."

Beep.

I frowned, grabbed my cell, and glanced at the screen.

Kyrell: St. James and his group are here.

I pocketed the damn thing.

"It's time, isn't it?" she asked.

I fixed on those eyes and gave a slow nod. She straightened her spine. "Then let's get this over with."

I didn't have time to respond, not that I knew what I'd say. Her fingers grazed my arm as she strode past, heading for the door. In an instant, it was open and the faint voices of my men and her sisters invaded.

"Where is she?" the feisty one barked. "Where is my sister?"

"I'm here." Helene called and stepped out into the hallway, followed closely by a massive motherfucker. A bodyguard for Vivienne, no doubt.

I followed her, catching careful glances from my men, then daggers from her family. Riven and Kane waited. Thomas was nowhere to be seen...again. My little brother was starting to worry me.

"Are we ready?" As he asked, St. James watched his woman carefully.

He should. The daggers she was throwing with her stare might get her into trouble. I lowered my gaze to her big round stomach and gave a nod. "Yeah."

St. James stepped closer, drawing my focus. He didn't like me looking at his woman. I glanced toward the movement as the Sons stepped in, scanned my men, and headed our way. Carven and Colt drew my men's attention but none more than Riven's.

A sea of red came through the doorway as one by one the Daughters stepped in, their gazes fixed on my brothers.

"You know what you have to do?" Kane asked as he walked along each one, touching them gently on the shoulder.

He'd been prepping them since he arrived, making sure they knew what to do. All we needed was for them to get inside, then they were free. One wrapped her arm around her middle, another shifted suspiciously closer to Kyrell. He stared straight ahead, eyes fixed on Kane.

But Helene was the one who stepped forward, wrapped her arms around her sister, and jerked a glare at St. James. "She's not involved in this, *right?*"

He scowled and shook his head. "I told her she's to follow a safe distance behind, with Guild."

"Make sure you do." Helene forced her sister's gaze to hers. "You need to protect those babies."

Bab*ies?*

Huh.

I didn't have time to ponder which one was the father as the dark-haired son moved closer to her, eyeballing me like he had a problem. I met that stare and stilled. Something not quite human moved behind those dark blue eyes, something that made me wary. That *never* happened.

"Okay." Kane glanced around the room. "Sounds like we're ready."

"Almost," St. James muttered as the deep, throaty growl of a muscle car invaded.

The Bankses were here. Car doors opened as the engine died.

"Now we go," St. James declared.

"Boss."

I lifted my gaze, nodded to the others, and headed toward Thad.

"What is it?"

"We lost Kyrell," he murmured.

I glanced toward the door as Nick Banks and his brothers strode through, dressed in black khakis and double shoulder holsters packing some pretty nice armor. "Find him," I growled, not looking away.

Thad disappeared. This was not a good time for anyone, much less Kyrell, to go MIA.

"Hunter." Nick Banks nodded my way, watching Thad walk out. "Everything good here?"

"As good as it's ever going to be," I answered and headed out.

The others followed, as did the Daughters. Two of my men dragged Harmon's man from the workshop to the truck. Deep purple hues were cast along the horizon, as though this night knew bruises and blood would follow.

Riven followed Harmon's man, his gaze stony as the passenger door was opened. I headed toward them, watching as Davies pulled out a burner cell and held it out toward the guard.

"Make the call," Davies muttered. "You fuck this up and it be your life on the line."

Movement came in the corner of my eye. The Daughters, Helene, her sisters, and everyone else stood around the rear of the truck, watching us intently.

But then Kyrell came striding through them, looking pissed off.

"What is it?" I asked.

He just shook his head. "Nothing to worry about. Let's just get this done."

He took over, grabbed the cell, and shoved it into the guy's hand. "Make the call." Then he crowded the guy hard. "You want your family to see you alive, don't you?"

The guard looked scared as he took the cell. Trembling fingers hit the wrong button, not once but twice, until the schmuck moaned and tried for the third time.

We all waited, listening in as the call was answered and the panic played out. What do you know, the idiot played it out, using the panic in his own tone to trigger that bastard Coulter on the other end.

I could hear him roaring from here.

"Those fucking women better be alive, Childs, or I'll fucking have your head!" The asshole held out the cell at the scream. Heavy breaths followed, reaching my ears until, *"I need a proof of life. Helene...I want to hear her."*

The asshole lifted his gaze, desperately seeking the one woman he shouldn't look at. My gut clenched. All I saw was his skull buckling under the force of my fingers.

"The fuck he is," Riven whispered under his breath.

But she came, playing the one part she should *never* have had to play...*a Daughter.*

He pushed the cell toward her when she neared. *"Speak!"* He roared loud enough for her to know Coulter was listening.

She grabbed the cell, closed her eyes for a second, then opened them and lifted the phone to her ear. "What?"

I stepped closer. We all did. Riven, Kane, even Thomas shifted behind us, coming closer.

"Fuck you," she snarled, her voice trembling with fear. *"FUCK YOU!"*

It was exactly what Coulter would want to hear. She shoved the cell back at the guard and strode away. Vivienne and Ryth were waiting, pulling her into their arms in silence while the rest of it played out.

We got the address. That was all that mattered.

The goddamn address of where they were.

The call ended and the asshole handed it back to Kyrell, meeting his stare.

"Let's go," I commanded, turning around to the most precious cargo I'd ever carried. Nick and Tobias pulled on black balaclavas with stark white skulls painted on them as Ryth shrugged off the long black trench coat covering the red lace lingerie she wore.

One of the Daughters had been too damaged. Even after Kane spent three hours with her, she hadn't surfaced from a near catatonic state. We'd needed someone to take her place...and Ryth was that someone. Only now her stepbrothers had insisted on taking the place of some of my men.

I didn't know them.

I didn't trust them.

But as Tobias turned his head and met my stare, I knew they'd be just as ruthless as my mercenaries. Maybe even more so.

The Daughters were loaded into the back as the guard climbed into the driver's seat, Helene and Ryth along with them. Night was coming on fast, darkening that beaten and battered hue to lights out. Stars sparkled instead as the truck's engine started and Riven and Kyrell climbed in.

"Easy," St. James urged, helping one of the Daughters into the back. I almost didn't recognize him with the stark white skulled balaclava over his face, black cargos, and a black, high-necked vest strapped with gleaming Sigs.

He helped them inside and turned his head, watching the Sons climb into one Explorer and Vivienne and the bodyguard into the other before he turned back.

I strode forward after they were all inside, gripped the edge of the cargo hold, and lunged. I pushed upwards and my boots hit with a *thud*. I watched the door close in front of me.

Then darkness.

Darkness and fear and underneath that, hope...

I turned around in the dark as the lock on the outside of the door slammed into place with a *bang*.

"Hunter," she called. I closed my eyes for a second as my pulse boomed louder than it should.

"I'm right here." I opened my eyes and stepped forward, finding her in the dark.

I'd know her anywhere.

Even in the back of a truck heading to our fate.

I reached out and my hand brushed hers as I murmured once more, "I'm right here."

FIFTEEN

Helene

THE TRUCK BOUNCED AND JOSTLED, THROWING US AROUND inside the back of the truck. I staggered and hit something hard and *warm*. His arm wrapped around my waist and pulled me against him. I reached behind for balance and felt the rush of his warm breath against my ear.

"I've got you," the mountain at my back whispered.

Heat radiated from his body and into mine. In the terror and dark, that hunger still rose. I opened my hand, released my desperate hold on his pants, and gripped his thigh, my fingers sliding downwards.

"Keep doing that, Helene, and you're going to take my mind off what I'm supposed to be doing here."

My pulse raced at the thought of that.

All that power.

All that...

Hunger.

At the tips of my fingers.

I could make a man like that fall to his knees.

Still, I pulled my hand away, focusing on the darkness as the truck bounced, turning onto streets once more. The more I stared into the dark, the sharper my vision became, until I could make out the larger shapes inside the gloom. Two men crowded a small form. I didn't need to call out to her to know it was Ryth. With both Nick and Tobias at her side, there was no way they were letting my sister out of their sight.

It was just how I needed it to be.

The last thing I wanted was my sisters dragged into this any more than they already were. But we'd had no choice. My heart still ached for the Daughter we'd left behind.

I'd held her hand and talked to her, trying to coax her into reality, but she'd refused to surface, staying instead in the darkness of her mind.

Get her to the table.

The memory of the nightmare surfaced. Midnight waves crashed, spilling into my mouth as I plunged down into the terror. My grip clenched around Hunter's thigh. Somehow, he knew that was more than pleasure. It was survival. He moved closer, his hard body pressed against my back. The brush of his gun at my side made it feel all surreal.

You're mine.

Coulter's words returned from the call.

You hear me? I'm not done with you, Helene. Not by a long shot.

I had a part to play now, a decoy for Coulter and his men, and I was banking on the fact I was all he was thinking about.

My stomach clenched, my thighs pressed together. I'd be happier if I had a gun, but they couldn't risk it. Not until we were inside. Hunter was expecting an armed compound, not unlike the one we'd just left. He said most of the men would be gone, just some pulled back as soon as the call was made. But most would be too far into the wind to come back quickly.

Silence filled the rest of the truck, not even the other Daughters made a sound, leaving only the eerie growl of the truck's engine to fill the space. Still, I couldn't stop myself from glancing toward the closed divider at the front of the cargo hold.

I wanted more than anything to see Riven. My cheeks burned with the betrayal. I was standing outside now. My loyalties had somehow shifted. I turned my head, finding that white skull mask in the gloom, knowing there was no going back now. Not even if I wanted to.

The truck swerved suddenly, throwing me back. The strong muscles of Hunter's arm tensed, driving me against him. His other hand flew out, slamming against the truck to brace us. That dark, midnight stare fixed on mine, triggering that desire once more.

There was no avoiding it now. Not with my body pressed hard against his. One slight shift of my stance, and I caressed the hard outline of his cock. The truck straightened and he dropped his hand, brushing my hair from my eyes.

"We're almost there." The crackle came through his earpiece.

But the mountain never looked away.

It was Nick who did, turning to find us in the dark.

My pulse skipped and I shifted my focus to the truck as it slowed.

"I'll be right behind you, my little fighter," Hunter murmured. "They won't get a goddamn chance to touch you."

My heart was in my mouth, pounding in my ears as the truck geared down.

Faint voices reached me and not the voices of soldiers...it was *women*. Laughter. Excitement. The faint sound of car doors closing reached me and as the truck slowed to a crawl, there was...*music?*

"What the fuck is going on?" I whispered.

Nick and Tobias both drew their guns, and pushed my sister behind them.

From the other side of the truck the giant outline of London St. James stepped forward. "What the fuck is happening out there, Hunter?"

"Hell if I know."

The truck slowed to a crawl, then slowly came to a jarring stop. My head snapped forward and my teeth gnashed.

"Kyrell," Hunter snarled. "I need a SITREP *now!*"

But his command went unanswered. All we could do was stare at the front of the truck in the dark as the front doors opened. Riven's growl reached me, his bark of anger and disgust echoed. Still, I couldn't understand a word he said.

Panic filled me.

One that echoed throughout the space. I tracked the sound of heavy footsteps before the lock on the rear door opened with a squeal and the door was thrown up.

The sparkling headlights of expensive cars bounced off gleaming bumpers. Rolls-Royces and Lamborghinis drove in a tight circle of an expansive driveway behind us, pulled up outside the towering sandstone columns of a very expensive house, and stopped.

"Hunter." Riven stood at the back of the truck and stared up at us. "You're not going to believe what we're seeing."

I stepped forward, drawn by the opulence of Bentleys and sleek black Maseratis.

"Helene," Hunter urged. "Wait, we don't know what—"

"Riven?" a redheaded woman called as she strode along the veered off driveway toward us.

He turned, watching as she lifted her gaze to the interior of the truck. The Daughters reacted around me, shifting uncomfortably as her gaze stopped at me.

Her smile was quick and genuine, fixed on me as though she was a long-lost friend. The only problem was, I had no idea who the fuck she was.

"We've been expecting you." She waved her hand for us to climb out. "All of you. Please, if you'll follow me."

"Hunter." Riven's warning tone ripped out.

The mountain was there, striding out of the darkness behind me.

There wasn't a fucking flinch in her eyes. Not even as Hunter lowered himself out of the back of the truck and towered over her. "Who the fuck are you?"

That smile never wavered as she met his stare. "Who is of no importance. What's really important is family." Her focus shifted to the back of the truck once more.

I knew who she looked at, even without turning my head.

"No," I stepped closer. "You don't get to look at her."

"Don't you agree, Riven?" She swung that ravenous stare back to him. "Family. Just like your sister."

Riven lunged, grabbing her around the throat. "What the fuck did you just stay to me? *You* don't fucking know my sister, do you hear me? *You. Don't. Know. Her.*"

Her eyes sparkled. "Don't I? If you want to see her, then I suggest you get our precious cargo out of that filthy truck and follow me."

Riven said nothing, not even as she tore away from his grasp. He just let her go with a look of pure astonishment.

"You're fucking lying," he growled. "That's all you people do is lie."

"Am I?" She grinned and lifted her cell. Her gaze went to the screen.

It felt like my heart stuttered and broke as I waited. But before the life squeezed out of me, she raised her hand and the cell to him.

I couldn't see it.

I took a step forward.

Still...I couldn't see.

Riven wrenched a sickened stare at her. "Who the fuck is that?"

Her grin only grew wider as she took a step forward. "Look closer, Principal. Don't you recognise your own kin?"

He swayed and his face turned ashen. For a second, I thought he was going to faint.

"Hunter," Riven croaked. "Do whatever she says."

Kyrell stepped around the back of the truck, but he kept on walking past Riven to stop at her side.

That smile was chilling now. Deep red lips curled tight at the edges as she reached out and gently placed a hand on Kyrell's arm. "Good work, Dane."

The betraying bastard had the gall to smirk.

"You sonofabitch," Hunter growled as he lunged down, his boots slamming into the driveway before he rose. "You're a dead man, Kyrell. Mark my words. You won't see sunrise."

Kyrell had the gall to chuckle and shake his head. "Commander, nothing speaks louder than money and these guys, my friend, have a fuckton of it."

Hunter strode forward, grabbed him by the front of his shirt and yanked him forward until Kyrell faced his glare. "I'm *not* your Commander and I sure as *hell* am not your fucking friend."

One look toward the bitch with all the power and he shoved Kyrell backwards.

"Riven," I called his name but even he had no plan for this.

None of us did.

He couldn't look at me, just shook his head. Whatever he saw on that screen rocked him in a way I'd never seen before.

"You." The bitch wrenched her stare at me. "You want to see your sister and her babies?" She lifted the cell in her hand for us to see. "Then you'll do exactly as I said."

All I saw was the overhead view of a black four-wheel drive, the faint shadow of a man behind the wheel with a woman in the passenger's seat.

"Fucking *bitch.*" London strode forward and lunged from the rear of the truck to land beside Hunter.

But Kyrell was already moving, drawing his gun and taking aim until he pressed the muzzle against London's head.

"You can't get to them." London stared at the cell. "They're too fast. They'll outrun you."

But she wasn't shaken. "Let's see if they can outrun a missile from one of our fighter pilots in the sky.

That stilled him.

So much so that the color drained from his face.

"No." I shook my head. "*No!* You leave her alone. You leave *all* of them alone. You want me, right? That's what you want. You want me, then here I am."

"Helene, *no.*" Riven took a step forward, hitting Kyrell's arm, forcing the muzzle of his gun to move from London's head.

But there was no way out of this.

For my sisters, I'd endure anything.

"We want all the Daughters." The woman turned her gaze to the front of the truck and gave a nod.

From the side, soldiers dressed in black came, two pointing guns at Nick and Tobias as they shielded my sister.

"I promise you no harm will come to them," the bitch started. "Unless you force our hand. You don't want to do that, do you, Helene?"

No.

No, I didn't want to do that.

I swallowed hard and shook my head, taking a slow step forward.

"Helene," Ryth called behind me.

I couldn't stop, nor could I look at her. If I did, I'd crumble. So I stepped forward, bent, and gripped the edge of the truck, then *jumped.* "You leave my sister out of this." I rose and met her stare. "Do you hear me? You leave my sister out of this."

The bitch just smiled. "I'm afraid that can't happen, Helene."

One nod and her men rushed forward, lunging and jumping into the back of the truck.

Bang!

I jumped at the sound of the gunshot and stumbled to the side, watching as one of her men hit the floor. Tobias stepped forward, his savage gaze fixed on the man lying with a hole in his chest. "You lay a hand on her and you're fucking dead."

"WAIT!" The woman held up her hands. "Wait now! You won't be harmed. My men are here to escort you, nothing more."

"Then tell them to back the fuck up." Tobias wrenched that savage glare her way. "Before I put a bullet in the next one."

Nick was at his side.

"Easy." She held up her hands, nodding at her men.

They all backed up, giving Nick and Tobias a wide berth. There was no way out of this but to the end. We all knew that. Nick strode forward then jumped down. Tobias followed, turning for my sister the moment his boots hit the ground.

"It's okay, baby." He reached up for her as she knelt, sliding her bare feet over the edge.

One heave and she stood next to me.

"Get the others." The bitch commanded and her men moved in, helping Daughter after Daughter out of the back of the truck.

"This way," Kyrell called.

Ryth looked my way and reached out her hand.

I hated myself for putting her in this position.

But I needed her even more.

I hooked her slender fingers and her palm hit mine.

It felt like fate had brought us here.

That undeniable push had once driven me in front of a speeding car. It drove me again, forcing me to turn and follow the others into that place that looked too pretty to be Hell.

Then again...*what was Hell but money and power and the dark, terrifying things it bought?*

SIXTEEN

Riven

"Move." Hunter's backstabbing second in command drove his gun against the middle of my back, shoving me forward.

My head snapped backwards, teeth gnashing as I stumbled, the ugly fucking bitch's heels clacking as she walked ahead. I wrenched my gaze over my shoulder to Hunter, then back to the asshole glaring at me. For the tenth time in as many seconds, I thought of rushing him and taking my goddamn chances. If it was just brute strength, then I was more than sure we'd be able to take them.

But it wasn't just our lives in the balance now, was it?

"Keep walking, asshole," the bearded bastard ordered.

But I swear, if Hunter didn't shoot this motherfucker, then I would.

My gaze shifted to Helene, who moved protectively in front of her sister. Even in the face of her own fucking danger, she protected her kin. I glanced to the Bankses. Nick had his arm around Ryth, guarding her with his body, whereas his brother was looking for the next bastard to kill.

I'd heard they were fucking savage...but Christ!

Between them and the Sons, there wouldn't be a person standing after this was done. No one left to interrogate, anyway. I turned back and followed the Daughters into the opulent hallway, glancing at the glass wall that divided the garage space. Fuck, even the floors gleamed. I'd thought I knew all the heavy hitters in Hale's arsenal of the depraved. Looked like I'd been wrong. Still, all I could see in my head was the video footage of the woman on the screen the bitch had shoved into my face.

No.

Not a woman...

A stranger.

Don't you recognize your own kin?

I winced and kept walking as the door closed behind us with a hiss and a soft *thud*. Locks clicked, triggering my pulse to race. Looked like we were in this to the bitter fucking end.

"Stop fucking looking around and keep going!" the bastard behind us demanded.

"Fuck *you*," Helene snarled.

I stepped aside, looking behind to see Hunter's ex-man step between her and her sister, driving Helene forward...and into me. She reached for my hand and it felt like the most natural thing in the world to take it.

Protect her.

That's all that hummed in my veins, making sure she got out of this alive.

No matter what it took.

A soldier opened a side door leading into the garage, leaving the bitch to nod before she walked through.

"Through to the other side." He pointed across the space and glared at the rest of us. "To *that* door."

We had no choice but to follow as she strode ahead and stepped through the far door. I was almost there, almost to the door with Helene's hand in mine, when she smiled and slammed the door shut behind her with a *thud*.

My ears suddenly ached, until they popped with a flash of pain. The entire room had sealed and a low hiss started, followed with a bitter tang in the air.

What the f—

I spun around, searching high up for the vents where the sound came from.

"What the fuck is that?" London yelled.

And the blood drained from my face.

"Gas," Nick roared, shoving Ryth to the ground under him. *"That's fucking gas!"*

The door we'd passed through closed with a thud, the soft seal closing us in with that foul stench. I clamped my hand over Helene's mouth. "Breathe slowly," I demanded and pushed her low.

"You *motherfuckers!*" Tobias lunged, driving his shoulder into the glass door.

But the thing didn't even shudder.

The bitch stepped closer, and pressed some kind of button beside the door. Her voice echoed through the speakers in the garage. "I thought you might appreciate the lengths we're going to here."

I took a step, feeling the garage waver. Hard breaths only drew whatever shit they were pumping through the vents deeper into my lungs. I tried to keep it together. "What the fuck did you say?" My words were slurred and felt strange.

"This is after all, your brother's finest work," she continued.

"*What?*" I whispered, standing in the middle of the garage as the lights went out and plunged us into darkness.

OWNED.

The word was neon white, somehow coming from the glass goddamn walls.

OBEY.

CONTROL.

A cold sweat raced along my spine making my gut clench. "No," I shook my head. "*No.*"

But that bitch just smirked and slowly released the button.

"*Fuck you!*" Helene ran and lunged, slamming her fists against the glass. "*Let us out. LET US OUT!*"

"I'm afraid I can't do that, Helene," she said, her faint words reaching us even without a speaker.

Hunter unleashed a roar, then drove his shoulder into the glass along with Tobias Banks.

Chaos..

That's all it was.

The Daughters started crying and wailing.

Bang!

Tobias shot at the glass.

"*NO!*" I screamed and lunged for Helene, grabbing her as the bullet hit the glass and ricocheted. Someone screamed. A piercing, sickening wail. I spun, searching the bodies through the white mist and caught the sickening look of shock from his brother, Nick.

"Ryth?" Tobias stumbled forward. "*RYTH!*"

Helene took a step, pulling out of my arms.

"Baby, *no,*" I slurred as the room started to tilt.

Screams followed.

Screams and under that...

OBEY.

CONTROL.

OWNED.

"Nightieeee niiiiiigggggghhhhhttt, Prinnnnncipppppaaaaal." That's bitch's warped words, invaded as my knees buckled and I hit the sleek, gleaming floor.

I tried to reach for Helene as she crawled for her sister, but she never made it, almost reaching her as she plunged to the floor.

Thud!

Thud!

Bodies dropped all around me.

I tried to hold on, unable to do anything but suck in that bitter air, drawing it deeper into me.

OWNED.

Get to her. I dragged myself forward, using the last strength I had left.

OBEY.

I reached out, grasped her bare ankle, and dragged myself forward another tiny bit.

Hunter slumped to the floor against the glass wall. My eyes watered, blurring my vision even more. Still, all I saw was her.

"Helene," I croaked, sliding myself against her, one hand over her back as I plunged into the dark, that last neon white word blazing in my mind.

CONTROL.

SEVENTEEN

Kane

"*KANE!*" Thomas hissed for the third time in as many minutes.

Still, I ignored him, scanning those wearing expensive tuxedos and exquisite dresses as the well-connected climbed out of their Bentleys and made their way to the front of the house and I tried to find a way inside.

Only, there wasn't one. Not one I saw, anyway.

That clenched fist in my chest kept tightening and tightening and tightening.

I'd seen the back of the truck, glimpsed it before the large gate swung shut behind it. They were in there somewhere...but where...and who the fuck were these people? I swung my gaze back as the rich old fucks and their trophy wives with plastered-on smiles hanging on their arms headed inside.

I couldn't grab one.

Not exposed like this.

But I would if I could. I'd snap the old fuck's neck faster than he could blink if it meant it'd get me inside those walls. Only it wouldn't. That I knew.

"Hey, you got a cigarette?"

I straightened from where I stood under the tree and turned to watch one of the young wait staff heading my way. "Excuse me?"

He froze, turning pale as he glanced at Thomas. "Oh, fuck. Sorry, you're not one of *them*, are you?"

He glanced toward the house and the party.

Adrenaline hit me like a blow. "No." I shook my head and stepped out from the shadows. "No, I'm not one of them."

His shoulders relaxed. "Oh, thank fuck. For a minute there I thought I just lost my job. We aren't allowed to talk to them." He glanced their way again. "You know, the rich old fucks."

I couldn't help but smile, a little anyway. "No, I guess not."

"I need this job man. I got bills up to my fucking neck, if you know what I mean. Anyway." He shifted from one foot to the other and finally saw Thomas as he stepped out from behind me. Then he paled. "Oh, fuck. Sorry, Father. I mean. Jesus, I'm sorry" he stuttered and winced.

I jerked my gaze toward my brother. "Lose the fucking collar, Thomas."

He glanced from the kid to me and then nodded, working the buttons until he tugged the collar free.

"It's okay. It's his day off," I explained, wincing as I turned back to the kid. *His day off?* Fucking idiot.

"Oh," the kid said carefully. "That's okay then."

"But no," I said, taking a step toward him. "To answer your question. I don't have a cigarette. What I do have is a brother who's not well. Are you, Thom?" I swung back to him, meeting his stare.

He scowled, then finally caught on. "Yeah," he said slowly. "I think I ate something that doesn't agree with me."

"Probably those fucking fish eggs." The kid winced and nodded. "Those things look rank."

"Yes." I stepped closer. "He's supposed to be here to help with the speech. We came out here for him to have some fresh air, but I don't want him walking back through the front, you know in case he—"

"Chucks everywhere?" The kid turned pale.

I gave a nod, looked over my shoulder, and scowled.

Thomas moaned the most pathetic moan I'd ever heard and gripped his stomach, but he must've been convincing enough.

"I can let him in through the side entrance. It's for the staff, but being a priest and all...I'm sure they won't—"

I swung my arm back and reached behind me, grabbing my brother's shirt. "Thank you," I gushed as I pulled my brother forward, desperate to get inside. "Thank you very much."

It was one of the few damn times my brother's so-called calling actually fucking helped us. The kid stepped backwards, glancing from me to Thomas. "Oh, okay, sure."

We didn't give him another second to think about it, just ushered him back along the side of the mansion where he'd come from. The sounds of the party grew louder the closer we got. I yanked Thomas forward even harder, lengthening my stride, until the kid pressed his card against the digital lock scanner and the damn thing gave a beep before it opened.

We were inside in a heartbeat, nodding at the kid as he held open the door, then we left him behind. We made our way deeper inside, stepping out of the hallway that led to the back area of the house to where the party was in full swing.

I stepped to the side, leaving room for the waiters to pass carrying empty silver platters piled chest high on cupped hands. But I wasn't there for the champagne, nor was I there for the canapés. I stepped further into the house, nearing the expansive ballroom packed with the filthy fucking rich.

"They're obviously not in there. We should go," Thomas urged at my back.

But I couldn't leave, Not until I knew who they were. I shook my head, waved him off, and took another step, rounded the bottom of the stairs and moved closer.

I thought I recognized a face or two. An out of state senator and I was sure that was Congressman Peters hiding behind the outstretched palm leaves as he sat at the far end of the room. Yeah, the closer I came, the more I was sure that was him.

Laughter cracked out from the middle of the room. Deep, guttural laughter, that made my lip curl instinctively. I narrowed in on that sound and found Julius Harmon the center of attention. So that's whose house we stood in? Now I just wanted to trash the goddamn place.

Movement caught my eye as a woman cut through the tables, making a direct line for him. The redhead was in some kind of hurry, but stopped at his side and bent over to murmur in his ear. An old asshole from the table beside them reached out and placed his hand squarely on her ass.

I watched for her response. There was nothing, almost as though she expected that kind of attention in a place like this. *That's because they're not just here for the party...*

The thought stopped me cold.

Of course they weren't.

"Sonofa—" I whispered and stopped.

A woman sitting at Harmon's table rose, dropping her napkin to the table.

I froze.

My pulse was hammering as she lifted her head, her gaze moving to Harmon.

Familiar blue eyes were fixed on him.

I knew those eyes.

I saw those eyes in my dreams.

And my nightmares.

No.

I shook my head and stepped backwards.

No. That *can't* be.

I slammed into something, hard. Glasses clashed and clattered behind me, falling in a spectacular *crash* to the floor!

"*Shit!*" the waiter cried, trying to grab the glasses.

I turned back and watched the woman with dark hair and blue eyes look our way. My pulse boomed. It was her...*it was Melody.*

Harmon rose, staring at us, and the redhead's eyes widened before she scanned the room, waving men dressed discreetly in tuxedos forward from the outside of the room.

"We have to go." I spun around and started walking, meeting Thomas just outside the ballroom.

"What is it?" he asked.

I just grabbed his arm and scanned the rest of the lower floor, searching for a way out of here. There were guards at the exits. So there was only one way to go. I lifted my gaze along the stairs...*up.*

"The stairs." I shoved my brother, driving him forward. "*Now, Thom!*"

He lunged, taking the stairs two at a time. I was close behind, momentum and sheer desperation driving me forward. Only my mind was still frozen on the woman in the ballroom. The one who'd looked eerily like our sister.

But she couldn't be.

Because there was no way in hell our sister was sitting with a monster like Julius Harmon, not willingly, at least.

I drove myself higher, lunging up the stairs right behind my brother. He stopped at the first floor, scanning left and right, then kept going. My thighs were like lead, my chest was on fire.

"*Hey! You!*" someone called behind us.

I didn't turn around to look. Whichever way this went, it wasn't going to be good. "Find a way to get to them!" I gasped.

"What the fuck do you think I'm doing?" Thom sucked in hard breaths and scanned the landing as we stopped on the second floor.

The damn rooms were a blur, but along the wide hallway that wrapped around the outside of the rooms, I caught a glimpse of night. "There!" I stabbed my finger toward it.

He jerked his gaze to me, then down the stairs before his eyes widened. I risked a glance, to see four of the fuckers after us. We didn't wait around to chat, just lunged along the hallway and kept going.

Desperation filled me, a kind of sick, stabbing feeling I'd never felt before. But as I made for that hallway, it wasn't Riven's or Hunter's face I saw. Nor was it my sister I raced toward. It was Helene.

"Down here!" Thomas called.

I raced after him, knowing my steps were slowing like hell. Thom lunged through a cracked open door at the end of the hall and waited, slamming it closed behind me as I careened through.

Bang!

I sucked in hard breaths and stumbled, bracing myself on the end of a desk.

"*HEY!*" Someone beat against the door.

I flinched and turned to my brother. "We have to get the hell out of here."

But he was staring at something at the end of the room. He took a slow step forward.

"OPEN THE GODDAMN DOOR!" the asshole on the other side roared.

I spun around, desperately searching the windows for a way out. But Thom seemed unconcerned about the guards beating their fists and roaring threats through the door, all he cared about was the paintings hanging on the wall.

I strode toward the window as he slowly made his way toward them.

"We have to jump, you know that, right?" I searched the sill for the locks. But he never answered, pissing me off. I spun, barking, *"Thom!"*

But he was just staring at the damn painting and the pictures next to it.

Keys rattled outside the door. I unleashed a snarl, wrenching my focus back to the window and found the press lock on the side of the damn thing. One *click* and the window released, leaving me to shove the window upwards and turn.

Cold night air rushed in as I lunged, grabbed my goddamn brother, and hauled him away.

"Wait" He fought against me as the study door burst open.

All I saw was the glint of the gun as the guards rushed into the room, a gun pointed at my goddamn brother as he yanked some kind of stupid map from the wall.

"NO!" I screamed, spinning to grab a large crystal vase from the small table next to me, and threw it across the room.

The thing weighed a goddamn ton and hit the guard in the head. I didn't waste a single second rushing forward to grab Thom as he stumbled my way, his wide eyes still pinned on the paintings on the wall he'd left behind.

With a guttural roar, I shoved him through the window, then slammed into him hard as we slipped out the window on the second floor.

"The fuck you do!" the guard yelled behind me as he grabbed my shirt and yanked me backwards.

Movement came from a window two rooms down as another of Harmon's fucking men ducked out of the window onto a balcony and took aim. Thom froze, staring, as Coulter followed the guard out, dipping his head low until he straightened and adjusted his jacket.

He took one long look at both of us and clucked his tongue. "Now, this isn't where I left you, is it, Doctor?" He shifted that hateful glare to me. "No filthy loading dock, no gun pressed to your head. The only question is...what do I do with you now?"

"Sir," a call came from the open window Coulter had stepped through. "The auction, sir. It's time."

Coulter just gave a slow nod and turned back to me.

My stomach clenched as a sickening wave washed through me.

"I guess there's only one place for you to go, isn't there?" he said carefully.

Thomas stumbled forward and cast the map he'd torn from the wall out and into the dark. The night breeze caught it, causing it to flap and slip away, disappearing from view.

"Fuck!" the guard behind me snapped and pushed forward.

"Leave it," Coulter commanded. "I'm not missing this...not for all the world." He glanced at the asshole who had me by the shirt. "Bring them and if they give you any trouble, put a bullet in the Priest."

EIGHTEEN

Helene

My head rolled forward and my teeth gnashed, shocking me out of the washed-out gray blur of my mind.

"There she is." Warped words reached me.

A woman?

Her fingers were cruel as they grabbed my arm and twisted. Pain followed, the ache familiar and cruel. I tried to open my eyes, but they refused to budge, leaving my head to roll.

A crack of light slipped in, but it was the heaviness that held me under.

The heavy gray fog in my mind.

Fragments came to me.

A room...

A hiss of *something*.

Then nothing.

"Do you like it?" The woman asked, moving in close. "We took what they'd been giving out at The Order and had our chemist tweak it a little. I was told it gives a helluva rush."

Her face was blurred and her wide eyes were fixed on mine. "Looks like it does, doesn't it?"

I had no idea what she was even saying.

My tongue felt thick and alien as I licked arid lips and croaked, "Where am I?" I winced with the words, my throat sore and aching.

I tried to remember what had happened...but there was nothing, not even my own name came back to me. Just nothing but emptiness.

"Oh, honey, don't you remember? You're at your wedding," she said as she straightened.

Wedding?

My...wedding. I tried to hold my head up, keeping her stare as she straightened. "Here. Let me help you get dressed, we can't very well have you walking on stage dressed like that now, can we?"

I slowly looked down at the red lingerie I wore and scowled. "No," I slurred. "I guess not."

The woman turned around and walked to a chair, grabbing something black before she turned around and came back. I winced at the glaring fluorescent lights that hurt my eyes.

"Here we go." She slipped the shoulder strap down. "Let's get you fixed up."

She pulled the bodysuit down with a hard yank, spilling my breasts free. Cold air licked me, making my nipples tighten. She lowered her head, watching the reaction, then cruelly cupped my breast. "Fuck, you're beautiful."

Something inside me recoiled at her touch. I tried to shake my head and force myself up in the chair. This didn't feel right. None of it.

The door opened behind her with a hiss, and movement came at the corner of my eyes. High heels and a long, tight black skirt came into view. Bright lights made it hard for me to see.

"Isn't she beautiful, Mel?" the woman who cupped me asked.

I lifted my gaze to the strange woman, watching her come closer. She said nothing, just stared down at me.

"What...what is happening to me?" I whispered.

"You're getting sold, honey," the stranger murmured. "After all, it's not every day we have Weylyn King's daughter on the stage, is it?"

The woman in front of me smiled, then released my breast, tugging the red lingerie all the way down. "Lift."

I didn't move, trying to gather that slow, warped, insistent voice in my head. Still, it didn't matter. She lifted my leg, worked the red bodysuit free, and cast it aside.

The brunette watched us as the black bodysuit was slipped over my feet and worked up my legs.

No.

Don't do this.

Don't...

I lifted my head to say the words rolling around in my head and caught the shine of glass. Through the window a man hanging by his hands kicked and bucked, tearing at the bonds. His face was half-hidden in darkness. But there was a glimpse of his face, a tortured, terrified stare. Those eyes fixed on mine.

"We have a lot of men bidding for you tonight and some lucky man is going to take you home for you to obey his every command." She tugged the bodysuit over my stomach to cup my breasts. One hand was fed through the strap before the other followed.

"Who...who's is that man?" I whispered, trying desperately to remember anything other than the heavy fog in my head.

The woman stopped, then glanced over her shoulder, which only made the man more desperate, pulling his hands until his spine bowed and the buttons on his shirt ripped.

"Oh, him." She turned back, her lips curled into a tight smirk. "He's no one...no one you need to worry about."

His mouth was open, screaming words I couldn't hear. But I wanted to hear them...I was desperate to hear them. I pushed forward. "I need to go to him."

The room swayed as I stood from the chair.

"I don't think so, honey. That man is dangerous."

Dangerous? I shifted my gaze to him. The moment I did, that nagging sense of familiarity came rushing back. My heart boomed, flooding my veins with the rush.

"Let's go, princess." The redheaded woman gripped my arm and pulled me toward the door.

The brunette opened it, holding it for us to pass. But it was that man...the man with half a shadow for a face hanging there.

You want to scream? A man's growl filled my head. *Go ahead. I like the sound muffled against my hand.*

My steps suddenly stopped in the middle of the hallway. He lunged, the whites of his eyes almost neon in the dark. His mouth moved, stretching wide.

Hell...something. *Hell*...that's what he was screaming. Anguish was written all across his face as he savagely lunged until the shackles snapped taut.

No!

He screamed.

NO!

"Keep going, princess." The redhead murmured, pulling me forward.

I took a step and stopped as the glint of glass walls swayed.

"Easy now. We're almost there." The redhead glanced behind her. "Mel?"

"I'll be right there," the other woman murmured. "I have something to take care of first."

"Hmm. Your call." The hold around my arm tightened as I was pulled forward again.

I didn't want to go, didn't want to leave that man silently screaming in that room. But the more I stood upright, the harder it was to stay like that. I followed her, stumbling, until my knees buckled. I fell sideways, hitting the glass wall before I was grabbed and pulled upright.

"Christ, that shit is strong. Isn't it, princess?" She grunted, heaving me along the hallway.

The bright lights overhead swam. I couldn't even answer, just put one foot in front of the other until we came to another room...a room with more women.

"Here we are." The redhead unlocked the door and pushed it open.

There were two more like her, dressed immaculately in floor-length dresses. One blonde, the other chestnut brown. They rushed forward, grabbing my other arm.

But it was the huddled women dressed in the same red bodysuit I'd worn that held my focus. *Remember...why the fuck can't you remember?*

I stumbled forward.

Red.

Red lingerie.

Shadows falling across her as we stood in the back of a truck.

My pulse was booming as I yanked my arm free and lurched forward. I had to find her. The young woman...the one I had to protect.

"Looking for someone?" the redhead asked behind me as I staggered toward the women.

I grabbed each one, turning their faces toward me, searching for the one I needed to protect.

"Obey."

I stiffened at the word.

Heels clicked on the hard floor as the redhead stopped beside me.

"You know that word, right?" She brushed the hair over my ear, her tone softening. "Yeah, you know that word. Obey. Control." She moved close and whispered. *"Daughter."*

NINETEEN

Riven

---

*"NO! DON'T YOU FUCKING DARE TOUCH HER!
DON'T YOUUU TOUCHHH HERRRR!"*

I yanked, snatching my arms forward. My pulse was a fucking sledgehammer as I screamed and pulled against the steel cuffs around my wrists.

Through the glass window, I saw them in that room, watched helplessly as Helene slumped in the chair. That redheaded bitch turned to the male nurse beside her and gave a nod. There was nothing I could do but watch as they injected something into her veins.

They're not going to kill her...

The words were cruel fucking comfort as I watched the needle slide from her vein and the male nurse straighten. He left then, slipping out the door to her room, his steps soundless. I couldn't hear a goddamn thing. Not their voices or anything but the hiss of cold air being pumped into the vents above me. The same fucking vents they'd used to drug us with.

All because of me.

Stupid!

STUPID!

I sucked in hard breaths and lifted my gaze to the woman I loved slumped in a chair in the room on the other side of the glass. The drug had hit her harder. Of course it had, she was smaller...and susceptible...because of all the drugs in her system.

And whose goddamn fault was that?

A tortured sound ripped free as I hung suspended.

I shook my head, desperate to get it together and *think.*

But I couldn't remember a goddamn thing, not after I'd hit the concrete floor in that garage. The first thing I became aware of was that I was handcuffed. My focus returned to the room opposite us as that redheaded bitch leaned down to whisper something in her ear.

Helene's head rolled backwards, even from here I could see her eyelids flutter, trying to wake. My chest was a hollow fucking cage, one that arched and throbbed as that bitch tugged the strap of her red bodysuit down.

"No...*no you fucking don't,*" I warned as she spoke in soundless words.

Then with a yank, she pulled the rest of her lingerie down hard, spilling her breasts free. My balls tightened and revulsion ripped through me as I watched her kneel and cup Helene's breasts.

"You FUCKING CUNT!" I screamed, lunging against the bindings.

Helene's head rolled forwards. Her gaze sharpened as she fixed on that dead bitch's hands on her body. There was a lazy shake of her head as though deep down she knew that was wrong.

Exactly how she was when I had her cuffed to my goddamn sofa as I fucked her with my fingers.

I was no different...no fucking *different.*

"I WILL FUCKING KILL YOU!" I hollered and kicked, throwing myself forward until my cuffs clashed and bit into my wrists.

Slowly, Helene turned her gaze toward me as another woman stepped into the room behind them. I froze, watching this brunette close the door and move closer toward them. But Helene was fixed on me. I could see her lips move slowly, almost hear her mouth the words. *Who is he?*

The redheaded bitch looked my way, then smiled before saying. *He's dangerous.*

Dangerous?

DANGEROUS?

I yanked against the cuffs. I was going to kill that goddamn *BITCH!* I was going to fucking tear her *apart! Just let me get out of here.* I lunged until the tendons under my arms screamed in agony. But that was *nothing* compared to my heart being ripped from my body.

Because that's how this felt.

The bitch rose, dragging Helene with her, now dressed in black. *Black...she was about to be sold.* That chilling thought plunged all the way to my soul. Helene stumbled, but was held upright as they all headed for the door.

"DON'T GO!" I bellowed. *"DON'T GO WITH THEM, HELENE!"*

She lifted her head, her gaze fixed on mine as they stopped in the middle of the hallway. Then she was gone, being taken away from me...and leaving the brunette behind.

I shook my head, pulling against the cuffs as they disappeared. But the brunette stayed behind, slowly turning to me.

I froze.

No.

There was a shake of my head as she opened the door with a hiss...or it could've been a tremble.

My past stepped into the room, lifting the same brown eyes of my mother to mine.

"No," I whispered as she came closer, moving soundlessly like a ghost.

But Melody wasn't a ghost. She was real and she was standing right in front of me.

"Mel?" I whispered, terrified for her to answer.

"Yes, big brother. It's me."

Still, my mind refused to believe. "No," I stared at her. "It can't be you."

"Oh, I assure you it's me," she answered, holding my stare.

"How. Where?"

"How. Where?" she repeated. "Is that all you have to say?"

I lifted my gaze to the empty hallway. "Please," I whispered. "Don't do this."

Gone was the emptiness in her eyes when I turned back. There was only savagery now. Complete annihilating feminine rage. She stepped closer, searching my eyes. "Don't what? Sell your fucking whore?" Her lips curled and there was a sickening, throaty chuckle that spilled from her lips.

She stepped closer, so close I could smell her expensive perfume.

"Oh, believe me," she whispered. "I'll be walking her onto that stage and making sure she's sold to the most violent of them all. In fact, I think we have a record number of men bidding for your sweet Helene. I cannot wait until she's taken. They might even send me a video of the first time they fuck her. I hope the drugs wear off before then. I can't wait to watch her scream and fight...for a while anyway. I might even have it play out on the window for you. How would you like that, *big brother?* Would you like to watch the first time they force themselves inside her? I do hope there's a whole lot of them. They could all take turns...just like Coulter and his men did before."

Her smile grew wider.

Revulsion rolled through me, making me fall forward. I was going to be sick. I was going to...

"Why look so shocked, big brother? After all, this is what you do, right?" She leaned down, until the soft strands of her hair brushed my shoulder. "You groom them for sale. You *break them*."

"No." The word was a hoarse whisper. I closed my eyes as their faces came back to me. All the women we'd hurt. All the things we'd done. "We did it all for you." I lifted my head, meeting that cold, empty stare. "We did it all for you."

"What?" She tilted her ear toward me. "What did you say?"

"We did it for you. To find you."

Slowly she met my stare. "Oh, you stupid, *egoistical* fucking idiot. Did it *ever* occur to you that the reason why you couldn't find me was because *I* didn't *want* to be found?"

No...

No.

This wasn't my sister. This wasn't my...all the things I'd done for her.

"Isn't that what you wanted? To get rid of your painful annoying little sister?"

I shook my head.

"Do you even remember what you screamed at me? *Just DISAPPEAR!* That's what you said. You wanted me to disappear. Well, let me assure you, big brother. Your annoying little sister is dead and buried. You know...I didn't even fight when that sleek black car pulled up beside the playground where I sat crying after you screamed at me. I didn't even scream when a man climbed out and headed toward me. The same man you worked alongside all these years. No, I just took his hand and climbed inside Hale's car that day and I never looked back. I went with him willingly and later, I climbed into his bed."

My gut clenched. "No." The thought of her with *him.*

Her smile widened. "Every day he worked beside you, then he came home and fucked me until I could hardly walk and I fucking *loved* knowing all the sick, vile things you were doing was to get close to him. I loved knowing my disappearance was eating you alive."

"You...you *fucking* bitch."

That laugh came once more as she took a step backwards. "Oh, big brother. You don't know half of it. I'm going to enjoy watching the woman you've fallen in love with get violated tonight." She bit her lip and cupped her breasts, her perfectly manicured nails dragging across her hard nipples. "Yes, I think I'll enjoy it very...*very* much."

She turned...and my heart dropped into my stomach. "No... *no!*"

She yanked open the door.

"Please, Melody! Please MELODY! DON'T DO THIS DON'T DO THIS—"

The glass door closed with a *thud.*

Then she was gone.

I screamed for her. Screamed and lunged against my cuffs until I lost feeling in my hands and my voice was hoarse. But she never came back...she left me alone. And all those vile things I'd ever done came rushing back to me. Images filled my mind, images of what they would do to the woman I loved...

I dropped hard, hanging by my wrists alone as thick, heavy sobs filled me.

There was nothing they could do to me that was worse than this.

Nothing that would ever compare to my own...private...Hell.

Because, I'd done this.

I'd done it all.

TWENTY

Helene

I STUMBLED AS THEY LED ME AND THE OTHER DAUGHTERS along the hallway to a set of stairs, then climbed them to enter an expansive room, one lined with beauty stations and high chairs.

"Let's get you ready, shall we?" the redhead murmured, holding my arm.

I grabbed hold of the chair I was led to, climbed onto the seat, and closed my eyes. My head was still slow and swimming, my thoughts faded and too far away for me to grasp.

"Easy now," someone said.

I cracked open my eyes and watched someone dressed in white lean over and push a needle into a Daughter's arm, before pulling the plunger free. A nod from the redhead and he moved on to the next Daughter, disposed of the last needle and picked up a fresh one. That didn't feel right. I shifted to the Daughter who'd just been given the drug as her eyes rolled back in her head.

My hands trembled as I pushed up from the seat. "Wait..." I slurred, and lurched forward.

But the male nurse was already pushing the plunger all the way to the hilt, glancing up into the Daughter's eyes. But her eyes didn't close like the other one's had. Nor did she seem to slump into a washed-out delirium. No, instead her eyes shot open so wide I thought they'd burst. In an instant she lunged, unleashing the most terrifying banshee shriek I'd ever heard.

I stumbled backwards, narrowly missing them. But the redhead was hit so hard she flew backwards. Only it was the male nurse who took the brunt of her attack, falling backwards to land on the floor. She was on him in a blur, clawing his face and screaming.

My stomach clenched as she shoved her fingers into his eyes. One came free with a sickening *pop*. Then she wasn't the only one screaming. His roars were just as deafening, making the other Daughters in the room scramble backwards, pressing their backs against the wall.

The redhead and her guard tried their best to drag the Daughter free, but she was past the point of being in control of anything.

She clawed his face, tearing shreds of skin free until her focus fixed on the syringe in his hand. With a scream, she pried it free from his grip. There was no stopping her, no fighting it as she yanked it free, lifting it over her head. The redhead punched the side of the Daughter's head, yanking her hair as she tried to pull her free.

Even the guard unleashed a blow, hitting the Daughter in the side of her face. She fell sideways, sliding off the male nurse and into me. My knees buckled with the force, instantly dropping me to the floor and directly in her line of sight. But I wasn't her target. All she wanted was them.

With another chilling scream, she drove the syringe down with all she had, straight into the nurse's chest.

BANG!

Her head snapped toward me. Wetness splattered across my face as the Daughter slumped to the floor. Only the screams didn't stop, as the nurse clawed his protruding eyeball.

BANG!

He slumped and his hands dropped to the floor beside him. Terrifying silence rang in my ears as the redhead wiped her hands against her gown and straightened, turning her gaze from the two dead bodies on the floor in front of me.

"Right," she said, stilling the shake in her tone. "Now that's taken care of, let's get back to business."

One glance my way and she winced, then turned her focus to the others. "You." She pointed to one. "Over here."

Another woman stepped in carrying a small bag of makeup. The redhead snapped her gaze her way. "Start with that one. I want them to be perfect."

But I couldn't move, still on all fours staring at the vacant eyes of the Daughter in front of me...the one who was now missing half her head.

"Hurry," the redhead snapped. "I want her out in five."

I shoved against the floor, held onto the chair and slowly pulled myself upright. *Stop this...you have to stop this...*

The words were slow and distant, leaving me to glance back at the dead woman as though what'd just happened had been some fucked-up dream. But it wasn't a dream. That was real.

"Okay," the redhead snapped, glancing at the door as that familiar brunette walked in.

She looked my way, then took hold of the Daughter who had now been made up with deep red lips. "This way," she said, leading her out of the room.

"You, you're next." I watched as another one was selected.

She shook and wept, slumping hard as they forced her into the chair. Hairspray hissed, the sharp scent filling the room before her black hair was swept up and pinned, revealing her long neck. Makeup was next, just enough to make her lips stand out.

Then the brunette was back, glancing my way before she turned to the new made-up Daughter. "You, come."

I glanced at the door behind her, then slowly scanned the rest of the room, searching for a way out of this hell.

"I wouldn't if I were you."

I glanced back at the cruel woman who called the shots. She held my gaze. "You wouldn't make it, and it would be an absolute waste to have to kill you." She took a step forward. "Not only that, you don't want to make me go to the basement and drag your sister up here to take your place, do you?"

My sister...

The words caught my breath. Her face rushed back to me. Young, beautiful...with the most perfect birthmark on the edge of her cheek.

"Ryth," I whispered.

The bitch turned away, walking to where the next Daughter was in the seat, her hair being straightened this time with a hair iron.

But as I stared at the Daughter's hair being combed, my memories slowly came back to me. It wasn't just the truck this time. It was Ryth's face, and the two men she was with...*Tobias and Nick,* their names followed. Then another face rushed in to take their place. A man's face...a man I knew. One who thrashed and screamed, hanging by his hands tied over his head.

That man's dangerous...

I shook my head.

No.

No, he wasn't dangerous at all.

My breath caught as the brunette came back, her gaze narrowing in on me. "She's next." She commanded, then pointed my way.

I shook my head as they came for me, the redhead and her guard with the gun.

"Now, you're not going to give us trouble, are you, Helene?"

Helene...

My own name resounded in my head as the redhead grabbed my arm and pulled me forward.

"I think your sister was hurt," she said, searching my eyes for a flicker of recognition. "It looked serious. I guess that's what happens when you shoot at bulletproof glass. I do hope she gets to a doctor soon."

My heart hammered at the words.

There was a shake of her head.

"In the chair, Helene...*now*."

I eased down, my ass hitting the leather seat. The make-up artist flinched as she stared at my face, then bent over, yanking wipes from a container and cleaned the mess that had cooled against my cheeks. A comb was tugged through my hair before it was swept up.

"No. This one stays as she is."

The brunette stepped into the room and headed my way. "No hair, no makeup. I want them to see her raw." She stopped beside the chair. "The others went fast, they were cheap. But I expect there'll be a battle over you." She gripped my chin, turning my face toward her. "So fucking exciting."

I had no idea what she meant...but I knew it wasn't good.

Her fingers dug into my arm, bruising as she yanked me forward.

"My sister," I moaned to the redhead as I was dragged away. "Tell me...tell me where she is."

"I'll text it to you," she answered before she laughed.

That revolting sound stayed with me as I was pulled out of the room and turned right before I was forced up three more stairs. The hushed murmur of voices reached me as a heavy black curtain was yanked aside and I was forced forward and plunged into darkness.

"Keep going," she hissed.

Confused, I stepped forward until another set of heavy black curtains pulled away, leaving me standing in the center of a stage in the middle of a room filled with men and women sitting around tables at my feet.

"And here is the one you've been waiting for." The brunette's cruel grip tightened as she pushed me forward. "The problematic, pain in the goddamn ass known as Helene King. Now, I'm sure many of you have had your fair share of the kind of trouble this woman is notorious for...and don't forget, she is the eldest daughter of the benefactor of tonight's auction, Mr. Weylyn King himself. Where is he?" I couldn't move as she searched the crowd, then stilled. "There he is. Stand up, Mr. King. Stand up and let everyone see how much this stunning woman here resembles you."

Fear froze me to the spot.

All I saw were glinting lights and flickering candles.

Then there was movement...and in the back of the room a shrouded figure cloaked in shadows rose.

The drug that still raged in my system did little to dull the pain that ripped through my chest.

Lights glinted behind him, casting his face in darkness. But I didn't need to see it to know who the man was. Recognition raged inside me.

"So do we have anyone who would like to start the bidding?"

I couldn't even look at her as she spoke.

"Two million!" a man from the back called out.

"Three million" someone in front countered.

Ice ran through me at the sight as the man rose from his seat. I tore my focus from the man who was once my father to this man...and a ripple of terror tore through me.

*I know him...*I tried to fight the haze in my head. *I know him...I know...*

My body clenched. My pulse roared as he adjusted his tuxedo jacket.

"Coulter" the bitch at my side murmured. "I was wondering when you were going to spend your money."

I shook my head. "No." I stumbled backwards. *"No."*

Until I hit something big and hard. I spun around, coming face to face with a massive guard.

"Come on now, Helene," Coulter called from his table. "We were friends once. I'm sure we can be friends again...after all... you left my men desperate to get reacquainted."

The guard grabbed my arms and forced me backwards.

Instinct took over, causing me to yank my foot back and lash out, driving my heel into his knee. A *crunch* filled the air. He went down, grabbing his knee and roaring. All I saw was the darkness as I lunged.

"Stop her!" the brunette screamed.

Two more of the guards came out from behind the curtain. One I might've had a chance with...but two of them? There was no way I was getting out of that. They closed in, each one grabbing an arm. I kicked and screamed, throwing my body.

"RIVEN!" The name ripped from the depths of my soul. *"No... no...no. Riven! RIVEN!"*

They dragged me back to the stage past the guard still on the floor as he held his knee. My head snapped backwards as they wrenched me to the edge of the stage.

"As you can see," the bitch continued with a snarl. "There's still plenty of fight left in her. Do we have a bid higher than three million?"

"Three point five," someone called out.

"Four," Coulter called, those dark eyes fixed on mine. "Four million dollars."

The bitch turned her head. "Four million dollars? Surely, we can do better than that. How about we parade Ms. King around...let everyone see exactly what they're purchasing?"

Cold washed through me. I shook my head, yanking against the guards' grips. "No...*no.*"

"Get her down," she commanded. "Let's see if she's worth four million."

I bucked and dug my heels in, sliding against the stage as they dragged me toward the edge and with one hard *shove,* pushed me off.

I fell, my arms windmilling before I hit the floor. My knees buckled, dropping me. Agony flared, driving thunder through my head, making my thoughts even foggier with the drug.

My memories were still fragments.

Fragments and feelings. Both were just as terrifying as I pushed myself upwards and searched for an escape. Men and women stared at me, their beady glinting eyes full of ravenous hunger. The kind that made me sick.

Thud.

Heavy steps hit the floor beside me. I lunged the other way and careened into a round table, knocking flutes of champagne over. Drinks spilled but there were no cries of outrage.

No.

It was almost as though they expected it.

A cry tore free as I pushed away and ran, throwing myself right as more guards came from the edges of the room and made their way toward me. I searched for a weapon...anything I could use.

A grunt came before I was hit from behind and slammed forward, landing hard on a table in the middle of the room. Glasses flew sideways, flickering candles were snuffed out as I grasped the table to keep from falling and lifted my head.

Two men sat side by side. Their hands bound behind them. Guns were pointed at their heads.

"Helene?" one called my name.

He was familiar....so very familiar. *"Kane?"* I whispered, his name coming through that gray fog inside my head.

"Get her over here," my handler called.

I was yanked from the table, then dragged backwards. Memories slammed into me as I was pushed around to the other side of the table and forced to bend over it.

My face was slammed against the cold, hard surface. Tears came as I bucked, fighting against their hold.

Get her to the table...

Those chilling words found me. Resounding over and over and over in my head. *Get her to the table. Get her to the table. Get her...*I remembered now. Remembered their hands holding my legs open as greedy fingers were pushed inside.

"No! Get the FUCK OFF HER!" Kane roared, throwing himself forward. *"Stop this now...I SAID STOP THIS NOW!"*

Tears blurred their faces as I was held down, my hair fisted in a cruel grip as they kicked my legs apart.

"No!" I bucked, but the force of the grip smashed my cheek against the table.

All I saw was their faces. Kane...*Kane's face.* That's what I held onto, his bright blue eyes and perfect lips.

"Pull her ass wide," the bitch called in front of me. "Let's get a good look at what you can have. The bid stands at four million. Come on, gentlemen. I know you want to take the infamous King's Daughter for a ride."

I shoved and buckled, my cheek bruising as they ground my jaw against the surface. To my right someone shifted in the gloom. His face sharpened, that cold, detached stare fixed on me as Coulter tugged the crotch of his trousers and adjusted how he sat.

"Go on," he murmured. "Fight for me."

Those hard lips curled into a smirk. I bucked and screamed until fire exploded in the middle of my chest.

"I'LL FUCKING KILL YOU!" Kane roared. *"I'LL FUCKING KILL YOU ALL!"*

"Four million," the brunette called out behind me. "Do I have anything higher? Four million...going once..."

TWENTY-ONE

Riven

No! *NONONONO!*

"Take me!" I croaked. *"Just take me...please, Mel. I'm begging you."*

But my pleas went unanswered, fading to nothing in the empty room where I hung suspended by the cuffs around my wrists. Movement came in the corner of my eye as a group of guards passed the large window.

"Wait!" I screamed, then coughed, my throat on fire. *"I'LL PAY! DO YOU HEAR ME? I'LL PAYYYY!"*

But they kept walking, oblivious to my demands as though they never heard.

I sucked in hard breaths which only inflamed the burn in the back of my throat. I tried to swallow, but my mouth was bone dry.

"I'll pay." The words were nothing but air as I closed my eyes. "Whatever you want. Just don't...don't hurt her."

I'm going to enjoy watching the woman you've fallen in love with get violated tonight...

A moan ripped free, wretched and burning. I swallowed the sting like molten lava, leaving it to well inside that gaping hole in my chest.

I hated her.

Still, I hated myself more.

My hands were numb, swallowed by the pain as the metal shackles wore against my wrists. But if I had a blade, I'd cut them off. I'd do anything as long as I could get to her.

Helene...

Please, forgive me.

Because there was no way I'd *ever* forgive myself.

I opened my eyes, seeing movement from the corner of the window once more. Three more guards chatted and slowly walked past.

"Please, for fuck's sake, I'll pay," I hissed. *"I'll pay whatever you want."*

Just like the others, they never turned...nor did they hear me, until one stumbled forward, then to the side, slamming into the window.

The glint of a knife came, whipping through the air end-over-end to bury in the other guard's chest. He stumbled backwards, then looked down to see nothing but the hilt. Transfixed, I could only stare as the last guard palmed his weapon and spun. Only he didn't have a chance to fire.

The largest of the two shadows lunged, driving his fist into the guard's face. Harmon's man was no slouch, stocky and built. But he was still no match for the raw, unhinged force of this man as he drove his fist over and over into the bloody mess he'd left behind.

Until there was no fighting done.

Only the beating of an unconscious man.

Then those two men turned toward me...and I knew instantly who they were.

The Sons.

My breath left me as Carven bent down, disappearing for a second before he rose, then came toward me. A card was pressed against the door, letting it open with a hiss.

"Please," I whispered, pulling on the cuffs. "Get me out of here."

"Where is London?" Carven stepped closer, those intense blue eyes fixed on me.

It took me a second to understand what he was saying. I shook my head, drawing a curl of his lip. He stepped closer until he stood right in front of me. "I *said,* where the fuck is London?"

"I don't know," I croaked. "We were drugged, knocked out, and when I came to..."

He turned instantly, striding away, *leaving me behind.*

"*Wait!*" I roared, stopping him at the door.

He didn't care about me. He cared about little, that was easy to see. Programmed since birth, then trained to be the perfect killer, his loyalty could *never* be bought. It was earned. London St. James had earned it and so had their daughter, Vivienne.

Careful.

That voice inside my head whispered.

They knew what had happened within the walls of The Order. They *knew* what I did to the woman they loved. The woman carrying their children. One wrong word and he would run that blade across my neck and leave me hanging like a side of beef.

Still I had to *try*.

"They'll rape her again," I pleaded. "They'll rape her and it'll be all my fault. I know you owe me nothing, less than nothing. But I'm begging you. I'm begging you with all I have left. *Please* let me fight for her."

"And die?" the Son asked, then slowly turned. "Would you die for her? Would you sacrifice your kin...your blood...your fucking soul?"

He took one step toward me.

I knew that was how he felt about Vivienne, that complete annihilation of everything he ever was and ever could be until there was nothing left but one driving *need*.

The need to protect her.

The *need* to love her.

Even if she never loved me back.

"Yes," I answered as though there was only ever one answer. "Yes, I'd die. Yes, I'd do whatever it took. Kill me, give me a gun. I'll be her weapon until my last breath."

Something primal raged in the Son's blue eyes.

He turned around, leaving the room, and my heart dropped... until he stopped, bent over, then rose and returned, stopping just inside the door. "Live or die, I don't care. I would've come for you anyway after what you did to what belongs to me. But now...now I'm thinking I might let you live just so I can watch the utter destruction you'll unleash."

He tossed something through the air. Metal glinted under the lights as they sailed through the air. They were keys...*Jesus CHRIST THEY WERE KEYS!* I lunged forward, my mouth opening as wide as I could and gnashed down hard, catching the cold metal between my teeth.

"Good luck, Principal. But don't think this is over between us. You *will* still pay for what you did to the woman we love. You face us with honesty and remorse and you might just survive."

I'd never felt true fear before.

Not the kind that rendered you unable to think. All I could do was hold his gaze with the keys clamped between my teeth, then slowly nod.

That fire in my throat flared as I swallowed. Then they were gone, stepping over the bodies of the guards in the hallway and lunged, slipping from view.

They were coming for me.

There was a damn good chance I wouldn't survive. But I couldn't think about that now. All I cared about was Helene. I turned my head, working the keys between my teeth and rose up on my toes, but still, I couldn't get close. My hands were numb and throbbing. But I gripped the cuffs and heaved with all I had.

The tendons in my arms were screaming as I inched the key in my mouth to the lock. The tip slipped into the lock. I shoved my entire body forward, driving it all the way inside, then twisted my head, snapping open the lock.

My dead hand dropped. For a second, I couldn't move. Then adrenaline hit me. I jerked my gaze to the hallway, then hurriedly yanked the key from the cuff and worked the other.

Until I dropped like a stone to the floor. Agony was a sledgehammer blow through my knees. But I shoved upwards and lunged for the doorway, skidding as I stopped at the pool of blood around the guard.

His gun was all I wanted. I bent over his body and yanked his weapon free, then turned to the others. I snatched a second weapon and an access card free before I shoved upwards.

Minutes...that's all I had now.

Those I was losing fast.

I stumbled, then pushed into a run, heading to where I didn't know. I ran past the open door of another room, one that haunted me. They were here, that's all I knew. I felt it in the pit of my stomach. Darkened steps rose to my left as I raced along the corridor. The faint sound of a voice called out. A female's voice...

I climbed, taking them two at a time until I slammed face first into a heavy black curtain. Panic roared. I thrashed, slapping the goddamn thing from my face and stumbled as I slipped through.

"GET THE FUCK OFF HER!" Kane's roar hit me instantly.

I gripped the gun, that merciless hunger burning as I headed for the sound. Helene's muffled screams rang out, as did the excited murmurs of the others in the room. I slammed into the second black curtain, throwing it aside as my brother howled his fury.

Faces...that's all I saw.

There were fifty or sixty of them all sitting at tables. I swept my gaze around the room, narrowing in on my brothers.

"I'LL FUCKING KILL YOU! I'LL FUCKING KILL YOU! I'LL KILL YOU ALL." Kane bucked and screamed, with his hands bound behind him. Thomas sat there, staring wildly around the room, searching for a way out.

"Four million," my sister called, drawing my focus to the table where they held Helene down. "Do I have anything higher? Four million...going once...going twice."

Then I saw him as he slowly rose from the seat in front of her... Coulter.

Rage ripped through me. Consuming, ravening *rage*.

I lifted the gun, taking aim just as Thomas suddenly shoved upwards, tearing away from the guard at his back. His eyes were wide, fixed on movement that came from the corner of the room.

"Going three times," my cunt of a sister called out.

I saw the movement as men dressed in black invaded. *The fuck you are!* I ground my jaw, wrenching my attention back to Coulter and took aim again.

Until Helene moved, stepping right into my path. I froze, watching her scan the crowd, then she stopped.

Something sailed through the air.

BOOM!

The detonation was brutal. Men and women flew through the air. Chairs became missiles slamming into those sitting outside the last zone.

BOOM!

I lunged as more were thrown forward. Screams followed. Chilling, shrill screams that grew in crescendo. All I cared about was her, and my brothers a close second. With my pulse booming in my ears, I lunged from the stage, my frantic eyes scanning the table where Helene had been a second ago.

Kane charged forward, slamming into a man in his way. Thomas was a second behind him, his gaze lifting to find mine.

"Riven!" he screamed.

Crack!

I squeezed the trigger as the guard who'd held them prisoner took aim. The shot hit him in the shoulder, spinning him.

I shoved a woman aside. "Get the *fuck out of my way!*"

All I cared about was finding her. I yanked and shoved as those who came to sate their depraved needs ran for their lives.

"Find the Daughters!"

I jerked my gaze to the roar as I was slammed and knocked sideways. As I straightened, so did the assassin in black. He stared at me with the same empty, detached stare Carven had minutes ago. That same shiver of fear found me. I glanced at the others he'd come with, knowing instantly *what* they were.

"You." The Son turned his attention back to Helene, huddled on the floor under the table. "Come with me."

"No," I growled, shaking my head as I strode forward, putting myself between him and her. "She doesn't belong to you. This one is mine."

Kane and Thomas stumbled forward, pushing in to stand next to me while chaos raged all around us.

"She is a Daughter, isn't she?" The Son looked from me to her.

"Not yours, she isn't," Kane stated. "There's more." He gave a jerk of his head toward the stage. "Where she came from."

The Son glanced at the stage, then turned back again., that merciless stare finding Helene who still huddled, seemingly unaware, on the floor.

"She *doesn't* belong to you," I repeated, imploring him with a stare.

I knew without a doubt that if he wanted her, there was nothing I or my brothers could do to stop it. I just prayed he didn't.

He scowled, then took a step backwards as the sound of gunfire started in that room behind the curtain.

"You'd better hurry," Kane urged. "Sounds like they could do with a savior."

There was a curl of the Son's lip before he spun on his heel and lunged away.

A hard heavy breath tore out of me with a *whoosh*. I sucked in the air and strode forward, bending down to pull Helene up from the floor. "It's me...*Helene, it's me!*"

I wasn't at all sure she heard me, she was staring at me as though she couldn't see a goddamn thing. *Those motherfucking bastards.* The last thing I wanted to do was manhandle her. Fuck knows she'd had enough of that to last her a goddamn lifetime. But there was no time to worry about that now. I needed to get her out of there...and fast.

I grabbed her as gently as I could, pulling her up from the floor as others trampled around us. "Come on, Trouble."

"Baby." I slid my hands to her cheeks and stared into her eyes. "Can you hear me?"

She looked as though she didn't hear a thing.

For a second, I thought I'd lost her...until slowly, she lifted her gaze and those dark brown eyes met mine.

"You came," she said softly. I'd never been decimated by two simple words...until now.

My chest throbbed with the ache as I cupped her perfect face. "I will *always* come for you, Helene. Do you hear me? I will always come."

She swallowed hard and as though my words released some kind of spell, I saw life once again move into her eyes.

"Can you walk?" Kane asked her, then met my stare. "We need to get out of here."

Helene just nodded. I turned around, scanning the decimated tables and chairs before I grabbed a black suit jacket from the ground and wrapped it around her shoulders. "Let's get the hell out of here."

But there was no way we were heading where those vile motherfuckers crushed each other in an attempt to get through the single door.

"Come on." I pulled her against me and scanned the way I'd come. I'd rather take my chances with anyone else than with the Sons of The Order. But right now there weren't a whole lot of fucking options. "Stay close," I urged and pulled her with me back toward the stage.

I scanned what remained of the crowd as I stepped over a woman who was dead and the pathetic bastard next to her, searching for any sign of Coulter. Part of me wanted to see those stony fucking eyes fixed wide as he lay amongst the dead. But he wasn't anywhere I could see as I turned and lifted Helene up onto the stage.

My brothers were next, their hands still cuffed behind them, leaving them to slide along the edge and slowly push to their knees. I hauled myself up, my body shaking with the effort. "We need to get you out of those cuffs."

A piercing female scream came from behind the curtain. I shot forward, shoving it aside. But I was no white fucking knight... not for her at least. "Let's go, baby. Back the way you came."

Helene moved fast, scurrying back through the second curtain before my brothers followed. The thud of her feet on the stairs was the only thing I tracked.

"Please..." I whispered as Thomas shoved past, careening after her, followed by Kane. "Let us make it out of here alive."

TWENTY-TWO

Helene

My knees buckled as I hit the last stair. Still, I kept going, slamming my hands against the wall to push off once more.

"Who the fuck were they?" Kane barked close behind me.

Screams still filled the cramped air all around us, coming from those still fighting for a way out, and others fighting for their lives.

"Sons." Riven grunted as all four of us hurtled along the hallway.

There was a man dressed in a tux and his companion standing in our way. He swiveled as we raced toward him.

"Don't..." he lifted his hand, his eyes wide. *"Don't!"*

Bang!

I stumbled, careening forward as he crumpled to the ground in front of me, blood instantly seeping through his white shirt. His companion just sucked in a massive breath and unleashed a scream that resounded through my head.

"Hey!" Kane grabbed her, yanking her forward. "That piece of shit deserved to die, maybe you do too. I don't know. But what I do know is that if you don't get out of here right now, you'll be following him. Do you understand?"

She jerked those wide eyes up to him, the piercing scream dying instantly. She glanced behind him at the man who'd just killed her partner and sucked in hard breaths.

"So I suggest you start looking for a way out of this." Kane lowered his gaze to the dead rich fuck. "Then, if I were you, I'd clean out the fucker's bank accounts."

That made her snap to attention. She looked down at her dying lover, then lunged, tearing past us with a renewed desperation to get out of there.

"Always the fucking same." Kane muttered, gripping my arm gently and drove me forward. "Keep going, baby."

We left them behind, making our way along the hallway and past the rooms they'd kept us in. Three guards were dead outside the open door where they'd had Riven handcuffed and chained like a goddamn animal. I glanced over my shoulder before I glanced at the gaping wound in the guard's neck after being sliced from ear to ear. Maybe an animal is exactly what was needed.

We kept hurrying until gunfire came in the distance.

"Stop." Riven growled. "We all can't be out in the open like this."

Kane's grip tightened as he turned. "What are you suggesting?"

Riven glanced at a small hallway up ahead. "I think Helene and Thomas should wait here until we find a way out of here. All of us stumbling around this fucking place makes us sitting ducks in the open."

I shook my head. I didn't like that idea. We needed to stay together, especially because I still couldn't get my head cleared. I winced, feeling the hallway blur around me.

"It's safer this way." Riven brushed his fingers along my jaw. "We'll be back before you know it."

He didn't give me any chance to argue, just turned to Kane, then glanced at Thomas. "Protect her." He commanded before he turned away.

One nod from Kane and he followed, leaving us behind. I tried not to look at Thomas, feeling the weight of his stare. Instead, I slid along the wall, slipping deeper into the mouth of the hallway.

How long would they take?

I closed my eyes and prayed. I just wanted to get out of there. I just wanted to—

"Someone's coming." Thomas muttered.

I yanked open my eyes, finding him backing up in front of me. I stared at his strong shoulders under his snug white shirt, then glanced at the corded muscles under his rolled-up sleeves. He wasn't tall like the others, was shorter and stockier...and different...something I couldn't quite put my finger on.

But as the sound of footsteps grew louder, he pushed into me, forcing us further back into the hall. I held my breath, watching as three men dressed in Armani rushed forward, their faces frantic as they searched for another way out.

Thomas's fists clenched. His entire body tensed, ready to take on all three of them.

Protect her.

Riven's command filled my head.

Of course he would...still, there was that *feeling* about the Priest and, as the sound of the three men faded, Thomas eased.

"You're not like the others, are you?" I murmured softly.

He stiffened, then slowly turned my way. I could count on one hand the number of times he'd actually looked me in the eye.

"Why?" He asked. "Because I'm not killing myself trying to fuck you?"

I searched his brown eyes. "Do you want to?"

His cheeks grew red before he glanced away. So, he did...

"It feels wrong." He whispered. "All wrong."

"It's okay." I touched his arm, causing him to jump before I pulled away.

He jerked back to stand on the other side of the hallway, and stared at me, mortified. "You can't touch me like that. The lightness...I can't" He winced, and rubbed his arm where we'd connected. "I find some sensory stimuli uncomfortable."

Almost like he couldn't handle the contact.

"It's okay." I searched his downcast gaze. "You'll get beaten up and take it, but one light touch brings you undone?"

He lifted his gaze. "You sound like Mel, she used to tease me too."

In a blinding second, I felt like an ass. "I'm sorry. That was... insensitive."

He gave a careful shrug. "It's part of the reason why I leapt into religion. There was structure there, it's an instruction manual on how to live my life the way society accepts."

"As long as that society is rich assholes who degrade and use women."

His eyes darkened. I saw in that moment the sacrifices he'd made to find his sister...the kind of sacrifices they'd *all* made.

"I hope you find her." I whispered. "For all your sakes."

His flinch was instant, his eyes grew wide. "You don't know?"

I held that panicked stare. "Know...what?"

His chest rose and fell hard. "That woman...the one who sold you...that was...that was our sister, Melody."

The floor seemed to drop out from under me. Reflex took over. I wrenched my hand away and stumbled backwards.

"No." I whispered, shaking my head. I could still feel her cruel grip and hear her callous laugh. There was no way *she* was their blood. No way...

"I didn't believe it myself. But it was her."

"Oh, God." I doubled over as my stomach rolled. I threw out my hand to the wall. I was going to be sick. Then his hand found me and his fingers clenched around mine.

"I got you," he murmured. "Whatever you need."

My vision blurred with tears as I lifted my gaze. All the awful goddamn things they'd done, only for her to be...whatever she'd become. "*Why?*" I whispered. "Why would she do that?"

"Why indeed?" he answered, that knowing stare boring into mine.

Stand up, Mr. King. Their sister's words rang in my head. *Stand up and let everyone see how much this stunning woman here resembles you.*

The tears kept coming, slipping down my cheeks as the memory of my father's betrayal sharpened.

Until the heavy thud of boots stole our focus. The sound of a two-way crackled in the air. The guard almost passed us, until he turned his head and caught sight of Thomas in the corner of his eye.

No!

He stopped, glanced over his shoulder, then moved closer, finding me standing further in the back. His scowl was instant as he took in the black lingerie I wore.

"You?" he muttered, then swung that glare back to Thomas.

There was a second where time was suspended. Then in a rush, Thomas unleashed a roar and lunged at the same time the guard went for his gun. Both men grappled, throwing each other to the side until they slammed against the wall. The guard was fast and trained, but Thomas was no slouch, grabbing his head in a lock and driving his knee into the guy's chest, knocking the wind out of him.

The attack triggered something in me. I lunged and landed on the guard's back as he tried to lift the gun and take aim.

"The fuck you do!" I screamed, throwing my arm around the bastard's neck.

My head was still foggy and my reaction was painfully slow. The scumbag's jacket flapped wildly as he fought. I wasn't anywhere near the ruthless woman I'd been mere months ago, but I gave it my all, yanking his head backward with all I had.

BANG!

The shot was deafening. I wrenched my wide eyes upwards as Thomas slowly met my gaze, his face growing pale.

"*No...*" I shook my head, unable to take my gaze off him. "*Nononono...no!*"

But it was the guard under me who crumpled to the floor, carrying me with him. I fell, slamming my head against the wall until all I saw were stars...and Thomas as he towered over me with the gun in his hand.

The hot, metallic scent of blood filled the air, clinging cloyingly to my nose as I slowly looked down. All I saw was the uniform, just like the ones at The Order.

Get her to the table.

I kicked frantically, shoving myself away from the body.

"He won't hurt you." Thomas gasped as he sucked in hard breaths, those intense brown eyes fixed on mine. "Not anymore."

I flinched as I leaned against the wall, until Thomas slowly reached his hand out. My pulse was pounding as I took it, then took a step forward and wrapped my arms around him.

He didn't move for a second, then slowly he folded his arms about me.

"You said I wasn't like the others." He murmured against my ear. "I'm not. I wasn't going to tell you because I didn't want you to freak out or...look at me differently."

I eased my hold and pulled back, eyeing that careful stare.

"I'm going to touch you," he said. "Just not the way you expect."

I tightened my arms around him and laid my cheek on his shoulder. "This feels pretty damn good to me."

Footsteps sounded, ruining the moment. I jerked my head upwards as Riven and Kane rushed into the hallway. Riven glanced at us, with my arms around his brother, then looked at the dead guard. "We found a way to...somewhere, but we have to move."

I moved away from Thomas, stepped over the guard's body, and headed to where Kane waited. All four of us hurried, turning right as the hallway wrapped back around the house.

"Here." Kane rushed toward what looked like an elevator and pressed a button.

I froze, glancing at him. "In an elevator?"

He shrugged. "Either we go up and we get out of here, or we go down and..."

"And we're fucked." Thomas finished, then shifted his focus my way. "I don't like this."

"Well." Riven snapped, striding forward as the doors opened. "Right now, we're out of options."

He stepped in and turned, staring at us.

"Fuck." Thomas snarled as Kane followed his brother.

We had no idea what was down there. The Sons...the Order... *Coulter?*

A shiver ran through me. Riven threw out his hand as the doors started to close, holding them open. "Coming, Trouble?"

I had no choice but to follow. We were like the tide and the moon now, there was no one without the other.

I stepped inside and Riven lowered his hand, letting the doors closed. One glance at the buttons and I knew with a sinking feeling there was no way we were going up. The only buttons for this elevator were down.

"Shit." Kane muttered as we sank.

I shot him a glare. "That's it?"

He gave a wince, then a shrug. "Better than that fucking room... and the Sons." He glanced at Riven. "Where the fuck did they come from?"

Riven just stared straight ahead at the doors. "How the hell should I know?"

Kane gave a *humph* as we jerked to a halt and the doors opened. "You know something." He answered as Riven strode out. Thomas followed, leaving Kane to press his hand against the small of my back, steering me out.

This was unlike any goddamn cellar I'd ever seen. I coughed, choking on the musty air, and slapped my hand across my mouth as I stared at the entire wall filled with expensive-as-fuck wine.

Dust coated the amber bottles. Riven glanced at the row, then plucked a bottle from toward the end. "Jesus, this must be worth two hundred thousand. Pity." He said as he hurled it across the aisle, leaving it to smash against the wall.

I stared at the mess spreading behind us as we turned and made our way deeper into the cellar.

"There has to be another way out of here." Riven searched the darkness. "Only an idiot would leave one way out with this kind of expense. We need to spread out."

"The fuck we do." Kane snapped. "We just did that, *remember?* Look how well that turned out."

I shook my head. No...I didn't want to do that. I didn't want to be away from any of them.

Let's see if she's worth four million.

My throat tightened, the words just a choked whisper as a shudder ripped through me. "*No...I don't...*"

BOOM!

The faint explosion sounded somewhere far above.

We waited...

"What the fuck was that?" Thomas whispered as we all looked up.

Riven shook his head as the ceiling and the walls trembled. "Nothing good, that's for sure."

"We need to get out." I took a step backwards and swept my gaze along the walls as the glass wine bottles clinked and clashed, one breaking with a *crash*. "We need to get out of here *now*."

All four of us took a step backwards.

BOOM!

The second detonation was even louder, as though someone was doing their best to bring the entire place to the ground. The only problem was...*we were deep in the belly of the beast... searching for a way out.*

"We have to go." Riven's voice was emotionless and cold.

But I knew different. I knew *him*.

He reached out and grasped my hand in his. "We have to go *NOW*."

All four of us swiveled, turning around as the wine bottles bounced and shuddered, some sliding from the shelves sunk into the walls.

Crash!

Crash...

CRASH!

But as we lunged back towards the only other way out of there, a roar came out of the dark tunnel the way we were headed. The deep, male sound was almost unrecognizable.

Until it wasn't...

Riven suddenly stopped, jerking me to a standstill. As Kane and Thomas kept running, leaving us behind, he turned his head.

"Riven?" I whispered. "Is that...?"

His strong fingers unfurled from around my hand and he stepped away. As the crashing wine bottles grew into a shattering crescendo, he said the words which filled me with dread. "That's my brother..." he met my stare. "It's Hunter."

TWENTY-THREE

Hunter

Buzzzzz...

Agony ripped through me. My body shuddered and trembled as four hundred volts of electricity tore through my muscles. My spine bowed, contracting so tightly, white sparks detonated behind my eyes until something in my neck went _crack_.

That white was neon.

Blinding.

Suffocating.

Until the washed-out haze slowly darkened to the gritty dark gray cell they kept me in.

"You sure are a big bastard." My tormentor growled, sucking in hard breaths.

The _thud...thud...thud_ of his steps broke through the panicked racing of my heart. A heart that was shuddering and booming in my chest. My head hung low, and drool slipped from my lips. I couldn't withstand this...not for much longer.

He gripped my hair and yanked, forcing my head upwards. Those dark eyes blurred as they fixed on me. I could barely make out his face. But his voice...no, that was something I'd never forget.

"You're a tough sonofabitch, just like she told me you would be. But I've had tougher. I've seen a man take this for weeks, until his mind snapped and he became...he became...*something else.*"

My head rolled, until the darkness ate away more than the edges of the room.

"No, you don't." He shook my head, the crunch in my neck stabbing. "You wake the fuck up. I'm not done with you, not by a long shot."

But I couldn't.

I knew that.

I just couldn't.

Buzzzz...

My body clenched and my balls tightened with the sound. I unleashed a roar, bellowing my rage and agony as that rod was driven into my stomach once more. My boots skidded, kicking as my body obeyed a new master and its name was pain.

"That's it!" he hollered and laughed. *"Dance for me, motherfucker!"*

I ground my teeth, fighting to hold on as the room shuddered and shook all around me, until finally those jaws of agony released their hold and the beast that was the man stepped away.

The chains around my wrists shook and clanked. I slumped, putting all my weight on my shoulders.

Hard gasps filled my ears.

Until the *click* of a lock sounded and the spill of bright light washed in for a second, then it was gone again.

"He's still alive?"

I sucked in a breath and fire exploded in my chest, leaving me to cough and gasp until I thought I was choking to death.

"Does that answer your question?" The bastard muttered.

The *clack...clack...clack* of her heels resounded in the room. My head felt like it was made of lead, taking every ounce of energy to drag my gaze upwards until I looked into her eyes.

Those cold, unfathomable eyes.

She looked so much like our mother.

Distant.

Sad.

Unforgiving in the wake of our sister's disappearance.

From that fateful day she'd only had one child, and she'd been taken from her.

"Brother dearest." Her lips curled into a sneer.

I shook my head. "No." The word was a whisper. "You're... not...my...sister."

"Oh, I'm sure you're regretting that now, aren't you?"

Regret.

That was something I'd never had when it came to her. It was all anger. All rage. Directed at the one person I blamed for it all...*Riven.*

She opened her hand. "Give it to me."

My tormentor scowled and looked her way. "I don't think..."

She snapped her gaze toward him. "I don't *pay* you to think, do I?"

Pay?

I shook my head as the guard handed over the rod.

"*No.*" I croaked as she took the rod that buzzed and hummed in her grip, her painted red nails so out of place on something designed to torture.

Or, maybe it wasn't?

Maybe, this was *exactly* the kind of thing my sister enjoyed.

Breaking.

Destroying.

Controlling.

I lowered my gaze to that rod, watching the sparks inside light up as she moved closer.

"You see, brother dearest, I never wanted your family anyway. I was always destined for this one of my own."

Agony turned to rage. One that became something savage inside me. I'd never had rage for her, never had rage for a woman in my entire life. They were always the ones to protect, the ones to care for...until now.

Now...this one—the one who was supposed to be my blood—was different.

"He's going to die, you know that, don't you?"

She stilled, a crease carving between her brows. She knew what I was talking about. I saw it all play out in those brown eyes, before that smile was back again. Her lips curled wider. "You think you can get anywhere near him? Then...think again."

She drove that rod into my stomach, giving me all the voltage it had. I threw my head backwards, unleashing a roar that burned through my body. My stomach clenched. My insides jerked and quivered, tightening until I couldn't take anymore.

Then with a jerk she tore away, leaving my feet to tap and kick as I slumped, my shoulders screaming with all my weight.

"I will destroy you." She said through her heavy breaths. "Everyone you care about. Everyone *they* care about. I will take that white fucking knight need you have to protect and I'll tear it apart, until there's nothing left but despair. That's what *I* will do to you. But Hale...Hale already has what he wants."

A terrified, desperate scream echoed, growing louder before the door to my cell was thrown open.

"You fucking *bite* me again, you goddamn bitch, and I'll put a fucking bullet through that belly of yours!" A guard bellowed as he shoved a *very* pregnant woman into the room in front of me.

At first my mind refused to work.

I stared at her as she straightened, breathing hard and holding onto her swollen stomach.

"Hunter?" She called my name.

I just stared at her and tried to remember who she was...

Until the woman jerked a savage glare toward my sister. "I have no idea who the fuck you are...but you're about to know who *I* am real quickly. London St. James and the Sons will tear this place apart to find me...and you along with it."

The guard who'd dragged her in rubbed his hand and limped forward. "That fucking bitch is goddamn crazy."

"Oh, buddy," her lips curled, baring her teeth. "You have *no idea*."

"I know who you are, Vivienne." My sister turned on her.

I shook my head, my thoughts coming back to me now. I knew her...*Vivienne...Helene's Vivienne*.

"No." I croaked and shook my head. "Whatever you're planning, you're not doing that."

Vivienne's eyes widened as she took in the rod in my sister's hand, the one that hummed with the electrical current. She spun, terrified now, as she settled her gaze on the bastard who'd tortured me.

"You." She whispered, her face growing pale. "You did this... you did this to my Colt."

The brutal guard just smiled.

Through the blur, my sister smiled.

Then with a scream, the hurricane of a woman lunged. She clawed his face, raking her nails along his cheek before he had a chance to stumble backwards. Pregnant or not, that one was a force...just like her sister.

I hung there, unable to take my eyes off her, until Melody strode forward and shoved that rod against her belly.

"Make one more move and I'll shove four hundred volts through this belly of yours and right into your baby."

Vivienne froze instantly, then turned her head. Wild strands of her hair settled across her eyes. Still, she saw my sister clearly.

"Now, we don't want you to go into labor, now do we? Not until we have everything prepared.

I'd never seen a shade more sickening than gray, but the woman turned it now.

Sallow and terrified, her eyes widened instantly. "What do you mean, *prepared?*"

"Hale and I want everything ready for when we have our babies."

Vivienne stumbled backwards, her fingers splayed wide over her stomach. "No." She whimpered and shook her head. "I won't let that happen."

"Honey, you won't be around to stop it, now will you?"

Evil.

That's what my sister was.

Pure. Fucking. Evil.

There was no fight in Vivienne anymore. There was nothing but terror as the guard strode forward and grabbed her arm once more.

"If you take them, you'd better kill me." She finally whispered, staring into Melody's eyes. "Because I won't stop, and neither will those I love. I won't stop until I burn your world to the ground. You have no idea who you're dealing with...but you will soon." The guard jerked her forward. "You will soon."

"Take her along the tunnel to the car. Don't stop for anything, do you hear me? Not until you get to Hale."

Vivienne's eyes shimmered with tears. She shook her head, her gaze moving to me.

"No." I pulled on the cuffs, my arms burning and spent. Still, I had to try. "Don't you fucking dare—"

The sonofabitch who liked to torture grabbed the rod from my sister and strode forward.

I tensed my body, throwing myself toward the guard as he dragged Vivienne from the room. *"No NOOO!"*

Bang!

The door slammed shut. They were gone, leaving a gaping hole of desperation behind. *"DON'T YOU FUCKING TOUCH HER...DO YOU HEAR ME! DON'T YOU TOUCH HERRRR!"* My sister stepped closer and reached up, gently brushing her fingers along my jaw. I jerked away from her touch. "Get the fuck away from me. You're no sister of mine."

Rage found me as I met her gaze.

Excitement sparkled in her eyes.

She was right.

In a single blow, she'd killed any kind of need I had to protect her.

Now I just wanted her dead.

And Hale along with her.

"Farewell, brother. It was nice knowing you, however brief it was."

Then she stepped away, nodding to my tormentor as she turned and headed for the door.

The hinges squealed before it closed again with a *thud*.

"I guess it's just you and me now."

I sucked in heavy breaths.

Buzzz...buzzz.

My stomach clenched with the sound.

That rod was all I could see as he stepped closer and muttered. "Let's just see how long you last."

TWENTY-FOUR

Helene

THAT FAINT, BESTIAL SCREAM CAME ONCE MORE, reaching out through this underground hell to find us. Riven swiveled around, scanning every inch of where we stood, trying to get a bead on Hunter's location.

Seconds passed until I grabbed his arm. "Can you find him?"

The ceiling above trembled...and another wine bottle behind us broke.

There was panic in those deep gray eyes as they turned to me. "We have to keep going." He found my hand, grasped it tightly, and started walking back along where we'd come from until we passed the elevator and headed into the darkness.

"We can't just leave him." I hissed. "Riven...*Riven!*"

But Riven never slowed, instead he clenched my grip tighter, dragging me along. As though he was saying *I will get you out of here, one way or another...I will get you out.*

The only problem was...there were people we loved still in there.

Thomas and Kane said nothing as we headed along the darkened hall with only the deep rumble of the crumbling mansion above to fill the void. I was scared, terrified in fact. Still, we were together. There was no way I wanted to be alone. Thomas glanced my way, moving closer until he walked next to me, his arm occasionally brushing mine.

I didn't expect the contact, but I hadn't expected him either. Not the way he comforted me in ways no one else had. He met my gaze, but that stony stare spoke to me now. He wasn't cold or hateful, he was...different.

I brushed my fingers against the back of his hand until the deep rumble from above drew my focus. But the dark tunnel in front of us blurred. I stumbled, my heart lunging, until a strong hand clamped around my arm.

"Easy. You okay?" Thomas's brows narrowed.

I nodded, forcing a smile. "Just tripped." I answered, but my breaths were too fast and my eyes too wide.

He scowled even harder. "You can't lie to me."

I turned my focus to sidestepping the cracks racing across the floor and kept pushing, waiting for the drugs to subside. Flickers of memories hit me as Thomas focused on the path ahead. But I couldn't see the tight dark tunnel as it snaked up ahead. I was trapped in my head, forced back into the spotlight as I was shoved onto that stage. It was all I could see. The room. The crowd. Those ravenous stares fixed on me as I ran for my life.

My steps stuttered, the hold on my hand pulling me forward. Thomas looked behind as I tore my hand from his grasp. Those blue-gray eyes...eyes that looked so much like my sisters'.

"What is it?" Thomas stopped.

Riven glanced behind, found me, and stopped. "What?" He glanced around.

But the memories didn't stop, slamming into me over and over like waves crashing on the rocks. But I wasn't the rock. I was the water...*slam...slam...slam...*

"He was there. My father...he was there."

Riven glanced my way, then toward the tunnel up ahead before striding back and grabbing my shoulders. "Are you sure?"

Am I sure? My breath caught, then released in a gasp as the face of my father came rushing back. "Yeah," I answered, my stomach clenched in revulsion. "I'm sure."

Boom!

I stumbled sideways as the ground beneath us shook. Kane unleashed a cry as we all lunged for the wall, holding on.

"It's going to come down on us!" Kane bellowed.

"Help us!" A faint roar reached us. *"Someone fucking help us!"*

I jerked my gaze to Riven. He heard it this time. That was for sure. Even as the ground underneath us trembled again, all four of us surged forward.

"We're here!" Riven yelled.

"Here!" The sound came from somewhere in the distance. We threw up our hands, covering our eyes as the stony ceiling

cracked and crumbled, fine fragments falling all around us. "Can you hear us!" Riven surged forward.

"*Yeah!*" The response came.

The closer we got, the clearer the voice.

"Riven!" I shouted over the grumble of the aftershock. "That's—"

But he knew exactly who it was and as we ran, a darkened doorway came into view. One with bars across the top.

"*Tobias!*" I screamed as Riven skidded to a stop in front of the door.

I slammed into him, grabbing hold of the bars and stared into those savage eyes. "It's us...thank God, we found you."

"Good...now *get us the fuck out of here!*" He roared.

But beneath the aggression was something else, something only someone who knew him could see...*fear.*

"You're right, baby, look...she's here. Helene is here."

Only then did I hear Nick's low murmur. I looked past Tobias, who filled the doorway, to the feet and legs behind him.

"Ryth?"

I think your sister was hurt. It looked serious. I guess that's what happens when you shoot at bulletproof glass. I do hope she gets to a doctor soon.

"Show me." I whispered, staring at her feet. "Show me my sister."

Slowly, as though it took every ounce of his willpower, Tobias stepped aside.

There was blood on her side. Her face was turned toward me, or maybe it was Nick as he sat beside her. She winced, her brow glistening with sweat.

She was hurt. Cold washed through me...she was really hurt.

"Riven." I whispered, and grabbed the bars, yanking as hard as I could. "Get them out." I wrenched my gaze to him. *"GET THEM OUT!"*

He was frozen for a second, then glanced at the door and the lock. "We can't...there's no way we can get in there."

"She's fucking BLEEDING!" Tobias roared, grabbing the metal bars and yanking until I thought the corded tendons in his neck would snap.

A cry wrenched free, a sickening, wounded sound as I grasped the bars around his hands and yanked. But the thing wouldn't budge. It *wouldn't budge.*

"GET IT OPEN NOOOWWWW!"

I stopped, seeing the utter panic in Tobias's eyes.

"Please." I whispered, holding onto the bars, desperately staring at the bottom half of my sister as she lay on the floor of that cell. "Please, I'll do anything. I'll do anything."

"Then get the hell outta the way." The command came from somewhere behind us.

I spun around at the same time Riven did, staring into the piercing blue eyes of the Son, Carven.

"Carven?" I whispered, taking in the blood splatter across his cheek, then looked at his hands. "What the hell happened?"

He gripped a block of explosive with bloodied hands.

I knew exactly what he'd done.

He'd killed one of those who'd come to destroy everything.

He didn't answer, just looked at Tobias, his brow rising with an unspoken question as he lifted his hand.

"No." I shook my head. "No, you can't. You'll kill them."

The keypad wrapped around the brick of C4 was brand new, the numbers fresh and black, shimmering in the faint light.

"How?" I whispered.

"How do you think?" He said, looking down.

"Who are they?" Riven asked.

Those blue eyes were crystal clear as he answered. "Rogue Sons who are only after one thing."

Riven stiffened and his skin went pale as he glanced toward me.

You, come with me. The Son had commanded. Riven had stopped him. *She doesn't belong to you. This one is mine.*

She's a Daughter, isn't she? The Son had asked, turning those cold, killer eyes to me.

A shiver tore through me as I lifted my gaze from that block of C4 in Carven's bloody hands. What kind of man did it take to kill a born killer? *A more determined one...that's what.*

"It's the only way." Carven answered as the tunnel rumbled and shuddered around us.

"Do it." Tobias croaked. "Whatever you need to do, just do it. Get us the fuck out of here."

"You know this could kill you, right?" Carven met his stare.

Tobias looked over to where Nick cradled Ryth's head in his lap, then he turned back. "Set it up. Don't start the timer until we're ready."

I shook my head...*no*...*no*...*no*. I wanted them out but not like this. Tobias stepped away, then knelt beside her. "Little mouse, we need to move you. It's going to hurt. But you're strong, you're so fucking strong. I know you are. I watched you give birth to our son."

She looked up at him, then gave a nod. Nick eased out, holding her head like she was made of glass. I guess to them, she was.

"I'm okay." She croaked, holding onto him as he eased to his feet and picked her up.

"We need her against the far wall." Tobias urged.

Carven went to work, placing the C4 against the door.

"Helene," Riven gripped my arm and pulled me backwards. "Baby, we need to step back."

It was the last thing I wanted to do. Still, I let him lead me away, further back along the tunnel where we'd come from and let Carven work.

This wasn't right. None of it. But as I stepped backwards, the image of our father's face came back. My throat tightened, thickening until it was hard to breathe. My betraying goddamn father. There were no words he could say that could justify any of this.

The truth was as annihilating as the explosive Carven fixed to the front of the cell door.

"Trouble." Riven pulled me back a little further.

I let him draw me into his arms and turn me around. My arms went around his back as he pressed me against the stone wall out of the blast zone.

I lifted my gaze to his, to that animalistic rage that rippled deep inside, and my arms tightened around him.

"Hands over your ears, baby." He urged.

I wrapped my elbows around him, my palms clamped over my ears.

"Ready!" Carven yelled. *"Five...four...three...two...BOOM!"*

I screamed with the sound. Not because of the blast, but because my future was in that cell. The moment the dust and the smoke started to fall, I tore away from Riven, dipped under his hold, and raced forward, to that dark, frigid cell.

"Ryth!" I screamed and raced for the blown open door. *"RYTH!"*

Carven caught me the moment I plunged inside.

His icy blue eyes fixed on mine. He was so...mechanical. So ruthless. So uncaring, until he lifted his gaze to the cloud of dust as it settled...and out of that murky gloom came Tobias, carrying my sister in his arms.

Only then did the Son let me go.

I tore out of his hold. *"Ryth! Is she alive? IS SHE ALIVE?"*

Tobias stumbled, but his hold around her was like a rock, cradling her against his chest.

She coughed, her hand going to her mouth before she wrapped her arms around her stepbrother.

"Oh, God...oh, thank God." I gasped, coming to a stop in front of them.

Ryth turned her gaze my way and reached her dainty hand to me.

"Get her out of here." Carven ordered, pointing up ahead. "There's a small tunnel that way." He pointed the way we'd been heading. "It takes you around the front of the property and comes out near the driveway."

BOOM!

Another detonation rocked the tunnel, casting dust and rocks from the cracked ceiling up ahead.

"Carven!" A roar came in the darkness.

We all stared as in the distance came Colt...and beside him London.

"London?" Carven took a step forward.

The tunnel rumbled, shaking and shuddering. Behind us in the gloom something went *crash!*

"Look out!" Riven roared.

I was hit from behind and lifted. Everything happened in a blur. Panic. Power. Riven swung me around and out of the path as part of the tunnel ceiling dropped and smashed against the floor in the exact same spot where I'd been standing.

"Fuck!" Tobias looked up, searching the ceiling of the now fragile tunnel we stood in.

But London didn't search for the next falling missile. He scowled, looking at his cell. The screen was alight. Even from here I could see message after message scrolling.

"We're getting her out." Tobias stepped over the rubble, with Nick following, striding ahead.

"You'd better hurry." Carven muttered, staring at London as he lifted the cell to his ear. "What is it?"

London shook his head, wrenching the cell away to snarl. "There's like ten fucking voicemails from Guild, but there's no fucking reception."

In an instant, Colt paled. He shook his head as both London and Carven looked at him.

"What is it?" I stepped forward as my stomach sank. *"What is it?"*

There was only one thing it could be. The woman we all loved...my spitfire of a sister...*Vivienne.*

"Go." Carven. *"GO!"*

London spun and lunged. Colt followed...and did Carven, leaving us standing outside the cell.

They ran, overtaking Tobias and Nick as they carried Ryth out. Then all of them were running as the tunnel groaned around us

Crash! A portion of ceiling fell behind us.

"We have to get out of here!" Kane bellowed.

"No—" I started until Riven cut me off.

"Not without Hunter." He commanded. "We're not leaving without him."

"Then we *have to go...now!*" Kane stumbled backwards as another chunk of stone fell from the ceiling, crashing to the floor behind us. *"Run!"* He roared. *"RUN!"*

TWENTY-FIVE

Hunter

The place rumbled and shook. Chunks of the ceiling crashed to the floor all around us. But I couldn't care... no, the encroaching darkness took care of that. I hung by my arms. My head dropped forward and warmth trickled from my mouth. I tried to close my lips, but my body refused to work.

Another rumble came, this time closer and deeper, like we were wedged in the back of the throat of this beast.

"They bomb. They bomb and they bomb and they bomb."

I tried to open my eyes, tried to force my lids open. But there was nothing but the emptiness. Nothing but the pain...the pain that waits.

"Looks like you and I are going to die down here."

I wanted to care...but I couldn't.

Good.

"What?" He snarled, the stench of his sweat and excitement was sickening. "What did you say?"

I lifted my head, straining with everything I had to force my eyes open. Dull, yellow light spilled in. He was a darkened blur, moving closer, until his face sharpened.

"What the fuck did you say?"

"I said...good."

His lips curled, the whites of his eyes almost fucking neon. "Good? *Good?*" He roared as the basement around us rumbled and snarled.

An edge of the ceiling fell.

Crash!

He never flinched. He never even looked away, just stood there staring at me with his ugly fucking grin.

"*Good.*" He bellowed as he stepped away. "*GOOD!*"

My balls clenched and my pulse sped as he neared that fucking machine and turned a dial. "As long as the power stays on a little longer. Isn't that right, my friend? As long as the power stays on that...little...bit...longer."

Buzz.

I shook my head, my eyes widening as the rod in his hand hummed and buzzed. I shook my head as he turned toward me.

"No." I jerked, pulling on the unforgiving shackles around my wrists "*No.*"

He moved closer, reaching out to stab that thing into my side. I bucked, screaming as he drove that thing into my side until it felt like it was inside me, twisting and pulling. My head went backwards, the roar burning like fire.

"That's *it*! *THAT'S IT! DANCE, MOTHERFUCKER...DANCE!"*

I screamed until the room around me darkened, until there was no air left in my world...and the emptiness finally claimed me.

Slow.

Draining breaths found me, dragging me from the bleak oblivion.

"There he is."

A whimper ripped free with the sound of his voice. *No...no more...*

I was done.

I was so fucking done.

"Kill...me." The words came out an undistinguished mumble.

"What was that?" He growled.

A tremor roared all around us, shaking everything as the vibrations tore through the chains and into my arms until the ceiling gave way.

My arms dropped, letting me crash to the floor. Heavy stones hit me, slamming against my body, until one cracked my head.

Bright white sparks detonated behind my eyes.

"Jesus fucking Christ!" My tormentor roared.

I just lay there, unable to protect myself.

Slam!

Slam...

SLAM!

Each falling chunk of stone was like a fist battering my cheeks, my head, my body. Agony radiated, tearing through my eye. Warmth pooled in the corner before it ran down my nose.

"What...the...fuck?"

I thought it was Riven who spoke...but it couldn't be...because I was in Hell. I cracked open one eye...seeing the blur of darkness as he lunged across the room to land on the back of my tormentor.

Fists.

Rage...

Destruction.

That's what he was...pure *destruction.*

I forced my eyes open to find Riven with his arm around the bastard's neck...others rushed in. Soft hands, smooth...cradling. Her face swam, then sharpened as she moved into view.

"Hunter?" The angel spoke. *"Hunter, can you hear me?"*

But I couldn't answer. All I could do was lie there and watch my brother trying to kill the man who'd tortured me. Riven's dark eyes were black in the gloom. He looked like a demon. A vengeful, bestial demon.

I closed my eyes.

Maybe that's what I needed.

Demon.

"What, baby?" The angel asked. "What did you say?"

The image of Vivienne being dragged from the cell came rushing back to me. I opened my eyes to find Riven being driven backwards until he was slammed against the wall.

"I'll fucking KILL YOU!" My tormentor roared, that electric shock rod sparking in the gloom.

Helene wrenched her gaze toward them.

Everything moved in slow motion. One minute, Riven was the only one fighting the bastard who'd tried to kill me, then they were all there, rushing forward, attacking with fists and nails. I gathered the last burning need to get out of there alive and pushed upwards.

My arms shook violently, until they collapsed under the weight, sending me crashing back down. Screams were smothered by the roaring rumble of this fucking place crumbling around us.

I tried again, pushing upwards as they attacked the guard, disappearing under a hail of falling rock, until Riven reached out and picked up one of those rocks.

"NO!" The torturing bastard threw up his hand in a desperate attempt to protect his face.

But it was useless. My brother *was* wrath in that moment, those dark eyes wide as he brought that hunk of stone down with all the strength he had.

Crack!

The sound was sickening.

The guard fell...hitting the floor with a thud.

And the frenzy started. Kane and Thomas kicked and beat. Helene grabbed a rock of her own, unleashing it with chilling violence as she drove that rock into his head over and over. *"Fuck you!"* She howled. *"Fuck youuu!"*

Until there was nothing left to kill...

The guard's face was a bloodied mess. Unrecognizable. Slowly, Riven straightened, sucking in hard breaths before he suddenly lunged, grabbed Helene and hauled her sideways as a bigger chunk of stone fell from the ceiling and crashed to the floor right where she'd stood.

Her eyes were wide, staring at the mess, then she turned to Riven.

"We need to get out of here now!" Riven roared.

Kane and Thomas rushed toward me, dropping to the floor beside me. Kane lifted my cuffed hands, then glanced at the dead guard. "The key...we need the goddamn key."

He shoved upwards and was gone, hurrying to search the pockets of my tormentor.

"Sis-stt-er." I croaked, turning my gaze to Helene.

She moved closer.

Still, not close enough.

Agony ripped through my torn shoulder. I swallowed it down, crawling my fingers forward to snatch her hand. She flinched, jerked her gaze to mine, and scowled. I wanted to roar...to scream just like how Vivienne's voice screamed inside my head, tormenting me.

"*Si-st-er.*" Fire lashed my dry throat, snatching the word from my lips. *Sister...SISTER!* My lips stretched wide with the silent scream.

"What is he saying?" Helene wrenched a frantic gaze to Riven, standing behind her.

"He's saying sister." Thomas said, staring at him. "That's what he's saying."

"Sister?" She murmured, looking back at me.

"That *fucking bitch.*" Riven snapped, turning to step over the rubble. "She did this? *Of course she fucking did.* Goddamn bitch...*goddamn fucking bitch!*"

But that wasn't it...it wasn't the sister I cared about.

"No..." I pulled her close. "*Y-our...sis-ter.*"

The color drained from her face. There was a flicker of confusion before she whispered. "Ryth?"

I slowly shook my head.

"*Vivienne?*"

I nodded.

"Oh, *God.*" She rocked forward. "That's what the phone calls were, weren't they? They have her...they have *my sister.*"

She shot to her feet, stumbling away until she tripped over a chunk of stone and fell. Thomas was there instantly, catching her, pulling her against him as Kane rushed to me and dropped to his knees.

"We have to get out of here." He unlocked the cuffs, gently pulled them free off my wrists, and flung them across the cell. "Can you walk?"

I didn't know if I could, still I nodded. "You help. I'll try."

Thomas left Helene, strode forward, and grabbed one of my arms as Kane grabbed the other. My breath caught. My muscles were rock hard, spasmed tight. Still, I used them as best as I could, holding on as I slowly pushed upward.

I couldn't straighten, not at first. I was doubled over, holding on to both my brothers until I slowly forced myself upright.

"You good?" Kane asked.

My muscles were twitching and my nerves were fried, like every cell had been burned with a goddamn flamethrower. Still, I nodded.

"We need to get out of here." Riven demanded. "Everything else can wait. First things first, we need to track them down."

Helene nodded, panic in her eyes. She turned around, scrambling over the debris to race toward the door. I held onto Kane and leaned on Thomas, letting my little brother take my weight.

He was stronger than he looked, wrapping his arm around my middle. "I got you." He grunted.

We followed, two steps behind Helene and Riven.

Relief hit me as I stepped outside that dank piece of Hell. I sucked in the musty cold air, drawing it deep into my lungs and limped, following them as they hurried along some kind of tunnel. Vibrations kept shaking the place. We sidestepped fallen chunks of ceiling.

The place rumbled, quaking until Thomas stumbled to the wall and pulled me with him.

"The whole place is coming down!" He roared.

"We need to keep going!" Riven stabbed toward the darkness up ahead. *"That's our way out!"*

He grabbed Helene and surged forward. But he only took two steps before he stopped.

Flashlights cut through the darkness up ahead.

Two...three...then four beams cut through the gloom, heading our way.

"Here." Kane barked over the roar of the damn crumbling tunnel as he pointed to another dark open doorway. "Hurry!"

The last thing I wanted to do was step inside that room.

But Thomas was there, pulling me with him and back into a cell.

TWENTY-SIX

Helene

"*MOVE!*" KANE HISSED, DRIVING ALL OF US INTO THAT dark cell.

I didn't have time to argue, just stumbled as I was jostled forward and, in an instant, I was surrounded by the heat of four warm bodies. Heavy breaths blew against me, scattering my hair as I was pressed against the wall of the cell just inside the doorway.

The faint sound of footsteps echoed as the rumble of the collapsing tunnel died away. Voices followed. But I couldn't hear them, wedged between Thomas, Kane, and Hunter with Riven in front, facing the doorway.

I slowly lifted my gaze, finding the glint of their eyes.

My heart boomed. Warmth radiated between us.

Still, the faint bark of commands slipped into the cell. Only at that moment, I didn't care. Hunter reached up slowly, his curled fingers trembling as he brushed the strands of my hair from my face. Thomas's fingers dragged along my arm, then my neck before he reached around, cupping the base of my neck with his strong hand.

Even in the midst of utter destruction, we clung to the only glimmer of goodness we had...and that was each other. Thomas's hand tightened around my neck as Hunter curled his massive body, leaning on me. It was so natural to tilt my mouth toward him. For a blinding second, the horror could wait.

Warm, heavy breaths filled my ears, resounding all around me. I closed my eyes, comforted by the warmth of them as I waited for the moment our lips touched.

The kiss was soft, barely a brush, but the effect was instant, rippling through my body. I remembered his touch and his kindness. The way he'd defended me to his own kin. I opened my mouth for him, stoking our hunger.

"Jesus." Thomas murmured, his hold tightening around my neck.

I knew what he wanted, so I slowly pulled away and turned my head.

Thomas leaned closer, taking my mouth harder. His hard chest pressed against mine, pushing me against the stone.

"Fuck's sake." Riven snapped. "Can't you restrain yourselves for a goddamn second around her? You're fucking distracting me and I'm trying to listen."

Thomas pulled away, his honey brown eyes shimmering in the gloom before he turned away. Even though this wasn't the right time, we still needed it. A new surge of hope filled me.

"Server—" I caught the word.

Server? I gently pushed Thomas aside and stepped out from around them. What server?

All of us took a step closer to the doorway.

Another rumble shook the tunnel around us. It was barely a tremor, still it panicked the guards out there rushing past.

"We better not be fucking buried alive in this goddamn place."

"If we aren't, we're taking his precious servers."

"Damn right we are. Fuck him and his precious blackmailing files. Ain't nothing on those things that's worth killing ourselves over."

"Shut it." Another snapped. "Or it won't be the goddamn roof falling in that you'll need to worry about."

"Coulter must be paying you real fucking well, Conrad. Real fucking well."

"Move it." The guy who must be Conrad snapped.

"It's up ahead." Someone else called.

We moved closer to the doorway, Riven stepped to the side, straining to watch them, but the moment he turned back to us, I knew what he was thinking.

"No." I shook my head. "Don't look at me like that."

He scowled. "That server could be the key to everything." He hissed quietly. "I always knew Coulter would have access to the kind of information which could destroy all this."

"We don't have time." I urged. "Every second we stand here, my sister gets further and further away. She's the priority here."

He didn't like it. In fact, he looked like I'd just asked him to swallow a mouthful of broken glass.

It may as well have been like that for him.

His entire existence had been in the pursuit of finding where Hale had kept his sister and now...now that was over in the cruelest and most brutal way. Only, I couldn't let it be like that for my kin...no matter how enticing it was.

Riven slowly gave a nod. "You're right." He glanced at his brothers as though he was reminding himself the true reason for all this. "We'll get you out."

He waited for a heartbeat, then gently opened the cell door and peeked out, making sure the coast was clear before we all stepped out. I stayed right behind him, followed by Kane and Hunter. It wasn't until we were hurrying back along the tunnel that I felt the...*wrongness*.

I stopped and turned, finding Thomas gone. "Riven." I called, my voice rebounding in the space.

He spun around, then moved toward me, scanning the others. "Where the fuck is Thomas?"

Kane looked behind them. Hunter was slower, scanning the emptiness.

"Fuck." The Mountain snarled, limping as he took a step. "You go, I'll find him."

But I knew exactly where he was heading. "No. No, you can't."

"Go." Riven threw over his shoulder as he headed after Hunter. "Get out of here. I'll find you later."

Agony tore across my chest watching them disappear into the gloom. Thomas thought he could save us and destroy The Order. I knew it.

"Come on." Kane gently gripped my arm, pulling me forward as he took a step.

But I just couldn't go.

I couldn't leave them...not again.

"I can't." I pulled away from him. "I can't leave them behind."

"Goddamn him." Kane muttered.

We both turned around at the same time and hurried after them. We caught up to Hunter first, then Riven. A careful glance my way, and The Mountain nodded.

Flashlights bounced around the tunnel up ahead, then suddenly disappeared. My heart was in my mouth as I hurried, following them to the same spot. It was another tunnel...one that led to God knew where.

I shook my head. "We don't know what's in there..."

All I could see was one way in and no way out.

"He's my brother." Riven murmured. "I have no choice."

And in a single second, he was gone, slipping into the darkness.

I clenched my fists to my chest as anguish filled me.

Goddamn them. Hunter followed. Kane shook his head, that same desperation glinting in his eyes before he followed them in. I waited for a whole second, then took a blind leap of faith and followed. There was absolutely nothing. I reached out, found the wall, and forced myself to keep going.

But the tunnel took an abrupt turn to the right, and at the end, a light spilled out of a cracked open door, lighting the way forward. Thomas was there, standing at the open door, watching them inside before he turned his head to find the rest of us.

No.

I shook my head as Riven grabbed him silently by the shoulders and yanked him backwards, to stare into his eyes.

But Thomas just shook his head and looked at that room. The room where light spilled out and the muffled sounds of voices came. Riven dropped his hands, and pushed his brother behind him. As hurt as The Mountain was, his fist was clenched and ready. Kane reached behind himself, keeping me at his back as Riven slowly inched the door inward and stepped inside.

The light was glaring, causing me to blink as I stepped inside. Guards were busy pulling servers apart, taking the CPU's. That's all they wanted. They were so focused on that they didn't hear us, not until it was too late.

I surged forward as all four men lunged.

"What the fuck?" One of the guards roared, pushing upwards.

We attacked, rushing forward and lunging. I drove toward the guard sitting on the floor, yanking parts of the server open. He gripped the heavy metal case and shoved upward against the floor, only to swing it like a weapon at Riven.

The fuck you do!

Rage was the power I needed to carve through the murky haze of what remained of the drug in my system. I lunged, grabbing his hands and kept driving him around, using his own momentum against him, before I lifted my foot and drove it sideways against his knee.

Crack!

The impact was brutal, sending him crashing back to the floor. His screams were deafening as he dropped the CPU and grabbed his knee. *"YOU FUCKING BITCH!"*

I bent down, snatched the case from the floor beside him, and straightened. "That's right." I swung the metal device across my body and raised it into the air. "I am the bitch you tried to destroy."

One heave and I brought it down with all the strength I had. The CPU impacted the side of his head, slamming him into the wall. He slid down silently, blood streaming from his head as grunts and the sounds of brutal blows echoed all around me.

I swung around to find Hunter wrestling with the largest of them as another one who fought Thomas went for his gun.

"The fuck you do!" I screamed and lunged, swinging the CPU like a weapon once more.

Crunch.

Thud.

Thud.

Hunter unleashed a scream as I swung the device, driving it down on the guard's hand which gripped the gun. The weapon flew from his hand as Thomas unleashed a roar, slammed into him, and drove the guard backwards.

I bent down, grabbed the gun, and lifted it with shaking hands, stepping backwards as I scanned the room. "Stop...sto—" A hand clamped over my mouth.

I was yanked backwards against a hard chest.

"Now I know you don't want to squeeze that trigger, Helene." Coulter's voice filled my ears as he reached out and grasped my hand which held the gun. "You might just shoot someone you love."

He pulled it to the side, taking aim at Riven as his finger slipped around mine, curled around the trigger.

"Do what I say and no one gets hurt."

Riven spun, his dark eyes widening as he fixed on me.

My knees trembled. My body froze.

I shook my head.

No...this can't be happening.

As Coulter's men stepped around us, I dropped the CPU in my hand.

"We always seem to be interrupted." His breath was warm against my ear. "I believe the bid was still mine at four million dollars."

"Get the fuck off her!" Riven roared as he lunged forward.

But Coulter's men were there, driving a gun against his head.

"Please, try your best." Coulter urged. "I'd love nothing more than to splatter your brains all over this room."

"No." I shook my head as fear filled me. "Don't kill them." I begged, staring at the four men I loved. "Please...*please don't kill them.*"

Hunter surged forward, as did Kane and Thomas.

There was no way they were getting out of this alive.

I knew that...and so did Coulter.

TWENTY-SEVEN

Riven

THE BASTARD DECIDED TO DRAG HER FROM THE ROOM EVEN before he moved. I saw the moment he decided that. That flicker of hunger ignited like a fucking bonfire on the 4th of July.

The guard beside him took a step forward as the bleeding bastard on the ground in front of me pushed himself upwards on shaking legs and tossed the processing unit through the air for Coulter's man to catch it.

It was all they wanted.

"No." Hunter's growl was a husky bark as he drove himself forward.

But it was all too late.

I *knew* that, still agony ripped through me as Coulter yanked her backwards.

"No...NO!" I bellowed, shoving the asshole in my hands away as I lunged toward them.

"Riven!" She screamed for me, her scream muffled under his hand.

I was losing her again. *Failing her AGAIN!*

I swallowed down that howling rage and forced my gaze to her wide, panicked stare. *I'll find you,* I mouthed the words. *I. Will. Find. You.*

Then she was gone, stumbling backwards as the guard dragged her away from me.

But at the last second, I shifted my focus, burning that *dead motherfucker's* face into my mind. "I'm going to KILL YOU!" I hit the door as it closed with a *thud*.

My fists were brutal, slamming against the door before I drove my shoulder into the damn thing. *"DO YOU HEAR ME? I'M GOING TO FUCKING KILL YOU!"*

Rage rippled through me, plunging me all the way into that empty abyss. The one where I'd lived most of my goddamn life.

I'll fucking kill you.

I turned around, finding Coulter's men coming for me.

I will fucking KILL YOU ALL!

Coulter's men descended with fury and roars. I was grabbed by the biggest of them. His blow caught me on the side of the face, knocking me sideways until I slammed into the door. My breath flew out of me with a *whoosh*.

A second, that's all it took before I shoved against that door. I took his fist, swallowed down his blows, and all the time that seething, howling rage bellowed inside.

I turned to that big bastard as he grinned and came for me. My brothers' screams filled the room. I sidestepped his blow, swinging my fist across my chest to connect with him...until I was charged from behind.

One on one was one thing, but two of them?

Bring it on...

I shoved against the wall and stepped to the side, fixing my gaze on both of them. "You're going to die in this room. You get that, right?" I muttered.

Then the fast one lunged, driving me sideways as the big bastard swung. I dodged one, driving myself close enough to drive my knuckles into his side. The big bastard gave a grunt, then doubled over. It was all I needed. I swing my fist, ramming it through the air to connect with the underside of his chin.

His head snapped backwards, but it didn't matter. I was hit from the side, my feet lifting from the floor before I was slammed down.

Crunch.

Something in my ribs gave way. Agony ripped through me, blinding until I couldn't breathe. He was a shadow, rearing over me, sucking in hard breaths as he dropped down and straddled me.

"I'm not the one dying here." He said as he wrapped his hands around my throat. "You are."

Flickers of images filled my mind.

The image of my hands around another as I killed to protect the woman I loved. I tried to shove against the floor, knowing this was the end if I didn't move. I drove my feet against the floor, bucking my hips into the air. He fell sideways, his hold on my throat dragging me with him.

Until Hunter slammed into him with a guttural roar.

Bang!

A shot tore through the room. But I didn't have time to even care if I was hit. If I was moving, then I was fighting. I shoved against the floor, driving myself to where my brother raised his massive fist and drove it into the face of my attacker. But he was slow...and weak.

I unleashed a roar, dropped low, and rammed my body into the guard. Blinding, shooting, white-hot bolts of lightning tore through me. I couldn't breathe...couldn't think. Still, reflex took over. Helene's face filled my head.

As I swung my fist, all I saw was her.

Bang!

I bucked and stumbled sideways.

Deep down, I knew there was no escaping death this time, not as that punishing pain grew bolder, radiating from my thigh. Still, I stumbled forward, grabbed the bastard who'd attacked us, and cracked my head forward, slamming into his face.

Crunch.

He dropped hard, tearing his shirt out of my hold as he collapsed to the floor in front of me. I turned to Hunter. "You good?"

He winced, glanced at the blood streaming from the guard's face, and nodded. "Yeah."

"Good." I turned, to find Kane and Thomas battling two more of the motherfuckers with all they had.

But Thomas was still injured, spinning with the crack of a blow.

He stumbled and dropped to his knees. He drove out his hand to stop the fall and lifted his gaze.

The guard lifted his gun and pointed the muzzle at my brother kneeling on the floor.

I shoved forward.

"Don't you *fucking* move!" He swung the Glock my way, taking aim at my chest.

I opened my hands and limped forward. *That's the way...aim that at me.*

My knee shuddered, threatening to give way as I took another step. "There's no way out of here." I spoke carefully. "Not for you. Put the gun down and we'll let you live."

"Fuck you." He swung his wide, panicked stare around the room.

"*Hey!*" I barked, drawing his focus again. "On me, motherfucker."

The bastard jerked his focus back as I took another step.

"There's nothing here worth dying for." Kane urged, sucking in hard breaths from fighting. His lip was split, blood trailed from his nose. Still, he glanced my way and straightened, opening his hands. "Take a look around. There's nothing here. Coulter took what he wanted, and he left you behind to die."

"Shut the fuck up." The dead man snapped.

He was dead either way.

Maybe he knew that.

Still, if there was anyone who could get through to him, it was Kane.

"You have a family, and so do we. Throw the gun down and I promise you, we'll let you leave."

The tunnel rumbled around us, shaking more dust free from the ceiling.

"This place could come down any second." Kane urged, lifting his gaze as a crack raced along the ceiling and down the wall.

Panic filled me. I glanced at Kane and saw the same fear in him. The walls shuddered and shook again. A chunk of stone came away, falling to the floor in the corner.

"You want to be here when it falls?" Kane swung his gaze to the guard and stepped closer, opening his hands in a movement of surrender.

What the fuck was he doing?

I shook my head and scowled.

But my brother couldn't see what I saw. Not the way the guard adjusted his grip, or the way he turned that panicked stare back to Thomas. He was going to shoot him. He was going to...

With a roar, I leaped and slammed into him.

BOOM!

The shot was deafening.

"You. Don't. Fucking. Kill. My. Brothers!" I roared as I drove my fist down.

We hit the floor hard and I didn't waste a goddamn second, punching my knuckles into his face over and over again.

A numbness washed over me. All I saw was her face, those dark brown eyes fucking haunting me as I turned back.

Thump!

Crunch.

Thump!

Crack.

Thump!

Thump!

THUMP!

I couldn't stop, even if I wanted to...and I didn't want to.

"Riven."

Blood splatter hit my cheek. All I saw was red as I drove my fury down once more.

"Riven."

I jerked upwards, finding Kane standing over me looking down.

The dust-filled air that fell from the ceiling was like razor blades, but I sucked it down anyway. "Yeah?"

My brother looked at the mess underneath me. "He's dead."

I shifted my gaze, finally seeing the sickening sight for what it was...it was blood and bone and emptiness. I couldn't even release him, my knuckles were fixed around his shirt.

"Easy now." Kane urged.

He knew I didn't like that goddamn placating tone. Still, he used it.

I shook my head, shifting my focus to Hunter, who stood over the last guard lying dead at his feet, his neck canted at an unnatural angle.

Thomas stood on the other side of the room, staring at me in shock. It wasn't something I enjoyed, to be inhuman and violent in front of my blood. Still, it had been necessary. I reached over and pulled my fingers to release their hold on the body's shirty as the stony dust rained down even harder from above.

Boom!

The faint explosion was distant, but still chilling.

"We need to find a key." Kane moved, dropping next to a guard. *"Hurry! We need that goddamn key."*

But the moment he said the words, the ceiling came crashing down. I was hit from behind and slammed to the floor.

"Riven!" Kane roared.

But darkness slammed into me.

One minute I was awake...and the next I was out.

TWENTY-EIGHT

Helene

"*GET THE FUCK OFF ME!*" I tore out of Coulter's arms and ran for my life.

But I couldn't see a thing, running blindly with my hands stretched out, until a roar came from behind me.

"*Get her!*" Coulter's roar echoed all around me.

Footsteps followed, the heavy *thud...thud...thudthudthud* made my pulse race. But as they dragged me from that tight tunnel, a sickening *crack had* come from that room.

I stopped, stared into the darkness, and tried to understand what had just happened. My mind conjured terrifying bloody images. A bullet hole in the middle of Riven's chest. Hunter falling with a neat hole in the side of his head. The images snatched the fight out of me, turning me to prey.

"There you are." Coulter's man yanked me backwards until he hauled me over his shoulder.

Fight!

FIGHT!

I kicked, feebly at first, before reality backhanded me across the face and I drove my fist into the side of his head over his ear. Snatches of the past rose with the movement. I'd hit Riven like that the night he'd abducted me, and as I remembered the hostile stare he'd given me, I knew I loved him.

I'd give anything to earn that wrath once more.

But this wasn't Riven...this was someone far worse.

"Put me DOWN!" I bucked until I ripped from his hold and fell, hitting the floor hard.

Agony cut through my thigh and tore into my back. But I didn't have time to care. I shoved upwards, my feet slipping on the slick stone floor. I crashed back down. The cold, throbbing agony found me again as tears filled my eyes.

Get to them...

GET TO THEM!

But the moment I lunged, the guard lunged to the side, tormenting me as I tried to find a way around him.

"Uh, uh." He clucked his tongue.

"Cuff her." Coulter commanded.

Instantly, the guard lunged, grabbed me around the waist, and wrenched me backwards.

"You want to act like an animal, Helene?" Coulter's dark eyes found me. "Then you'll be treated like one. Don't forget, *I own you.*"

Four million dollars.

I shook my head as cold, hard steel snapped around my wrists. The tears that had threatened to fall slid warm down my cheeks.

"Bought and paid for." He said, his gaze sliding down my body. "You can bet I'll get my money's worth, as well."

Fuck you. My mind breathed hate, even as tears ran down my cheeks as I stared at him in the dark. *Fuck. You.*

"Sir." Came a voice behind him.

Through the shimmering blur, two more guards stepped around him and moved toward the wall. It took me a moment to understand what was happening. But as soon as I saw the wires and the block of explosives, I knew.

"It was *you?*" I jerked my gaze to him. "All of this? *It was you?*"

He leveled that sinister stare at me. "You mean the rogue Sons? No. That wasn't me. But why the fuck not take advantage of the castle crumbling all around me? I might very well take a page out of Hale's playbook and go to ground. How would you like that, Helene? Just you and me living in seclusion while the rest of the world thinks we're dead. I could devote my time to you then. One...hundred...percent, while you're alive, that is. Then, I'd have to find a new mouse to play with. Your youngest sister, Ryth, looks a lot like you, you know."

My stomach rolled until I thought I was going to be sick. I shook my head. "No...I won't allow that."

But my words fell flat as a small *beep* chimed and the guards rose from the edge of the tunnel wall. Neon red numbers counted down.

"Everyone back." Coulter commanded.

The guard came for me, grabbed me around the waist again, and hauled me backwards.

"BOMB!" I screamed. "RIVEN! IT'S A BOMBBBB!"

My throat burned with the roar.

But Coulter just chuckled. "I don't think they can hear you, my love. Still, you want to scream until your voice gives out, then go right ahead. But save a little fight for me. I have a feeling before this night is out, you're going to need it."

A shrill, scalding sound ripped free. I thrashed, trying to tear out of the guard's hold. But he just kept dragging me backwards.

"Everyone get back!" Coulter's command echoed. "Now!"

"It's a BOMB!" I howled. "Riven, IT'S A BOMB!"

I didn't know if they heard me. Please, I begged inside my mind. Please, let them survive.

The tiny red blinking numbers drew my focus as Coulter and his men headed back out of the tunnel in the dark, listening to the place rumble and shudder all around us. As my tears fell, that cruel bitch Fate dragged her sharpened nails along my spine. She moved closer, whispering in my ear.

Feel familiar?

I shook my head as the words resounded in my head and, as they dragged me further and further away from that ticking display, I remembered another time when I'd waited for an explosion.

The Order.

I was the one who'd destroyed that building to get my father free...and I'd paid the consequences for it. My back twinged as though by reflex. I'd attached a brick of C4 to the inside of that building and blew the wall out as I'd carried my father out of there. The same father who'd just sat there and watched me be violated in front of a room full of strangers...the father who'd sat by while I was sold to this—I found Coulter striding alongside us in the dark—*this...monster*.

The guard yanked me harder, dragging me as we rounded the curve of the tunnels and I lost sight of the tiny red blinking light of the timer. My bare feet skidded on the cold stone floor. Goosebumps raced along my spine.

"Stop this." I jerked my gaze to Coulter. "Stop and I'll...*I'll go with you*."

He stopped instantly, and the guard followed, leaving me to catch my own footing. I gripped the guard's arm around my chest, my pulse racing along with my breaths. Still, that howling desperation filled me.

"I'll do it." I whispered, my stomach sinking. "I'll do whatever you want."

His eyes glinted in the gloom as they fixed on me. I had him. I really had him. *Please...*I whispered. *Please*.

A slow, deep chuckle spilled from his mouth and resounded all around me. "If you had anything to bargain with, I might be tempted. Might, being the operative word choice there." He took a step, coming closer, and leaned down until I flinched away. "But if you haven't noticed already, Helene, you're already mine."

"No." I shook my head, that fear building inside.

"I can't stop thinking about that night." Coulter murmured. "I can't seem to get you out of my head." I jerked away from his touch as he brushed a coil of my hair around my ear. "I plan on getting reacquainted very soon, Helene."

My body trembled. "I-I'll fight y-you." I stuttered.

I sounded like someone else at that moment, someone weak and full of terror.

"I really hope you do." He answered and stepped away, nodding to the guard at my back. "I look forward to it."

I shook my head. This couldn't be happening. "*NO!*"

Moonlight spilled into the entrance of the tunnel, the faint glow growing brighter until we were finally out and I was cast aside and thrown to the ground.

I hit the dirt and the sticks hard, landing on my hands and knees. Agony throbbed along my thighs. But I curled my fingers, digging into the dirt, and shoved upwards. My movements were slow, the drug still lingering in my system, making me stumble as I swung around and lunged for the tunnel.

But the guard was right in front of me, grinning as he sidestepped.

"You don't want to go in there." He shook his head.

"Get the *fuck out of my way!*" I screamed, desperately trying to find a way around him.

"You'll miss all the fun." Coulter gripped the CPU and stared into the gaping tunnel mouth. "Five...four...three...two...*one.*"

BOOM!

The detonation was brutal, quaking the ground beneath my feet. Leaves shook from the trees around us, falling like rain. I took a step, then had to throw out my hands to stop from falling. Car alarms blared to life all around the towering mansion.

"Look at that!" Coulter bellowed, his eyes wide, shining with excitement as he turned toward us.

All I could see was the suffocating dust that spewed from the mouth of that tunnel, imagining the men I loved crushed to death.

Even if they survived the collapse, there was no way they'd survive the choking air.

My knees finally gave way, crashing me to the ground. I sat there staring into the darkness, knowing this was the end. For them...and for me.

"Oh, come on now." Coulter said above me. "Why the tears? Think of it this way, at least you finally got the revenge you wanted all along for your sisters. That *is* what you wanted, wasn't it, Helene? That's what your father told me, in confidence, mind you. He said you were planning on hunting The Principal, The Teacher, and the Priest for the vile things they did in those walls."

My heart rippled with agony at the words.

Coulter came closer, standing over me. His hand landed on the back of my head, gently pushing me against his leg. "*I* am your savior, Helene. I am the one who reminded you of your true path. You wavered, but I was right there ready to make it right. You are mine, Helene. I knew the first time I saw you, Fate had brought you to me. A true Daughter of The Order, one perfectly made to be mine."

"I'd rather die." I whispered, meeting that stare.

Coulter slowly straightened, pulling his hand from my head before he stepped away. "I don't pay good money for bad investments, Helene...instead, I hire that investment out to anyone willing to pay me over and over *and over* until I recoup my loss. You don't want that, do you, Helene? You don't want to be a *bad investment*."

My body core clenched at those sickening words.

I knew exactly what he meant.

He'd whore me out to any fucking vile bastard who'd ever wanted a plaything of The Order.

Get her to the table...

Hold her down.

I'd already had a taste of what kind of things men like Coulter craved. I'd barely survived it once before. I was almost certain I wouldn't again.

"Now be a good whore and maybe I'll let you see your sister."

My breath caught. I jerked my gaze to his.

"Now I get a reaction." He murmured, searching my eyes. "You do want that, don't you?"

"Vivienne?" I whispered.

Sister.

Hunter's choked pleas returned to me. I'd thought he was trying to warn us about Ryth...but he hadn't been. He'd been trying to tell us they had my sister, Vivienne. One who was *very, very pregnant* and far away from London or the Sons.

They'd whisk her out of the country and go underground so fast no one would have a chance to track her down...no matter how good they were.

That's what men like Coulter and Hale did.

They made women like us disappear.

I slowly forced myself to stand. There was nothing I could do for the men I loved anymore...as crushing as that was, I had to push it aside. Later, I'd find a blade to end this horror, but right now my sister needed me.

I *could* still save her.

I could still save *someone*.

"Take me." I whispered. "Take me to her now."

There was a tight curl of his lips. In that moment, he knew he'd won. "Good girl." He nodded and glanced at the guard. "Remove her cuffs, we won't be needing them anymore. She'll do exactly as she's told."

I didn't look away from Coulter, not even as my wrists were yanked upwards and the steel shackles removed. Coulter stepped close, grasped the back of my neck and dragged me closer.

"Now, kiss me." He commanded. "Make it fucking good, your sister's and her babies' lives are on the line."

TWENTY-NINE

Riven

BOOM!

The explosion shook the entire room, throwing me backwards until I landed hard on my ass. Cracks the size of my fist opened up in the ceiling overhead and only grew wider. This was bad... this was *very fucking bad.* I jerked my gaze left, scanning near where I sat and grabbed the nearest thing I could find.

The dead body of the guard weighed a ton, yet I heaved it upwards as the first chunk of the ceiling came crashing down.

"DOWN!" Hunter roared.

I ducked, threw my arms over my head, and cowered under Coulter's dead man.

Thud!

Thud

Thud!

Chunks of stone crashed down all around me until I couldn't breathe with the weight. The air turned choking, like a rag over my mouth, smothering me until I felt something inside me slip and darkness moved in.

"Riven!"

My name echoed faintly. But I couldn't move. I couldn't even breathe, trapped under that crushing weight with the vast nothingness coming at me fast.

"RIVEN!" That roar grew louder.

Something shifted from on top of me. A deep, guttural grunt was followed by a roar before the body I lay under was pulled aside.

"Are you alive?"

Short, sharp breaths gave me a little air, but it was enough. My eyes fluttered open, letting me stare into my brother's eyes. "Unfortunately."

The smile was instant. Kane just shook his head. "If you're making wise cracks, then you're alive."

"Yay me." I croaked.

Through the choking air, movement came from deeper in the room. Thomas appeared through the haze for a second, then stumbled sideways and fell, hitting the floor hard. For a second, he couldn't get up.

"There was...an explosion." Thomas choked and gasped, the fine dust coating his lashes and hair. He looked gray all over.

"No...fucking...shit." I forced out the words and rolled, driving myself up onto my elbows, and looked around the room.

The place was fucking destroyed. Chunks of the ceiling had given way all around me. But it looked like I'd taken the worst of it. Hunter stood above me. It was him who'd lifted the heavy rocks free, and that alone hit me harder than any goddamn boulder could have.

"Helene." I croaked, waiting for the room to stop spinning around me.

"She can't be far." Kane stepped over the rubble. "If we hurry."

A shadow reared over me. Hunter stepped close and reached out, waiting for me to take his hand. From the corner of my eye, I saw my brothers' reaction as they stopped and stared. Thomas rose as I took my youngest brother's hand and let him lift me from the rubble.

Never in my life had I thought we would protect and defend or even tolerate being in the same room as each other. But here we were...and it was all because of *her,* our walking hurricane. My seductive Trouble.

I released his hand and yanked my shirt up, covering my nose and mouth. It took me a second to realize just how vulnerable Hunter had been. He didn't show his face because of one thing and one thing alone...because he looked exactly like me. Those dark eyes reflected back at me and the hard planes of his cheeks mirrored my own. He'd truly hated me so much that for all these years, he despised his own reflection. I was the one thing he truly hated, the one thing that would force him to hide his face from the rest of the world...

I carried that, knowing it wasn't the only cruel twist of Fate between us. First there had been our sister's disappearance, then there was the blame.

Nothing could save me from the actions of my past. But there was one thing that could change my future...one blinding, consuming light. A woman who gave herself to all of us... *Helene.*

"We need to find her." I choked out the words. "And kill that motherfucker once and for all."

I swung my gaze to the dark, gaping hole that'd moments ago been the doorway. The door was gone, fallen from the frame in the crash as the rock gave way. I stumbled forward, climbing over the ruins until I stepped through the doorway and stared at the rocks piled high in front of us.

Panic flared for a second as I stared at the utter destruction.

"Fuck." Kane muttered behind me.

Never a truer word was spoken. My knees shook as I stumbled toward the massive mountain of stone and began to haul them free one by one. Barely a heartbeat later and they were all there, squeezing around me, reaching up to pull boulder after boulder free until there was space enough for us to climb over.

The moment we were free, we clambered over the rest of the fallen wall to get out of that tiny space and back into the main tunnel...but it didn't matter.

It didn't matter at all.

I stopped, my heart booming in the back of my throat, and stared at the walls and ceiling that had crumbled in around the blast zone. They hadn't wanted us to survive that. They hadn't wanted us alive.

"No." Kane stumbled forward as desperation hit me.

I crumbled, falling to my knees, and bowed my head.

I'd failed her...

Again.

There was no way we were getting out of there. No way we'd ever see the light of day again, until a cold, crisp burst of air hit me.

"Riven." Thomas called as he stumbled onto a mound of rocks.

Grief weighed me down, but I lifted my gaze to where my brother pointed at the stone ceiling. "There."

I couldn't see a damn thing. But I could feel it, and the moment I breathed in that clean, night air, I pushed upwards. My feet slipped on the rocks as I battled to get to him.

High above us, the glimmer of stars shone through. "What the fuck is that?"

Thomas smiled, his grin growing wider by the second. "That, brother, is a sign."

I hadn't believed in miracles, not until one stepped in front of my car. But if I believed in her, then I guess I believed *something* was out there beyond all of us. I lowered my focus to the looming stone wall in front of me. But there was still a mountain to climb.

"We just need to find a way out of here." Thomas added.

He had his faith and I had my rage. One I tapped into now as I stumbled forward and bent down, grasping the boulder at my feet and tore it from the wall.

Hold on, Trouble...just hold the fuck on.

We're coming.

THIRTY

Helene

HEADLIGHTS SPLASHED ACROSS THE GROUND AT MY FEET as a sleek black sedan pulled up behind us and the car doors opened.

"Get her to the car." Coulter commanded and stepped away.

I jerked my gaze to the mouth of that tunnel as a fresh wave of agony tore through me. I'd give anything to kick and fight and claw my way through the destroyed tunnel back to them. Even if they'd survived the blast, even if they'd crawled out of that room, they'd never get through the destroyed tunnel.

"Helene." Coulter murmured. "Your sister is waiting."

A shiver raced along my spine as I thought of her at the hands of these vile pieces of shit. I'd give anything to fight for the men I loved, but my sister needed me more.

It took all my strength to turn away and ignore the smug curl of Coulter's lips as I stepped toward the waiting car. The guard crowded me, gripping my arm as he drove me to the waiting open back door. But he needn't have bothered, there was no fighting, not anymore.

I climbed in and slid across to the other side before Coulter followed. The guard shut the door, then climbed into the front while the driver slipped behind the wheel. We were pulling away before I knew it. That consuming pang of agony made me turn and look behind us. The clump of towering trees where we'd left was empty. But it was the mansion that drew my focus and the jagged edge of the stone wall that had caved in.

"Don't worry." Coulter muttered. "I have plenty more mansions for you to despise."

My stomach sank at the words. I fought the desperate need to lunge for the door and throw myself out of the car...even if it was moving.

My fingers curled, aching for the feel of a cold, steel razor. Anything to find some kind of...

You seek release. Kane's words were conjured from the past. *You crave that rush. Let us be that for you now. Use us, take whatever you need.*

I turned away from the ruins and clenched my fists until my knuckles ached. Trees blurred outside the tinted windows as we flew down the long driveway and turned. But that need for the razor had died away. I had let them fill that hunger. I'd let them fill that void inside with their darkness and control.

Only now...that was over.

Coulter reached over and grasped my arm with one hand and the inside of my thigh with the other, then yanked me across the leather seat until I slammed hard against him. His hand stayed on my thigh as the car accelerated, skirted the heart of the city, and headed north.

The city lights sparkled, a couple laughed as they walked hand in hand along the street. They may as well be another galaxy away from where I sat with that monster's hand possessively on my thigh. "Where are you taking me?"

"Someplace they'll never come looking for you."

A shiver of fear ripped through me as the city lights grew sparse and finally fell far behind. Darkness crowded in and the towering apartment buildings and sparkling clubs were gone. Out that far, there was nothing but the highway. Cold moved through me and goosebumps raced up my arms, making me shiver. Coulter spread his fingers wider, the heat of his palm melting into my thigh.

"Don't worry. You'll be warm soon enough." He captured my chin and turned my gaze toward him. "You are mine now, Helene. Every scream of rage and agony that comes from these beautiful lips belongs to me. You will learn I can be a gentle master, if you obey."

I yanked away from his hold. "And if I don't?"

Those infernal eyes hardened. "Then this...partnership will be very hard on you. Very hard indeed."

I shivered, even though his hand was hot like a brand on my thigh. *Hard on me?* That'd been his threat. I knew better than anyone exactly just what he was capable of and that chilled me to the bone.

Headlights glinted against the towering ten-foot fence surrounding a facility the government owned outside the city, but as we skirted the barrier to whatever they kept away from prying eyes, I felt the sedan slow.

"What the fuck is going on?" I murmured, glancing at the driver.

He met my panicked stare in the rear-view mirror before pulling into the military base and stopped outside the guard hut. I looked behind us as a car drove past. The window rolled down and the driver handed over ID to the armed soldier, who grabbed the card, scanned the details, and stepped closer to glance into the back seat.

Help me!

Please, help me!

The scream rose as the soldier gave a nod. "Mr. Coulter."

"Open the gate, Morgan." Coulter demanded. "Have the others arrived?"

"Yes, sir. About thirty minutes ago."

Coulter just gave a nod and settled back against the seat. "Good."

The guard stepped away, allowing the window to rise as the gate in front of us rolled open.

WARNING

U.S. PROPERTY

NO TRESPASSING

VIOLATORS WILL BE PROSECUTED.

I stared at the warning signs as the car rolled through the gate and accelerated. I looked behind us at the guard hut as it disappeared. "What the hell is this?"

My captor just met my stare, saying nothing. This couldn't be happening...this couldn't be...*someplace they'll never come looking for you.* That's what he'd said.

He'd told the truth.

No one would look here.

After all...this was the government we were talking about. The car swept around a rise and dipped into a valley until I saw the bright lights of some kind of huge hangar, with the nose of a sleek jet peeking out as it slowly headed for a landing strip.

Vivienne...

Vivienne was on that plane.

"No." I whispered and lunged across the seat, clawing the door handle as the car came to a stop.

"Sir?" The guard barked as I clambered free.

"Let her go." Coulter commanded.

I didn't care, wild horses couldn't have held me back.

"*VIVIENNE!*" I screamed as I stumbled out of the car and ran. My voice flew back to slap my face and the wind snatched my hair.

There were armed soldiers all around the hangar, but I didn't care. My bare feet stung as they slapped against the asphalt. I was almost naked, dressed in nothing but thin lace. Still, I felt that fire in my belly as I sidestepped the soldier and ran along the side of the hangar after the jet.

Red lights flashed and the engines roared as they propelled the expensive plane around to face the runway.

"NO!" I screamed, waving my hands like a fool.

A blur of movement came from my right before I was hit.

"NO! NOOOO!" I shrieked, kicking and thrashing, clawing the soldier's arms as they wrapped around my middle.

"ENOUGH!" He roared, lifting my feet from the hard surface and dragging me backwards.

I threw my head back, cracking the back of my skull against his forehead. His hold slipped, allowing me to crash back down to the ground.

The jet's engines were deafening as it powered ahead, picking up speed. I pumped my arms, driving myself forward as I ran, not for my life, but for hers...but it was too late. The sleek Gulfstream's front wheels lifted and it rose slowly.

"No." I cried one last time as I dropped my hands, but momentum still took me, smacking my feet against the runway until they were on fire.

I stopped, my shoulders curling as suffocating sobs consumed me. *No...nonono. I'm sorry, Vivienne...I'm so fucking sorry.* My knees buckled, sending me crashing down. Agony flared through my knees as they hit the ground. Still, it was nothing compared to the grief that pummeled my chest.

I'd failed her.

I rocked forward, pressing my forehead to the hard surface until I drew in the choking, sickening scent of the pavement. Until hands found me once more, wrapping around my waist only to haul me up like a child. Tears streamed down my face as the soldier shook me.

"Stand the fuck *up!*" He roared.

I slammed my feet down and spun, then worked the pathetic wetness in my mouth and *spat*. The spittle hit his cheek and slid down. The soldier's lips curled and rage flared as he yanked his hand up. I couldn't help but flinch.

"Enough." Coulter commanded. "Take her to the hangar.'

The soldier sucked in hard breaths, trying to leash his anger, and slowly lowered his hand. Instead, he grabbed my arm and yanked me forward hard enough to slam into him.

"Give me a fucking excuse," he snarled in my ear. "I dare you."

Stunned, I careened forward as he dragged me back toward the hangar. Each step was flaying the soles of my feet. I limped, biting down on my whimpers. I wouldn't break, not in front of them. But as I was shoved forward, I turned my head to find the blinking lights of the jet as it climbed into the sky. Heading where, I didn't know.

But what I did know was they'd won.

They'd taken.

They'd ruined.

They'd controlled.

They'd...*beaten us.*

They'd beaten us all.

I was shoved toward the glaring lights of the hangar and the two other luxury private jets waiting to take any one of these vile bastards anywhere they wanted. Maybe it was Coulter? Maybe I was the next one to be ripped away from the only family I was willing to die for.

"Move." The soldier shoved my shoulder.

I stumbled forward, biting the insides of my cheeks to try to stem the flow of tears, and rounded the rear of the jet...and walked straight into Haelstrom Hale.

He stood there, staring at me with that same detached, holier-than-thou smugness. One I'd seen before. But now...now this was all too real.

"Helene." He murmured my name.

The soldier grabbed my arm, his fingers bruising. "Sorry, sir." He gave me a hard yank. "This one got away from me."

"Did she now?" Hale's brow rose.

"Take her to the house." Coulter commanded, striding toward us.

He handed over a CPU to Hale as the glare of headlights came through the open door of the hangar.

"No!" I shook my head, staring at that drive in Hale's hand as the soldier dragged me backwards. *"You can't fucking do this! YOU CAN'T DO THIS!"*

But they just stood there, watching me with that same almost amused stare like this was...entertaining to them.

"Fuck you!" Tears blurred those smug stares. *"FUCK YOU!"*

The solider yanked me hard again, making my head snap forward, and I bit my tongue. The heady taste of blood bloomed in my mouth. I swallowed it down, along with the pain and the burn in the back of my throat.

A black Mercedes four-wheel drive pulled up. The engine died and the driver's door opened. I caught sight of Harmon as the driver climbed out and opened his door. He lifted his gaze as he stepped out, catching sight of me as the soldier thrust me forward.

There was no humanity in his eyes. No warmth. No...*nothing*. Just greed and power and the kind of depraved detachment only men like him could have.

"Walk or I'll drag you by the fucking hair." The solder barked.

I stumbled forward, leaving them behind, turned my focus to where we were heading, and realised this was no military compound. This was a *lie*.

A house loomed in the distance, sprawling and commanding and curled around the private landing strip. But as I was pushed toward that house, I caught movement in the dark. The soldier yanked my arm, stopping me instantly. Out of the darkness they came. Two men, moving soundlessly, split up and flanked us.

"Daughter." One of them murmured.

But it was the soldier who reacted, stiffening and watching them from the corner of his eye. "You were supposed to be gone." He said carefully.

A shudder raced through me as the two men came closer, moving with sleek, soundless, purposeful strides. I knew instantly who they were.

They were Sons.

"And you were supposed to be reassigned." One of them said. "I told you the next time I saw you, it would be the last."

I yanked my arm from the soldier's hold and took a step backwards, until I slammed into another of them, one I hadn't even seen at my back. I spun around, meeting a threatening stare. A surge of adrenaline tore through me at the connection. My body reacted instantly, slowing my breaths as he looked at me.

"I've never seen you before." He murmured, searching my eyes. "What is your name?"

"Helene." I answered instantly.

I'd never had that kind of reaction to a male before. I'd never felt so...*obedient.*

"Helene." He slowly repeated.

The shiver that raced through me moved deeper until it felt like I was freezing. He lifted his hand, brushing the back of his curled fingers against my cheek. The contact was electric.

"I don't think—" The soldier started.

The Son in front of me moved faster than I'd ever seen before, lunging forward to grab him around the throat. "Do you wish to finish that sentence?"

The soldier's eyes widened. Fear shone before he shook his head. One hard shove and the Son pushed him away.

"I'll be seeing you, *Helene.*" He swung that ravening stare back to me, taking in every contour of my face, before he stepped backwards and turned away.

They were gone in an instant. Here one minute and gone the next. For a second, I didn't move...I *couldn't*.

"Goddamn *motherfuckers.*" The soldier snarled and straightened. "Think they fucking run the place." He jerked that savagery my way. "What the *fuck* are you looking at?"

I didn't know as I stared into the darkness where they'd disappeared. I'd never felt anything like that before. Not desire. Not love. Not anything I could put my finger on. But there had been a connection there. One that both chilled me to the bone and filled me with hope.

"Come *on.*"

My arms throbbed from his grip, still the asshole dug them in deeper, shoving me along the path to the sweeping manor that stretched all around us. Immaculate gardens were filled with the sweetest scented flowers I'd ever encountered. Still, they wouldn't smother the rot of the place. Nothing could do that.

I had a fair idea whose place this was. The house. The government warning signs. The private runway which was designed to get him out of the country at a moment's notice.

There was no way that this wasn't Hale's house.

The one he'd hid away in after his 'death'.

The soldier pushed me toward the front door, then reached around and shoved it open.

"Inside." He commanded.

Reflex made me lash out, grip the doorframe and hold on. My pulse was booming. One step...one step and it'd be over for good. Some part of me still clung to the hope Riven would come.

I'll find you.

Those were the last words he'd said to me. Mouthed silently as I was dragged from that room. My breaths sped, panicked.

"Take a step, *Daughter.*" The soldier leaned down to growl in my ear. "Or I'll tear your fingernails from this fucking entrance and throw you."

He would. That I knew.

Still...*I couldn't.*

He tore my hold from the doorframe, then shoved me so hard I flew forward. I landed hard on the Italian marble tiles. The brutal *thud* of the impact tore through my shoulder and into my neck. He was a darkened blur, bearing down on me. All I saw was his hands as he grasped a handful of my hair and dragged me to my feet.

"*You will fucking obey me!*" He roared in my face.

I bucked, grasping his hand around my hair as my scalp burned. "Stop it...*stop it!*"

He dragged me, kicking and fighting, along the hallway from the entrance to where a set of dark wooden double doors were closed.

A hard *thud* and he pushed them open. "Get the fuck inside." He shoved me.

I stumbled in, catching the glow of soft amber lights that spilled around the room through the sheen of my tears. Movement came from a murky corner. I barely caught it as someone turned and looked at me.

"Helene?" Came the whimper. "*Oh, my God! HELENE!*"

I stopped, staring, stunned as Vivienne stumbled forward, one hand wrapped around her belly, the other thrown out toward me. For a second, I didn't understand. I shook my head, my tears drying on my cheeks.

"You're not real." The words were hollow as she pulled me hard against her. *"You're not real."*

"I'm r-real." She cried, clawing me so hard her nails stung.

I wrapped my arms around her, still expecting my touch to meet nothing but air as the cruel fantasy dissipated. But that didn't happen. Instead, when I touched her, I felt warmth...and the sweet swollen life inside her.

I burst into a wave of fresh tears, holding onto her. "I thought you were gone. I thought you were taken from me. The jet...the *jet.*"

"It wasn't me." She reached up, cradled my face, and stared into my eyes. "Look at me. It wasn't me."

Outside the room the front door gave a *thud.*

Footsteps sounded, headed our way.

"What the fuck do they want with us, then?" I whispered.

"I don't know." My sister turned her head as the double doors opened. "I guess we're about to find out."

THIRTY-ONE

Riven

———

I HEAVED THE BOULDERS FROM THE PILE AND TWISTED TO drop them beside me. We were building our fucking way out of there out of the ruins of the tunnel, one or two boulder-stairs at a time. Those stars far overhead sparkled that little bit brighter, and the crisp wash of fresh air was so goddamn addicting it made me work faster, grabbing the next massive chunk of stone from Hunter as he grabbed it from Kane and handed it over.

"Careful!" Kane bellowed, making me jerk my gaze toward him.

The wall in front of me shook, the stones clashing against each other. *No...NO!* I lunged, grabbing them as one below gave way, slipping free. The rest followed, crashing to the ground.

Kane lunged, driving Thomas sideways.

Boom!

They crashed to the ground in the exact place where Thomas had stood. Dust billowed upwards, leaving my brothers to cough and splutter, yanking their shirts up and over their noses.

Fuck!

FUCK!

I wrenched my focus back to the gaping hole in the goddamn wall in front of me and wobbled. The chunk of wall under my feet was perched precariously at best. *You'd better hold, motherfucker. Do you hear me? You'd better hold.*

Her wide eyes haunted me as I bent, balancing my weight, and reached out. "Again."

There was no argument, not even a moment of hesitation. They knew what we fought for. Make no mistake, every second we stood here fighting to get out of this grave was a battle. Thomas lifted a boulder, his body straining as he heaved it up to Kane, then to Hunter who had the task of lifting it the highest, over his head to me.

I grabbed it, the muscles of my back screaming as I moved it into place, trying to find a secure footing. Stone by stone we rebuilt the wall, until it stretched above as close as we dared to that gaping chasm above.

Screams from the other partygoers echoed and the desperate sounds of roaring engines followed as they ran for their lives. *Good. I hope they all fucking die.* Some came for canapés and Dom Perignon and to rub shoulders with the city's elite, but the select few were there for a far more sinister reason...until it all blew to hell.

"Thomas." I muttered staring at the hole above us, then looked down at him. "You're first."

He shook his head. "No, Hunter is first."

But Kane was having none of it. He grabbed him by the shoulders. "I need you up there to help the rest of us, okay? Think of Helene. That's all you need to focus on. I'll be right behind you."

Thomas gave a nod, letting Kane step away.

My brother climbed the stones, moving up from Kane to Hunter, who steadied him until he reached me.

"You good?" I gripped his arm.

His face was pale, his stare haunted. Still, he gave a nod and helped me maintain my balance as he bent down. "If this all goes to hell," I grabbed his ankles, letting him hold onto my shoulders. "You make sure you find her. Whatever else happens."

"I will." His voice was a croak. "I promise."

That was all I needed. My body howled, protesting in violent shudders as I lifted my brother, drawing on every ounce of strength I had.

My stomach tensed, my breath holding in my lungs as I heaved him higher, pushing him with all I had. He was a heavy motherfucker. My face burned, the pressure in my head booming. With one last savage cry, I drove him up as hard as I could, and threw him through that hole.

He was gone, kicking out his feet frantically, and was free. Desperation soared inside me. *"Thom! THOM!"*

"I'm here!" He called, then peeked over the edge of the hole. "The edge is soft, but it'll hold."

My pulse raced as I turned. "Kane!"

But I didn't need to yell. My brother was already moving around Hunter. As much as my body wanted to give up, my mind didn't let it.

"You ready?" I asked.

"As much as I'll ever be." He muttered.

I didn't bother to wait. Each panicked thrashing in my chest was another second she could be further from me. My arms trembled as I gripped Kane's ankles and lifted. He placed his hand on my shoulder and reached for Thomas with the other. I drove all my strength into my thighs, feeling them tense as I unleashed a grunt and heaved him skyward.

He was out, kicking chunks of dirt from the edge free and straight into my face. I jerked my gaze away, spitting the taste of it out.

"Brother." Hunter murmured from close to me.

I found him at my side.

"Let me lift you." He said. "I'm too heavy."

"No." I shook my head. "That's not going to happen."

There was something brewing between us, a kind of truce. Maybe it was even more than that. My chest swelled with love.

"Get the fuck out of this damn hole," I commanded. "Then grab me."

"I will...brother."

Fuck. That word hit me hard, making my breaths deepen. I used that desperation as I bent and grabbed him. Fuck, he weighted a ton. I couldn't do it...I couldn't...

I'll. Find. You.

My own words resounded in my head. I'd do whatever it took to do exactly that. A roar tore from somewhere deep in my belly. I drove upwards with all I had. But I couldn't get him anywhere near the edge. Kane and Thomas were there, hanging over Hunter as he reached for them.

Cries came from my brothers. I lifted Hunter's feet again, pushing him the last few inches until Thomas and Kane grabbed him and pulled. I stumbled, barely catching myself as his weight left me and he was through.

It took a second, but then Hunter was back, reaching for my hand as he leaned down. "Your turn. You trust me, right?"

I met his stare, then nodded. My thighs felt like they were made of lead and I had nothing left in the tank. Still, I reached down, grabbed whatever rage or fear I had inside me, and bent my knees. With a brutal roar I lunged, driving my heels down into the stone wall.

Crack. Something under me gave way.

All I saw was my brothers.

And her.

Always her.

Strong fingers closed around my hand and pulled. My wrists and arms screamed with strain. But I clawed their hold with all I had.

Hunter howled, driving himself backwards and finally dragged me free of that hell. The moment I was out, I rolled, catching my breath then slowly pushed upwards, looking around through the trees to where men and women dressed in Armani and Chanel still ran for their lives.

Boom!

The ground rocked under me. The edges of that gaping hole crumbled to fall in.

"Get back!" Hunter roared.

I kicked, frantically driving my boots into the ground, and scurried away from that hole as fast as possible. A hard shove and I pushed to my feet. My damn legs shook. I thought it was just from exhaustion, but it wasn't. Leaves fell in waves from the trees and a fresh burst of guests' screams sounded as they hurried for their cars.

"We move, *now.*" Hunter roared.

I pushed forward, merging with my brothers as we headed for the corner of Coulter's mansion. The gaping hole from the caved in tunnel was at the rear of the house...what was left if it, anyway.

The side stone wall had been blown out. Smoke billowed out from inside. The bitter stench of C4 hung in the air. I lunged forward, driving myself behind Hunter, and rounded the corner...and slammed into two men dressed in black, carrying a backpack of explosives.

One of them gave a grunt, stumbling before he lifted that merciless stare to Hunter. I knew him...it was the one from before. The Son who...came for them.

"You." He took in Kane and Thomas, then back to Hunter until he scowled. "Where is she? Where is the Daughter?"

This one doesn't belong to you...

She's a Daughter, isn't she?

"They took her."

He jerked that unwavering stare my way. "And you just let her...be *taken?*" He spat as though the idea of that repulsed him.

Hunter scowled, narrowing in on the asshole. But it was the icy rage that rose inside me. "No. I didn't just *let her be taken.* We're going to find her."

The Son scanned Thomas and Kane before he settled back on me. "Only if I don't find her first."

"What did you just say?" I murmured.

The Son just glanced at Hunter. "Hunter." He gave a nod. "You can stop watching those rich fucks in the chat rooms. You won't find us that way."

"Is that so? Tell me, how *can* I find you?"

The Son took a step backwards, grabbing the shoulder strap on the pack full of explosives. "You don't...*we* find *you.*"

Then he was gone, slipping around the corner of the house.

"Motherfucker." I lunged, heading after him.

Exhausted or not, I was going to beat that asshole to death with that bag of c-fucking-4. But the moment I rounded the destroyed corner of the mansion, I saw nothing. He was gone...

just like that. I scanned the trees as Hunter and the others found me.

"Did you hear what that bastard said?" I muttered, then met my brother's stare.

That same savage stare scanned the trees as well behind me. "I heard." He said.

He liked it as much as I had.

"So we make sure we find her...first." He added.

I gave a nod and kept walking, lengthening my stride until I slammed into an older fuck and his goddamn trophy wife. I lunged, grabbing the asshole by his jacket. "Give me *your fucking phone!*"

His eyes shot wide, hesitating for a second.

It was a second I didn't have. I yanked my fist back and unleashed, driving my aching knuckles into the slimy asshole's face. *Crunch.* The blood that came from his nose was instant, as was the piercing, high-pitched squeal that came from his mouth.

He shoved his hand into his jacket pocket. *"Here...HERE!"* He shrieked.

I snatched the thing from his hand, pressed the button and lifted the camera to his tortured stare.

Ding.

The phone unlocked.

"Thank you." I muttered, focusing on punching in the numbers.

"Keys." Hunter demanded.

The guy actually started to shake his head until Hunter unleashed a low snarl. Then the asshole let out a moan, one hand holding his bloody nose as he shoved the keys to his Bentley at Hunter. "Take it...just *get the fuck out of my way.*"

Hunter snatched them from his hand. "Go."

But I was too busy trying to remember the one fucking number I needed right now. But I couldn't fucking remember. I spun, meeting Thomas' gaze.

"Thom, I need..."

He spoke before I finished, rattling off London St. James' number like it was written in front of him. I punched in the digits, listening to the cell ring before it was answered.

"Who the fuck is this?"

"It's Riven." I started. "We're out. Do you have a bead on Viv's location."

"No." He snarled. "Why...*do you?*"

He thought I had something to do with this? Anger seethed for a second before I stilled. I guessed I deserved that. "No." I answered. "But they've taken Helene, as well. My...my sister and Coulter."

Jesus fucking Christ.

When I said the words 'my sister', it made my fucking stomach roll. No wonder St. James didn't trust me.

"Motherfuckers." London snarled. "I'm going to kill those fucking assholes. Blood or not. They're going to die."

I lifted my gaze to the haunted expression in Hunter's eyes. "Not if I get to them first. Tell me where you are. We'll meet."

"You sure you want to do that?" He said carefully. "Colt and Carven are...*hunting*."

A shiver raced along my spine. "Yes." I answered. "Tell me where you are...and bring guns."

THIRTY-TWO

Helene

FOOTSTEPS THUDDED, COMING TO A STOP OUTSIDE THE double doors before they slowly opened. Hale was the first one through, scanning the room with that scrutinizing stare before he settled on Vivienne and me. Melody was next, quiet and obedient, stepping behind him to perch on the back of a brown leather sofa in the middle of the expansive library.

But it was Coulter I was wary of, watching him like you would a viper that slithered across your path as he made his way to a neat, expensive bar at the edge of the room.

"Vivienne. Helene." Hale called. "It's nice to finally meet both of you."

I dragged my focus from my rapist, to the man he worked for... the man he *looked up to*. The man who was supposed to be dead but was still very much alive. A sickening wave washed through me, forcing me to take a step, moving in front of my sister.

"Let my sister go." I shook my head. "She has nothing to do with any of this. Whatever *plans* you have, they don't concern her."

"Helene," she hissed at my back.

I reached behind, grasping her hand. Her manicured nails stung as they clawed my hand for a hold.

But I took that sharp, cutting flare, gripped her hand, and kept trying. "She has nothing you need. Nothing you want. Whatever it is you're planning, you have me. Take that...take that and let her go."

My fingers were crushed, the knuckles grinding with her panic and fear.

I knew what my words meant. I was giving myself up to whatever sick plans those bastards had. As terrifying as that was, knowing she was in that hell with me would be far more traumatic.

I could get through this...whatever hell this was, knowing she was away, safe, alive...protected.

"So devoted." Hale's eyes shone as they fixed on me. "And yet, you barely know her."

I clenched my jaw, then relaxed enough to force the words through. "I know her. I also know the men who love her. Men who won't *ever* stop looking for her. They tore the city apart looking for Colt before, so what do you think they'll do to find her, the mother of their children?"

A strangled sound came from my sister. Her hand shook in mine. I'd seen her fearless and savage, her face blood-splattered, and her eyes shining with the deadly gaze of a killer. But it wasn't rage that filled her now. Not in her condition. It was fear.

She was too close to giving birth.

And far too heavy to fight for her and her babies' lives.

But I wasn't. I wasn't and I wasn't taking no for an answer.

I released her hold, taking a step toward them, keeping my voice low. "You know who you're messing with, right? You know what you created. Have you seen Colt since you...since you tortured him? Do you know the kind of darkness you've brought out in him? A true killer...a *terrifying* beast of a man."

There was a quirk of Hale's lips as though he hadn't actually heard the truth of what Colt had become. But now he had... now he had and he—

The quirk curled, one corner of his mouth inched upwards and in an instant, the hope I had of scaring them to let my sister leave disappeared.

"I know." Hale whispered, grinning. "Because we made him that way. We will make more like him...so...many...*more.*" He looked behind me, fixing that ravenous stare on my sister. "Together we'll make a new Order. One that is better and stronger." He lifted the CPU in his hand. "And we will learn from the mistakes of our past. King's bloodline started the first Order, so we will use his bloodline again. Only, this time we'll use a little more...modification."

Modification?

A shiver tore through me. I shook my head as the double doors opened once more and a team of male nurses wearing white scrub pants and white shirts emblazoned with the name *NEW ORDER* on their top pockets hurried in.

"No." I shook my head. *"No."*

"Coulter." Hale commanded. "Will start the process. You will both become his to breed."

Breed? Revulsion slammed into me. I started to shake my head. The truth wedged in the back of my throat. *No. You will never breed with me. I made sure of that a long time ago.*

*I want children someday...*Riven's words rose like a slap.

"No. N-o fucking way." Vivienne took a step away, jerking her gaze to Coulter. "You come near me. You come near my babies and I'll fucking kill you. I'd rather die. I'd rather they—" She broke. Her tear-filled eyes blazed with hatred. "You will *not* touch my babies. You *will not.*"

"Are you really going to let this happen?" My pulse was booming as I found Melody's gaze. "You know how this turns out. How they use and take, just like they took your children. You must've cared for them. All those months feeling them growing and moving inside you. I know you loved them. Are you really going to let that happen to someone else? Are you really going to let them tear someone else apart?"

She scowled, then pushed off the back of the sofa, cutting across the nurses as she came close. My breath caught. Desperation boomed with my pulse as she stopped in front of me.

"Please." I begged. "Please, not her."

She had that same detached stare that Hale had. One that settled on me. "I can see why my brothers were so smitten with you. You took my place when they needed it. Someone to..." she reached up to brush the hair from my face, until I flinched from her touch. "Save." She finished. "Someone to save. Because they couldn't save me, could they? No...they couldn't save me."

White moved closer as the nurses stepped in behind her. Tears came. But they weren't tears of pain or the crushing guilt. They were from anger, from the shuddering, controlling anger.

"You belong to the New Order now." She murmured, then glanced at Vivienne. "Both of you do. Your master owns everything. You are, after all, a vessel." She dropped her hand to her belly and I knew...I knew instantly *she was pregnant*.

"The fuck she does." I spat.

One nod and Melody smiled. Hale moved behind her, heading for the double doors. "Let me know how you progress, will you, Coulter." He cast over his shoulder. "Especially with the eldest. I cannot wait to see her round and full."

With that, he opened the double doors and Melody went after him, falling in line.

I stepped backwards, opening my arms to protect her as one of the nurses pulled a vial from one pocket and a syringe from the other. "No." I growled. "You come near her and I'll fucking kill you...*DO YOU HEAR ME? I'LL FUCKING KILL YOU.*"

"Easy now, Helene." Coulter cradled the glass of Scotch in his hand from the edge of the room. "It's just a little something to take the edge off."

Two nurses descended, moving in from both sides. I jerked my gaze around for a weapon, but there was nothing... nothing but books and fucking rugs. The soles of my feet screamed in agony as I lunged, driving myself toward the closest nurse.

"Fuck you!" Vivienne screamed behind me. *"FUCK YOU!"*

I attacked with fists and fury, slamming into the nearest nurse and swung my fist. Knuckles drove into his stomach. He tensed, still it wasn't enough, just unleashing an *oof*. But I didn't have time to attack again as Vivienne unleashed a scream, punching and slapping the second nurse.

"Motherfucker!" I shrieked as I stumbled sideways and then went for him.

I drove all my strength into him, knocking him off her, then leaped. "You *motherfucker! YOU MOTHERFUCKER!"*

The sting in my arm was instant. Hands gripped me, holding me steady. I jerked my gaze to the nurse at my side. The one who held the vial in his hand...and the other gripped the syringe embedded in my arm, with the plunger pushed all the way down.

"What?" I murmured, and looked down.

"Like I said," Coulter started. "Something to take the edge off."

I shook my head, my thoughts slow as I looked at the nurse underneath me. He had no needle. He *had...no...needle.*

"It's for me." My words were dull and empty.

Panic roared, punching all the way to the surface as the room wavered and spun.

"Helene!" My sister screamed my name as I pushed upwards and shoved away.

But the moment I took a step, my knees buckled, sending me crashing to the floor. Agony burst through my knees before I shoved against the cold tiles. Even those blurred under my hand.

"Easy now." Coulter gripped my arm and lifted, easing me upwards. "I've got you."

"Get the fuck off her!" Vivienne screamed, lunging toward me.

I shook my head and the room blurred even more. *"Noooo...."* I slurred, reaching for her. *"Take me...take me."* I met my sister's panicked gaze. *"Not her...not my—"*

The darkness closed over me before I could finish.

I tried to hold on.

I really did.

But there was nothing to hold onto as my knees refused to support me.

The last thing I remembered was Coulter's voice as he murmured in my ear. "See you soon, Helene...see you soon."

THIRTY-THREE

Riven

THE BENTLEY'S TIRES SQUEALED AS I TOOK THE CORNERS like a madman, wrenching the wheel, and jerked my gaze to Hunter, sitting beside me in the passenger seat. *"How much fucking further now?"* I barked.

He looked at the rich asshole's phone, then scanned the streets ahead. "It's just ahead."

Just ahead?

Still, it wasn't *here*. I clenched my fist and drove it against the steering wheel. *"Fuck!"*

Get to her.

Get...to...her.

The veins pulsed in my neck as I strangled the wheel. I tried to focus on the streets rushing toward me in a blur, but all I could hear was Thomas' constant mumbling in the back.

"Heavenly Father, I pray you guide us with your steady hand. Help us find our way to her and watch over her."

"Your God isn't fucking listening." I forced the words through clenched teeth. "And hasn't been for a long fucking time."

Hunter shot me a glare. One I ignored and glanced at the cell on his lap. The red marker flared on the street up ahead. I caught the shine of streetlights against the black sedan before I tapped the brakes and yanked the wheel. The bottom of the six-figure fucking car scraped as we hit the entrance of the parking lot hard and bounced.

My teeth gnashed. Kane gave a grunt behind me as I braked hard, skidding the sleek machine, and pulled up alongside the open trunk of the silver Audi.

I didn't bother to kill the engine, just shoved the car into park and climbed out, drawing in the icy night air. Doors slammed all around me as we rounded the rear of the vehicle and strode to where St. James waited beside his trunk.

"Guns?" I demanded.

He met my gaze with a look of unhinged rage, then jerked his head to the open trunk. "Take what you need."

What I needed was her.

Then Coulter in front of me.

That'd be the only thing that'd sate the hunger inside me. Blood. *So much fucking blood.*

"Do you have a bead on their location?" Hunter asked.

London gave a shake of his head, then lifted his gaze to the roar of an engine headed our way. "No, but they might."

The Explorer took the corner sideways, swinging hard before it mounted the curb. I held my breath, waiting for the impact as the four-wheel drive hurtled toward us...but it didn't hit. Instead, it came to a screeching halt a hair's breadth from the Bentley and both front doors were thrown open.

If there was ever a lethal looking duo, it was those two. Stark white hair stood out as the Son rounded the front of the vehicle and headed toward us. But it was the bigger one, moving soundlessly toward us, that drew my focus. He never made an impact. In fact, you could be forgiven for barely even registering him at all next to his twin brother. But make no mistake, this Son...was dangerous.

An unhinged gleam lingered in the male's eyes. Thick shoulders moved as he lengthened his stride, moving away from his brother to stand at the rear of the vehicles. Even Hunter watched him warily.

"Anything?" London turned to Carven, then glanced at Colt, before turning back.

Carven just shook his head without answering. I fought the flare of anger, keeping the fucking thing leashed as I took in the chest strap across Carven's chest. One loaded with honed, combat knives.

"He has to be somewhere." London turned on them. "Someone *has* to know something. Go back there, torture every motherfucker until they give us a location."

One nod.

That's all there was.

One, simple, fucking nod.

"And if no one there will give up Hale, then we'll track down every motherfucker until someone does. Men, women, I don't give a fuck. No one associated with The Order will survive this, not if I have anything to do with it."

A lump rose in my throat at the promise. I clenched my stomach, trapping that fluttering in my gut. Carven turned around, heading for the four-wheel drive once more, before he stopped. "Colt?"

We all glanced at the Son, who seemed to be pacing back and forth, his jaw clenched in desperation. The veins pulsed, almost black along the side of his neck. But it was that unhinged look of brutality that scared the fuck out of me.

I'd never seen anyone so...unstable.

"Son?" Hunter took a step toward him.

"Hunter." London commanded. "*Stop.*" He took a slow step, never taking his eyes off Colt, who clenched his fists, squeezing all the blood free until they were white. "That isn't Colt." He said carefully, glancing at Carven.

"What are you talking about?" My brother shot him a glare, lifting his hand to point. "He's *right there.*"

"That's not Colt." London muttered carefully and stepped toward him, lifting his hands in surrender. "*Easy now, Son. Easy, it's me...it's London.*"

That...man, that...hunter, whatever he was, lifted his gaze to London.

Lips curled and a look of condemned boding evil stared back.

"Heavenly Father..." Thomas started, and whatever that *thing* was, looked his way.

I jerked my gaze over my shoulder, glaring at him. *"Not now, Thom."* I hissed.

Goddamn idiot was about to get us all killed by friendly fire. I turned back. There was nothing friendly at all about the creature standing in front of us.

"Wildcat." The low rumble came from Colt. He shook his head, as though he was fighting with himself.

"Get him out of here, Carven." London urged. "Make him leash that goddamn thing. The last thing we need is the Beast unleashed."

But Carven actually looked nervous as he stepped toward his twin brother. "In the car, brother." He commanded. "You heard what London needs."

He blinked, then shook his head, lifting those clenched fists to drive them into the sides of his head.

"Dear God." Kane murmured, then strode forward, pushing London out of the way. "Can't you see? He's having a mental breakdown."

"Kane...NO!" London roared.

But it was too late. The deadly male lunged, driving his muscled frame through the air like he was built to fly, and slammed into my brother, driving him to the ground. Kane hit with *an oof* before Carven was there, slamming into Colt, driving him sideways. They fought, slamming into each other with brutal savagery. Colt got one punch in, slamming into the Son's mouth, then another. But Carven never reacted, even when blood slipped from the deep split. Instead, he turned his head, spat the blood onto the ground, and growled. "You *will* get yourself together, brother. She needs us. Do you *hear* me? *She...needs...us...*"

Those words had an impact, stopping the onslaught. Colt sucked in hard breaths, his dark blue eyes fixed on his brother.

"Wildcat." He grunted.

Carven sucked in a hard breath of his own and eased backwards, releasing his hold on his brother's shirt. "That's it. *Wildcat needs us.* So how about you get yourself into the car so we can find her?"

Colt drew in heavy breaths, those dark blue eyes slowly growing brighter. "Carven?" He asked, bewildered.

"It's okay." Carven shoved against the ground and rose, then cut Kane a blistering glare. "Saved you from being therapized to death is all."

Colt had no idea. I saw that now. No fucking idea as he followed his brother.

"You good?" London asked.

They both nodded, then headed for the four-wheel drive, climbing in to leave us behind.

"What the fuck was that?" Kane muttered as he shoved against the asphalt to stand.

"That was what The Order created." London muttered. "And thanks to you, we've lost precious time."

Kane flinched. Jesus, I'd thought I was a hard motherfucker. But I was nothing compared to St. James.

Headlights splashed over us, drawing London's gaze. He lifted a gun, taking aim.

"Easy." Hunter strode forward. "It's my men."

I cut him a glare, then watched as the black Hummer pulled up alongside the curb hard and came to a stop. Two men climbed out before headlights followed and another Explorer pulled in alongside.

"Can't very well drive around in a goddamn stolen Bentley all night, can we?" He said and strode toward his men.

"Cell." London handed one to me. "Stay in contact."

"Will do." I answered as I took it and headed after my brother.

We all climbed in the Explorer. I took the passenger seat, leaving Hunter to talk to his men before he climbed in behind the wheel, and winced. He was hurt, that was obvious, but pain would have to wait. We had Trouble to find.

"Do you have a plan?" I asked.

"No." He answered, shoving the four-wheel drive into gear.

"Great." I muttered, that torment seething under the surface. "So, what, we drive around until we fucking see them?"

He cut me a glare. "My men are scanning satellite footage of all cars leaving the house, but with the number of assholes running from the scene, that's going to take some time. If you have a better idea, then I'm all fucking ears."

I didn't and we both knew that.

"Goddamn it...*goddamn it!*" I screamed.

But it wasn't Helene's face I saw in my head. Nor was it Hale's.

It was the cruel, twisted smile of my sister.

My *fucking cunt of a sister.*

"I'm going to fucking kill her. Just so we're clear." I snarled, knowing how demented I sounded. "I'm going to kill our fucking sister."

THIRTY-FOUR

Helene

SCREAMS FILTERED IN. FAINT SHRIEKS OF TERROR I couldn't hold onto. But I—I *knew* that terrified shriek.

Vivienne.

My sister's name came like a gust of wind before it was snatched away. Terror slammed into me. I tried to fight through the darkness, cracking open my eyes to a blinding white light that glared down on me.

Cold pressed against my back, a hard surface. A blinding brilliance shone in my eyes.

"Easy, Helene." A murmur filled my ear. "We're almost done now."

Pressure came from the inside of my knee. I forced myself to hold on, driving my lids wider to look down. Someone gripped my thighs, spreading my legs wide as someone else moved in from the other side. Someone dressed in white. A sharp sting came from where he worked on me, all the way deep inside. I winced, then moaned with the agony.

"What...what are you doing to me?"

"Just a little sting." Another man murmured. "You'll be all fixed up soon."

I tried to shake my head, but it dropped backward instead, hitting the icy surface I lay on. I stared upwards, to the man holding my legs wide and I couldn't hold onto my body, not when that wave of nothingness swallowed me.

"You'll be good as new." Coulter's voice droned. "I'm going to put a baby in your belly, Helene. Do you hear me? I'm going to fuck you so hard you'll always be full of what's mine."

But that emptiness moved in, taking me back under once more until I floated away again.

Screams followed.

Faint screams.

I hit something hard, driving upwards toward that murky gray light.

"What?" The word was a slur as I forced my eyes open once more.

That darkness was so heavy, wrapping around me to hold me down.

"Get the fuck OFF ME!" Someone howled.

I knew that voice. I knew that—

With a roar, I drove myself upwards, bursting through that heavy weight that held me down.

Movement came from the corner of my vision as I cracked open my eyes. Through the murky wash of light in the corner of the room, someone fought for their life.

Help her. The faint words grew louder inside me. *Help her now!*

I blinked and forced open my eyes. My body weighed a ton as I lifted my head and drove numb limbs under me. "Get...*get off her!*" I slurred, my vision slowly sharpening.

Two men held my sister down as another one leaned over her. She kicked and bucked, her eyes wild and wide. *"NO... NO..NO!"* She screamed.

I shoved upwards, but my legs wouldn't work. *"Get..."* I slurred. *"Get the fuck off her!"*

My feet moved, letting me slowly drag them under me. I stumbled, falling forward as the nurse in front of Vivienne straightened and stepped away. I swung my fist, missing them completely as the nurses let her go and backed away.

There was blood on her stomach, bright and glaring. I swung around. *"GET THE FUCK AWAY FROM HER!"*

But they just watched me warily and moved back towards the door.

"What the fuck did you inject in my babies?" Vivienne screamed, tears sliding down her cheeks as she cradled her belly.

I spun around, my lips curling and lunged for them. But they yanked open the door and were gone in an instant. *Thud.* The door closed behind them, leaving us alone.

"Vivienne." I croaked and stumbled toward her, dropping to the floor at her side and stared at that bright blotch of blood on her soft white t-shirt. "Talk to me." I pleaded, lifting my gaze to hers.

"They injected something inside me. Into my stomach." She met my stare. "What the fuck was it?"

I shook my head, my own body stinging between my thighs as I closed them tight and reached out, gently touching her. "I don't know."

Tears shimmered in her eyes before she closed them and bowed her head. "My babies. Please, God, don't let me lose my babies."

My throat thickened instantly. I'd never wanted children, not after I'd started to delve into the sick bastards who made up The Order. I knew what they did to women, how they bred them, how they stole their babies hours after they were born.

I knew they were raised together until they were older, then they were divided. The Sons were trained to be killers and the Daughters...well, I knew first-hand what they did to them, selling them off to the men with the deepest pockets.

Men like Coulter.

Tears ran down her cheeks as my sister shuddered in agony. From the moment I'd met her, she'd been a force, earning her nickname, Wildcat. But that ferocity was long buried under pain and fear now as I sat there and watched my sister break.

Thick heavy sobs ripped from her lips. Her splayed hands roamed all over her swollen belly, searching for any sign of distress.

"I can't feel them." She shook her head and opened her eyes. "I can't feel them."

I shook my head, the tiny movements jarring. This wasn't happening...this wasn't.

"They took you." She said suddenly, wrenching her head up. "They took you...what did they do? Did they? *Did...they?*"

Get her to the table.

Those words pushed in. But I couldn't speak. My throat throbbed, aching and clenching, strangling anything I had to say. All I could do was breathe and clench my knees tighter and try to push away the pain.

I'm going to put a baby in your belly, Helene. Do you hear me? I'm going to fuck you so hard you'll always be full of what's mine. Acid punched all the way through my clenched throat. I pushed away from her and stumbled to the far corner of the room.

A bitter tang spilled from my lips. My knees shook, making me slam my hand against the wall to brace myself.

"What?" Vivienne asked. "What is it?"

Tears filled my eyes. I shook my head. Still, she shoved against the wall, painstakingly heaving herself to her feet.

"Helene."

I lifted my head as tears slipped free.

"Tell me."

How could I? How could I tell her the decision I'd made over a year ago when she was. WHEN SHE WAS WHAT???

"We're sisters. You can tell me anything. There's no judgement here. I think you know we're well past that now."

I swiped the back of my hand across my mouth and straightened. "Not sure about that."

She scowled and took another step forward, grabbing my chin. "Tell. Me."

I wanted to fight that need, knowing she was all I had. I couldn't ruin what we had. Not now. But to lie to her, especially now, would hurt her more. So, I took a breath and started. "Before I finally met you, when I was searching for you and found out about The Order, I had a minor surgery."

Her brow creased deeper. "Go on."

"I had myself sterilized." I said finally. "After seeing what they did, after what they *were doing,* there was no way I could live with myself if I brought a child into this world. Not knowing there were men like Hale and Coulter out there."

She paled in front of me, instantly turning a shade of gray. But then she straightened her spine. "I get it. Seriously, I do. It was the one thing that broke me when I found out the news myself. The one thing—" her voice broke. "The one thing London promised to protect us from."

Her hand went to her belly.

That was bloody and still.

Footsteps thudded outside the door. The *click* of a lock came before it swung inwards and in stepped our private tormentor, Coulter. Only this time he brought his men with him. Men whose gazes were fixed on me the moment they stepped into the room. Three went to the right, while one lingered beside the bastard.

I took a step, moving in front of Vivienne as Coulter glanced at the spill of acid and spittle left on the floor. But he didn't wince or look disgusted. In fact, his eyes glistened with hunger.

"Lights." He commanded.

In a heartbeat, the room darkened.

He stepped forward, making Vivienne whimper and move back. But I forced myself not to move, to protect her. My breaths were panicked. My pulse boomed in my ears. He looked behind me to Vivienne, then to her belly. "You'll take some time and that's okay. That, we have plenty of." Then he swung that chilling stare to me. "I have your sister to start with."

No...no...no...no.

Flashes of blinding lights filled the room, then came the music, booming so loud it made Vivienne scream and shove backwards until she hit the wall. She slammed her hands over her ears, but it was the neon white words that splashed across the walls in this secure room that drew my gaze.

Owned.

Slave.

Daughter.

Daughter.

DAUGHTER.

I rocked backwards on my heels. My pulse raced as I stared at those words. Movement came from the corner of my eye. I knew it was Coulter, but I couldn't look away, hypnotized by the words as they changed.

OBEY.

OBEY.

OBEY!

"Take off your clothes." Coulter murmured in my ear.

No. No fucking way. Get the fuck away from me. GET THE FUCK—

But my hand rose on its own, my finger sliding under the strap of my lingerie. *OBEY. OBEY. OBEY.* Cold air licked the tight peak of my nipple as I dragged my top down.

Tight lips curled even higher as Coulter turned to his men. "See, no fighting now."

Only I *was* fighting. He just couldn't see it. Images slammed into me as I stared at those hypnotizing words. Only it wasn't the images he wanted. It was me...

Me running through the halls of The Order with C4 in my hand.

Me fighting, driving my fist into one of the guard's faces as he came around the corner to find me.

Me blowing out the side wall.

I've got you! The words resounded in my head, pulled from the moment I'd carried my father out of that place and was forced to leave my sisters behind. Sisters I'd searched for. Sister's I'd killed for.

"That's it." Coulter traced my shoulder with the back of his curled fingers. *"So obedient now."*

Fuck you.

That savagery grew inside me as Coulter stepped around my back, his hand sliding around my neck until he grabbed my throat.

"Nooo." Vivienne's moan filtered through the booming music, the same one they played in The Order.

She shook her head, her hands clamped over her ears. She knew what they were doing...*she knew.*

I held onto that stare. Screams echoed in my head. I was fighting, desperately trying to hold on to the woman I'd once been. The woman they'd destroyed.

Get her to the table.

Those words slammed into me.

No.

I would not let that control take over.

Fight.

Fight!

FIGHT!

My mind held on to my sister, fixing my focus on her wide brown eyes and the blood stain on the front of her shirt.

"Look how easy she is now." Coulter called to his men.

He swung me around, my breasts bouncing as I spun. But as his men lowered their gazes, taking in my body, I became aware of the room. My gaze searched the darkened corners.

"Get the fuck off her!" Vivienne screamed. *"Get the FUCK OFF MY SISTER!"*

She stepped forward, desperation roaring in her eyes, until I gave her a small shake of my head, stopping her cold. I reached up and pushed my thumb under the edge of the black bodysuit I wore, the one Riven's sister had sold me in.

I didn't need her protecting me.

Because I didn't need that.

Not anymore.

THIRTY-FIVE

Riven

THIS WAS THE THIRD TIME WE'D DRIVEN THESE STREETS.

The.

Third.

Motherfucking.

Time.

I tried to leash that merciless side of myself, but I was losing the goddamn battle. "If we've had no sighting then, don't you think we should try somewhere else?"

Hunter jerked his gaze my way. His fists were white-knuckled around the wheel. "And where the fuck do you suggest we start?"

I *knew* where I wanted to start. Right where London had sent the Sons, right back to that goddamn party. "Not here. How's that?"

"We need a solid plan." Kane started behind me. "And we can't do that until we hear back from either Hunter's men or St. James."

"I need to hunt."

"What?" Hunter snarled, his voice nothing more than a growl.

One hard jerk of the wheel and I was thrown sideways, slamming into the door. *"Jesus fucking Christ!"* I roared, shoved myself upright and turned my head.

But Hunter was savage, glaring at the street ahead as he wrenched the wheel again, only this time throwing me toward him. *Are you trying to kill us?* I opened my mouth to say just that when I realized where we were...and where we were heading.

Opulent houses flashed past us as we tore along the familiar street. I knew *exactly* where we were. When I looked back at my brother, I saw that same desperate hunger I felt in me. My senses sharpened as we turned once more and sped back along the long road, passing a bank of police cars pulled up on the side of the road.

Red and blue lights flashed neon in the night. It wasn't until we were almost past that I saw what was really happening.

The District Commander stood at the front of the cars, talking to a lone man dressed in an expensive black and white tux. Shouting, more like. There was a lot of finger pointing from the lawman, along with a look of outright rage. My lips twitched as we flew past. There was no way the law was stepping foot on that property.

No doubt the guy in the tux was the most expensive lawyer in the city...if not the country.

Headlights splashed across us, blinding as we headed for the towering two-hundred-year-old forest that surrounded the expensive property.

"You want to hunt?" Hunter killed the lights and jerked the wheel, plunging us between the trees until we skidded to a stop. He looked my way, his dark eyes shimmering in the dimness. "Then go hunt."

I was frozen for a second, but that was all I needed. I yanked the handle, palmed the Sig Sauer I'd taken from St. James, and lunged out of the vehicle.

My boots hit the soft earth hard as I pushed off, driving myself toward the partly destroyed mansion once more. Smoke billowed out from the ruins. I gripped the gun and ran for the chaos. There were still men and women wandering around and others sitting on the endless expanse of the manicured gardens, unable to come to terms with what had just happened.

But they weren't the ones I was after. I wanted the bastards who'd run this auction. The ones who'd most likely run for their lives at the first explosion. But that didn't mean all was lost. If they weren't here, then there had to be someone to torture...my thoughts shifted to the lawyer who was right now at loggerheads with the police.

Someone like him.

A roar sounded as I ran across the front of the expensive mansion and headed for the opulent garages that spilled around the side and spread out at the back.

"*Easy!*" A male bellowed in a voice that sounded a little too familiar.

Only because I'd witnessed the same male fight mere minutes ago and as I ducked around the massive white pillars at the corner of the house, I came face-to-face with London's two kin once more.

The Sons.

Only it wasn't the cold-blooded ambush I expected. Two rich assholes lay on the ground, pushed up on their elbows. Blood streamed down the front of one asshole's face. His nose was crooked. No guessing how that happened. But the other guy was deathly pale, cowering and holding himself upright before he dragged his knees up and curled himself into a ball.

But they weren't the reason for the terrifying guttural screams that came from the blonde-haired killer as he paced back and forth in front of me...

No.

His brother was.

"*Colt!*" Carven lunged as the bigger of the twins wrenched his fist back and drove it into the side of the rich fuck's head.

"*HURT HER!*" He screamed, his eyes wide and bulging. "*HURT HER!*"

Carven grabbed his brother's wrists, fighting with him as he wrestled his fists back down. "*We don't know that!*"

I slowed, breathing hard, and neared, wrenching the muzzle of my gun to the sneaky suit who tried to scurry away on all fours.

"Uh-uh." I muttered and shook my head, stepping forward. The weasel-faced motherfucker slowly lifted his head until those beady eyes saw the barrel before shifting to me. "You're not going anywhere."

"Listen to me." Carven yanked his brother's arms down. *"LISTEN!"*

There was no man behind those eyes as Colt stared. That I knew. Footsteps came behind me as Colt wrenched his wrists out of Carven's grip. A wounded, bestial sound came from the Son I'd once thought was mute. His knees buckled, dropping him to the ground.

"What the hell set him off?" Kane asked, carefully stepping forward.

"Kane." I warned. "Don't."

Thud!

The Son slammed his fist onto the concrete so hard it split his knuckles. Blood bloomed, dripping as he unleashed a tortured moan and wrenched his fist high once more.

But the goddamn therapist in him didn't listen. "He's getting worse."

Carven shot him a murderous stare. "Yeah? *No shit.*"

The sneaky asshole in front of me had the good sense not to move. But it was the other weeping, pathetic excuse for a man that drew the unhinged Son's gaze.

Colt unleashed a snarl and lunged, clambering on all fours to slam the blubbering idiot against the ground and screamed into his face. *"They are...THEY ARE CHANGING!"*

What...the...fuck?

I winced as I lifted my other hand, reaching blindly into my pocket, not daring to move my gaze. One fast glance, and I pressed the main contact number St. James had given me, listening to the ring tone before it was answered.

"What is it?"

"Yeah." I started, staring as the Son pinned the poor fucker down and roared like a goddamn animal in his face, slamming his bloody fist against the ground.

"THEY ARE CHANGING!"

"You might want to get your ass here...like *now.*"

"What the fuck is going on?" St. James barked in my ear.

"Chaos." I answered. "Just get here." I lowered my hand and hung up the call.

"Colt." Carven urged, carefully moving closer. *"Buddy, it's me. Colt...COLT!"*

His brother wrenched his manic gaze upwards, that dangerous stare narrowing in on his brother as the ripe scent of fresh piss floated in the night air.

"Jesus." Kane muttered, looking down.

The dude under the disturbed Son had pissed himself in fear, the stench growing more pungent by the second. Colt swung that demented stare to the cowering dude, sniffed the air, then pushed off him.

"Run." Kane commanded the moment Colt shoved upwards and stalked toward his brother. The cowering bastard might be a spineless piece of shit but he wasn't stupid. He scrambled forward, shoved upwards, and scurried away, leaving the other guy staring after him in fear.

"Listen to me." Carven tried to soothe his brother. *"Stay with me."*

Colt shook his head. He clenched his bloody grip and stepped forward, that sickening, terrifying sound growing louder.

Kane wrenched his gaze to Hunter, then to me, imploring me with his stare. I ground my teeth and gave a small shake of my head. *No...fuck no.*

Do something, he mouthed.

I shook my head harder, and pointed my finger. *You. Do. Something.*

He wanted to. But the moment he took a step, Carven shook his head, stopping him cold.

"Look at me. You gotta leash it, do you hear me? You gotta leash *the Beast."*

The Beast? What the fuck kind of messed up situation was this?

I stared at the kid. Not a kid. A man. A barrel-chested man, with bulging arms and fists like fucking boulders, built like a goddamn fire truck. One who was about to tear this goddamn place apart and us along with it.

Tires squealed faintly at the edge of my focus. The soft *thud* of a car door followed. But I soon forgot about those sounds, focusing more on the Son as he turned and paced in front of his brother, taking mammoth strides that cut between us and his brother.

"You can't let it out." Carven urged.

Colt unleashed a snarl, raising those mangled bloody fists to slam against the sides of his head. He was going to tear this place apart, that was certain. But he was going to beat himself to death doing it.

"What the fuck is going on?" London snarled.

The slam of his boots crowded in. I turned then, taking in the air of barely contained rage in the man.

The man I'd once hated.

The man I once would've put a bullet in his head.

Until *her*.

Until...*Trouble*.

"He's going out of his mind." Carven wrenched a terrified gaze to the only man he'd ever known as a father. *"Look at him!"*

London lifted his hands and took a step forward. "Easy, Son... *easy*."

Colt had calmed down once before, pulling himself out of whatever mental anguish this was. But this...this was...*different*.

Colt's eyes sparkled in an unhinged and inhuman way. He was a madman in his movements. His lips curled, teeth bared, as he sucked in heavy draws of breath and stalked forward. A growl rumbled in his chest, throbbing like a living thing trapped in there.

"Changed." He snarled. *"Changed...changed...changed."*

"He keeps saying that." Carven shook his head, tormented. "He keeps saying they are changing or they're changed."

London scowled and took a step forward. "What are you saying, what's changed?"

A moan came from Colt. He raised a bloody fist and drove it into the side of his head before he threw his head back and roared.

I flinched at the sound.

"THEY! THEY! THEY CHANGE!!"

"They?" London whispered. "What do you mean *'they'?"*

Colt, or whatever that was, shook his head.

But London pressed him. *"What do you mean 'they'?"* He stepped forward, grabbing his Son by his shoulders. "Do you mean the babies? *Beast! DO YOU MEAN OUR BABIES?"*

"YES!" He bellowed. *"YES THE BABIES!"*

"Jesus Christ." London seemed to collapse. *"Jesus...fucking Christ."*

A pang of agony tore across my chest. London stumbled, almost falling to his knees until he slammed his hand against the wall to save himself. "The babies." He shook his head. *"It's the babies."*

But as tormenting as it was to witness, I couldn't care about his pain. Not right now...not then. "You...you can feel them, can't you?"

Colt lifted his head and that feral stare stopped on me in an instant.

That thunder boomed inside me. I was so selfish at that moment. So utterly fucking selfish. Still, I didn't care. I'd use anyone, hurt *anyone,* to get Helene back to me. "You can, can't you? You can *feel them."*

London turned back, that pained stare fixed on Colt before he stumbled forward. "Is that true? Can you...can the Beast feel them somehow?"

The Son just nodded.

"Then what the fuck are you waiting for?" I urged. *"Find them."*

THIRTY-SIX

Helene

"Owned." Coulter's eyes glistened in front of me. "That's what you are. I own you, Helene. I *own* every bit of you." He looked down, trailing his curled fingers down my bare arm. "I can feed you with my drugs. I can tie you to my bed and put a baby in your belly. How does that sound? You want to carry my child? Do you want to feel me riding you every night. I'll fuck the feel of the Principal out of you. How does that sound? By the time I'm done, you won't remember him at all. Only me...*only...me.*"

I fought the tremble, instead fixed on the sight of those words shining in his eyes, the ones splashed across the walls of the room and the spines of the books on the shelves.

OBEY.

MINE.

Fragments of my past collided with my present, to moments before all this started, when I wasn't broken, but was the kind of woman who'd led a Son to a boat storage yard to take him out

346

with one savage blow. The one who'd hauled a pack of C4 explosives into The Order, taking out as many guards as I could to rescue a man I loved...*once.*

Screams pierced my thoughts, causing me to look over to where Vivienne kicked and fought, wrestling two of Coulter's guards who tried to hold her.

But she refused to be held.

"GET THE FUCK OFF MY SISTER!" She screamed, turning on one of her attackers, driving her fists into his chest, forcing him backwards. He stumbled and his lips curled in a snarl of rage.

Still, I couldn't move, frozen by those blinding words and the drug that roared in my veins.

OBEY.

DAUGHTER.

Daughter. That was me. I belonged to him, to the one who gripped the back of my neck, forcing me to turn my gaze to his. I opened my mouth as he leaned down and his cold, cruel lips smashed mine against my teeth until my face throbbed with the pain.

"You sonofabitch! YOU SICK SONOFAGODDAMNBITCH!" Vivienne screamed.

Coulter pulled back, still holding my head in place. But in the corner of my eye, I saw her, hissing and fighting like a...*wildcat.*

"I'M GOING TO KILL YOU!" She howled, punching and thrashing, driving herself forward in a desperate attempt to get to me.

Because that's what love looked like.

That's what love was.

Desperate, and violent and feral.

Just like...Riven...Kane...Thomas...*and* Hunter. The men trapped in that tunnel. The men who'd died trying to save me.

"*FIGHT!*" My sister screeched. "*HELENE, FIGHT HIM!*"

"*For Christ's sake! Get her out of here!*" Coulter roared.

I didn't even flinch at his booming voice, didn't really hear him at all. I was numb, trying to block out the feel of Coulter's fingers as they dragged back upwards, cupping my breast, kneading the soft flesh to cruelly pinch my nipple.

"Mine," Coulter murmured as he lowered his head again.

"*No...NO!*" Vivienne screamed as his men dragged her toward the door. "*Why don't you fight him! HELENE! WHY DON'T YOU FIGHT!*"

"Don't listen to her." Coulter murmured as the warmth of his mouth closed around my nipple. "Gerard, move the papers on the desk."

Two of them moved instantly.

Get her to the table.

I trembled at those words. My core clenched tight as the guards dragged and fought my sister, shoving her forward with brutal blows. Papers fluttered from the desk to the floor and a stack of hardback books followed with a *thud* as Vivienne's head snapped backwards from the brutal assault and her knees gave way.

Everything happened in slow motion. The guard towered over her, shoving her even harder to the floor. My pulse sped as my widened eyes fixed on the sight as she was slammed against the floor and those words...those neon *fucking* words. *Mine. Owned. Obey...obey...obey.*

"That's the way."

I was moving before I realized it, pulled forward to the desk near the books, then I was lifted and placed at the edge.

"Lie down," Coulter commanded. "Lie all the way down." He licked his lips as I slowly lay back. "Four million dollars." He muttered. "I'm going to get my money's worth."

Heavy, gasping sobs drew my focus as, from the corner of my eye, Coulter fumbled with the zipper of his pants. I turned my head to watch as Vivienne pushed herself upwards on shaking arms. Her eyes glistened with tears, her face was ashen, but it was the blood on her shirt that riveted my eyes. The vibrant blotch was more sickening than a gunshot to the chest.

My babies! Her screams still resounded in my mind as Coulter moved, slowly taking a step toward me, his hand reaching all the way inside his trousers to pull his hard cock free.

"Open your mouth, Helene." His words were warped and slow as my mind shattered, breaking into a million tiny pieces.

I stood outside myself at that moment, watching as that version of me did exactly as he ordered. Coulter took another step and rounded the desk to stand beside me, blocking my view of my sister, until the glistening pink tip of his cock was all I saw.

"Open, Helene." He gripped my chin, forcing my mouth open. *"Open wide and take what I give you."*

Revulsion hit me, making my stomach clench until I knew I was going to be sick. But I was outside that body, looking down at myself. That version of me didn't suffer. That version of me didn't care.

"Helene!" Vivienne screamed my name. *"HELENE!"*

I jerked my gaze to her as Coulter drove his hips forward, guiding himself into my mouth.

No.

I jerked my focus to Vivienne as she shook her head, staring in horror. Her mouth moved, screaming...

But I couldn't hear her.

I couldn't hear anything.

My throat clenched as Coulter bucked his hips, driving all the way into my mouth. That revulsion slammed into panic, surging all the way through my body like a drug.

In a blinding moment, everything slammed together.

Vivienne.

Coulter.

And me...

I wasn't outside my body anymore. I was on that desk...on that *fucking desk with his cock shoved down my throat.*

Panic roared. My chest was on fire, caving in with the need to breathe.

"That's it!" Coulter moaned as he drove his cock harder into my mouth, cutting off my air. *"Suck it, you filthy fucking whore!"*

No!

No!

NO! I howled in my mind as I gnashed my teeth together and bit hard. The sharp incisors snapped down and carved all the way into that thick, throbbing flesh until with a *pop* of that vein, the metallic taste of blood filled my mouth.

Coulter jerked instantly, then looked down.

But he didn't see the drug-fuelled Daughter...

No.

He saw me.

I clenched even harder, shaking my head, gnawing what was left of his mangled flesh, until I gave a savage jerk of my head and tore his member free.

Screams came. Bloody, sickening screams, as I shoved against the desk and drove myself upwards. I didn't care that I was naked. Didn't care about the blood running down the back of my throat and out of my mouth as I turned my head and spat, dislodging that *thing* from between my teeth.

"YOU FUCKING BIT ME!" Coulter howled as he cupped the bleeding, spurting, wound between his legs and staggered backwards. "YOU BITCH. YOU FUCKING BITCH! I'LL KILL YOU! I'LL—"

I unleashed a scream and lunged, driving myself through the air until I *slammed* into him. His knees buckled, crumpling underneath him until we hit the floor. I attacked with an inhuman ferocity, driving my fist into those wide, unblinking eyes.

"You!" Thud. *"Fucking!"* Thud. *"MONSTER!"* I shrieked, and drove my fist into his face as hard as I could.

Crunch!

Blood shot out of his nose, but then my hair was fisted and yanked me back hard. Fire seared my scalp as I was dragged free and thrown to the side.

"Get him out NOW!" The guard above me roared.

But I wasn't done. I wasn't anywhere near done.

I twisted and drove my clenched fist up into his balls. With an agonized *oof,* he doubled over, releasing my hair. I scurried like a savage on all fours, grabbed one of the books discarded from the desk, and spun.

Vivienne screamed as one of the guards dragged her to her feet, lifting her until her spine bowed and her eyes widened.

"The fuck you do!" I roared and scrambled forward, launching myself toward him like a madwoman.

The heavy book in my hand became a weapon. One I drove through the air and into the guard's side.

He buckled sideways, screaming as he fell. But I didn't stop. I *couldn't* stop. I was neither the powerful woman nor the broken one anymore.

I was an animal.

A monster.

The *Daughter* they'd tried to ruin, only for her to become something else.

Something unhinged.

And dangerous.

I gripped the book with both hands and slammed it into him again until it slipped from my grasp as he buckled to the floor.

"Shoot her!" He screamed. *"Shoot the fucking BITCH!"*

Vivienne shoved forward, grabbed the book from the floor, and lifted it high over her head. With a chilling, terrifying scream, she brought it down with all her weight. It slammed into his throat, crushing his windpipe with a sickening *thunk!*

His eyes flew wide. His breath was caught in his lungs. Panic filled his stare as he clawed his throat.

"Choke on that, motherfucker." Vivienne snarled as she eased backwards.

"Call the *Sons!*" Coulter screamed as the three remaining guards grabbed him and lifted, dragging him toward the doors. *"CALL THE GODDAMN SONS!"*

On some level that broken part of me knew once they did, this would be all over. We'd never survive. No one could.

"Kill...*them.*" Vivienne moaned as she grabbed her stomach and looked down.

That bloody blotch on her white t-shirt grew larger. I stared at the mess, refusing to recognize it as a sign for whatever terror was coming.

They couldn't leave.

I *wouldn't let them.*

I took a step, my legs wanting to shake and my mind hazy.

"No." I took another step forward, moving between them and their salvation.

Out there was our deaths.

I knew that.

And I couldn't allow that to happen.

"You're not going anywhere." I faced them and clenched my fists. "Not alive, at least."

THIRTY-SEVEN

Riven
_____

FIND THEM.

Car alarms unleashed deafening squeals. Glaring orange lights flashed, lighting the way as we flew through the city streets, headed only God knew where.

The words still lingered, entwined in the desperation that howled like a fucking animal inside me. My hand was clenched around the edge of the window of London's car as he hunched behind the wheel and drove like a madman.

*It's the babies...*I winced and focused on the blur of movement outside as the Son's tormented stare filled my mind. *It's the babies.*

Thud.

The crunching blow came from the side of an expensive Mercedes parked outside an apartment block and another blaring sound was added to the mix.

"Jesus." I muttered, staring at the blur of a shadow.

I could barely see the Son as he ran along the city street faster than anything I'd ever seen in my entire life. I looked at the speedometer and the inching numbers as they crept higher. An ache moved through my chest. He couldn't keep this pace up, not for long. A few minutes at least. Ten at the tops. Still, I glanced at that shadow as it pushed harder, the Son leaning forward as he hurtled toward his goal.

Wind from the open window whipped my hair into a snarl. Fragments of dust and dirt blew into my eyes, blurring them instantly. *Goddamnit!* I swiped my hand across my face, blinking away the grime until I saw him once more...running now on all fours.

What the hell?

Had he tripped?

Had the Son fallen?

I jerked my gaze to London, searching for any sign of worry. If anything, he seemed to be pushing the Explorer harder.

"Maybe we should—" I started.

"No." Came the command from the backseat.

Carven sat behind me. Kane, Thomas, and Hunter were in the Explorer, behind us, whose headlights were blinding in our rear-view mirror. I hoped to God they were seeing this, because if I told them what was happening, they'd think I was insane.

But I wasn't insane.

I was...*amazed.*

We left the towering apartment buildings behind for the darkness of the trees and the night. The Son ran even faster, hunkered down on all fours.

"I hope to Christ he knows what he's doing." I forced through clenched teeth.

London said nothing. Instead, he turned his attention to the city street as it turned into the highway and headed for the restricted government zone. Still, Colt ran, hunkered down, pushing off with his massive thighs to run like a goddamn animal.

"Am I...am I seeing this right?" I murmured, glancing back at London.

"You are."

Only when I turned back, I could see the sheen of sweat that glistened in the moonlight. He veered left, lunged for the towering chainlink fence that surrounded the army compound, and slammed into the barrier, then speared his fingers through and climbed to the rows of razor wire around the top.

"No." I shook my head. *"He's going to get himself killed if he goes in there!"*

London was just as worried, looking over his shoulder as we left the Son behind.

"What the fuck?" I muttered.

But he said nothing, just yanked the wheel, veered the car toward the center of the road, then wrenched it and hurtled us toward the guard hut at the edge of the compound.

"Carven," London said coldly.

The killer was already moving, shoving open the door before the car had even stopped. I'd never seen anything like it. He was a goddamn specter. The stark white hair was the only thing I tracked as he rounded the rear of the vehicle and made for the guard.

"What?" The surprised mutter came from the soldier as he stepped out of the darkened hut and saw the Son headed for him.

He never stood a chance.

Not even to go for his gun.

Or even cry out.

One minute he was whole. The next, a dagger was embedded in the middle of his chest before it was wrenched free and dragged neatly across his throat.

He crumpled where he stood, hitting the ground before Carven stepped over him, picked up his shoulders, and dragged him back inside. The gates started rolling open before we knew it. London never waited, just slammed his foot against the accelerator and hurtled the four-wheel drive into the compound.

I braced my hand against the dashboard. "I hope to hell you know what you're doing."

"Me too, my friend." London murmured as the vehicle bounced on the uneven road. "Me too."

There was no time for pride. No time to feel anything other than that cold, honed rage. I gripped my Sig, my finger arching for the trigger. *Get to her...get to her...GET TO HER!*

The glint of lights shone in the distance.

"What the fuck is that?" I muttered.

The only answer from London was to push the Explorer harder until we were flying forward. The closer we came, the more desperate I became. Lights bounced off the nose of a sleek jet parked halfway out of a hangar.

"Not an army training camp, how's that?" London seethed.

I caught a glimpse of movement racing toward us, coming out of nowhere. It was Colt...but he was struggling. His steps were slower. Our headlights bounced off the blood on his hands. My mind went to the thick rows of razor wire along the top of the fence and I winced.

But he never stopped, just kept pushing himself toward that hangar. There was movement, a frenzied scurrying as armed guards ran...the only problem was, *it wasn't toward us.*

"What the fuck?" London yanked the wheel of the Explorer, making the lights splash over the back of the small army running hell for leather.

It wasn't until we passed the jet and the hangar that we saw what they were running toward. A massive house sprawled along a rise in the distance. The lights were on, the front door thrown open. That's where everyone was headed.

That's where she was...

My gut clenched.

A sickening wave of panic filled me as the headlights from Hunter's car behind us filled the interior. One of the guards in front of us suddenly stopped running and turned, our headlights blinding him for a second before Colt lunged, slamming into him.

"Stop the car." I demanded and stabbed my seatbelt release. "I said, *stop the goddamn car.*"

London braked hard, throwing me forward. I yanked the door handle and shoved. I was airborne before I knew it, desperate for the blows of my boots on the asphalt and the kick of the gun in my hand.

There were guards everywhere. Some turned toward us as Colt attacked with sickening rage, grabbing the guard by the throat and lifting his body into the air.

His barrel chest rose and fell hard with his heavy breaths. Still, that didn't stop him. He slammed the guard to the ground and drove his fist into the guy's face with the kind of force you'd expect from a vehicle collision.

Crack!

Blood spewed everywhere from the guard's nose and his mouth, it even trickled from the corners of his eyes. I looked away, not needing to see the rest. There was no surviving tonight. Not for them...or for us. Not if they'd hurt the women we loved.

I'd *welcome* death.

If it meant I'd never live a *fucking second without her.*

Car doors slammed behind me as I lifted my gun and took aim, squeezing off a shot as one of the mercenaries narrowed in on Carven.

Crack!

Carven looked over, seeing the guard dropping before he glanced over his shoulder. Those dark blue eyes found me a second before they turned back. He drove forward, pushing himself to sprint toward the house at full speed. Colt was a second behind, leaving the bloody mess he'd made to charge toward his brother.

I couldn't help but follow.

Crack!

The gun kicked in my hand as I squeezed off shot after shot. Only I didn't want to be out here. I glanced at the open front door as Carven plunged through. I wanted to be there.

Find her.

Find. Her.

FIND HER!

I unleashed a roar and pushed forward, ducking as gunshots were aimed at us.

Boom!

Colt never bothered to slow, he just charged, slammed into the half-open door of the house, and was gone.

"Fuck!" I bellowed and ran, racing up the sweeping stairs to the mansion.

Dirt shoe prints were everywhere. The immaculate gardens were now trampled, I saw as I lunged up the last stair and burst through the door.

Screams came from inside the house. A man's scream...and a woman's...*no. No...not a woman...women.*

"*I'll fucking KILL YOU!*" Came a shrill cry.

My pulse boomed. I knew that voice. I knew *that voice.*

"Vivienne?"

I charged forward, slamming into two soldiers as they came from another room in the house.

Crack!

Crack!

CRACK!

The barrage of gunfire came a second later from somewhere deeper inside. A bullet whizzed past, embedding into the wall not far from my head. I ducked and raced toward the sounds as Colt unleashed a savage howl of fury.

I charged forward and slammed into another soldier who'd turned toward me as he stood in the middle of the hallway, his gun in his hand.

"What the fuck—"

He didn't have time to finish before I fired. The shot hit him in the center of his forehead. Blood splatter arced through the air behind him as he dropped to the floor. Screams and sounds of chaos came from behind those double doors. A *thud* came as someone slammed into them as I lunged and pushed one door aside...and froze.

Bodies. Blood and butchery.

That's all there was.

Colt lunged and took out two other men who held a woman down as his brother went to work with his daggers, taking out two men at a time. But my focus wasn't on them, it was on the woman on the ground. One who was *very...very* pregnant.

Colt slammed his fist into the side of one attacker's head, knocking him out cold before he turned on the other.

"No." The guard's eyes widened. He shook his head frantically and tried to back away. "No, I didn't mean…"

But there was no escape. I glanced at Vivienne, who was bloodied and beaten, her shirt ripped and her eyes wild as she shoved to stand. Only she wobbled, her hand going to her belly, cradling it as Colt wrenched his gaze her way, scanned her from top to bottom, then turned back.

The guttural sound that came from that male chilled me to the bone. But I wasn't here for them…I pushed in, searching the rest of the room, and stopped.

A woman howled and raged at the far end of the library. One who was naked, straddling a man as she beat him with…*a book?*

Trouble.

I lunged forward as three men tried to drag her off him.

"The fuck you do." I lifted the gun and took aim, squeezing the trigger.

Crack!

I hit one guy, causing the two others to spin around and face me. But it wasn't just them. Two more stood at the edge of the room in front of an open single door near the shelves. They were dressed in black, no weapons that I could see. But that meant nothing. They stood there watching Helene as she lifted the mangled, bloody mess of a book over her head and brought it down once more.

Thud!

I swung my gun toward them, watching as one looked in my direction, piercing me with that detached, vacant stare.

They were Sons.

Sons.

But they weren't here to kill us. Not yet.

The honed killer turned his attention back to Helene, watching her with a look of...*pride.*

He was proud of her. Proud as she unleashed all her fury on that, that *thing*.

"Don't. *You. Fucking. Touch. My sister. Again!*" Helene slammed the book edge side down over and over in a sickening frenzied attack. One that made my stomach drop and my insides run cold.

She slowly rose on shaking legs, naked and heaving. Blood ran down her face and over her lips until she lifted her gore-splattered hand and swiped her mouth.

Then I looked down and saw the mess of the man she'd attacked. There wasn't much left of his face...but what little remained intact told me all I needed to know.

It was Coulter.

A smirk tugged the corner of my mouth. Helene didn't need saving. She never did. No, Hell hath no fury like a woman defending those she loves. And Trouble was that woman. She hadn't needed saving, she'd saved her own goddamn self.

A shiver of fear moved through me as I watched her. She was annihilating and terrifying all at once.

I'd never seen anything so goddamn beautiful in my entire life.

My pulse boomed, the sound deafening in my ears. I'd fallen for the woman...and I'd fallen hard.

One of the soldiers near her lunged and drove his fist into the side of her head with a *thud*. She staggered sideways as I dropped my shoulder and, with a roar, rushed that motherfucker, slamming into him. The stench of blood. The blistering burn of my own howling rage was too much and it spewed out of me as I drove the muzzle of my gun under the bastard's ribs and pulled the trigger.

Pop.

The muffled sound was instant. His eyes flew wide before he looked at me. There was a flicker of confusion, then a softness of surrender. One he never came back from.

Thud.

He crumpled to the floor as I turned, lifting my gun. My breaths were heaving as she turned her head to meet my gaze. That merciless rage in her eyes shone, then dulled as they widened. "Riven?"

"It's me, Trouble." I took a step toward her. "It's me."

Her knees trembled as she lurched forward, dropping the bloody book from her hand. It hit the floor with a *thud*. Then she was in my arms, wrapping her own around me.

She might be fury.

But even fury needed someone to watch her back. The heavy thud of footsteps came all around me. Movement came at my back, drawing my focus. Hunter was there, filling the doorway. Kane and Thomas were at his back as London pushed in, driving into the room behind us.

Only they weren't the only ones. Soldiers poured through the single door where the two Sons stood watching, only they didn't stop, pushing into the room all around me.

Screams of rage followed.

Crack!

Crack!

CRACK!

Gunfire was unleashed and bullets whipped past, narrowly missing. I spun, pushing her behind me. "Hold on, Trouble. Whatever happens...hold onto me."

THIRTY-EIGHT

Helene

HOLD ON, TROUBLE.

Hold onto me.

I reached out with cramped, aching fingers, brushing his back as he strode forward, then lunged at the stream of soldiers coming for us. *Protect. Protect. Protect.* That need howled inside me as I hurled myself toward one of them as he swung his fist at Riven's head.

"No!" My scream was inhuman, searing the back of my throat.

I slammed into Coulter's soldier, driving him away from the man I loved. Riven jerked a savage glare my way. His lips curled as he lifted his gun, took aim at the soldier and fired, shooting him in the chest.

Crack!

The asshole stumbled backwards, then looked down to the spreading bloody mess over his chest before he fell. But Riven didn't have time to aim once more before he was slammed by two of them, then lifted into the air.

No. The scream sounded in my head.

NO!

Crack!

The shot came from behind us. I looked over my shoulder to find Hunter, swinging his massive fist. The blur of movement was terrifying as bloody chaos filled the library all around me. Still there were more of Coulter's men as they pushed through the door.

Grunts and gunfire came from behind us. Sickening *crunch* of shattering bones were followed by guttural screams. The kind that stayed with you for a lifetime.

There were too many of them. Too many to *survive.* The shine of a gun came, drawing my gaze upwards as one of Coulter's men took aim. That savage gleam in his eyes fixed on me.

Get her to the table.

Those words resounded. Flickers of memories assaulted me and in the terror came his face. It was him...one of them from The Order. He smiled as he took aim, passing one of the Sons I'd met outside earlier that night when they'd dragged me in here. Only, as Coulter's soldier passed, the Son lifted his foot... and tripped him.

Crack.

The shot hit the floor.

Crack!

Another came, only this time it was from us. Kane strode forward, a gun in his hand. "I remember you." The doctor said, *crack!* He fired his gun once more. "But she won't...not anymore."

Kane slowly turned around, those clear green eyes dark with rage before another of the soldiers rushed him. The attack was sickening. I unleashed a scream, watching as Hunter charged them, tearing the bastard back who'd driven his fist into Kane's face, and unleashed one of his own.

I didn't wait for them to attack again. This time I dropped to my knees, searched the dead soldier for his gun, and found it trapped under his thigh.

Bang!

The weapon went off as I yanked it from his limp grasp, the bullet embedded in his leg before I had it in my hand.

"Get the fuck off him!" I yelled as I lifted the gun and fired.

Crack!

I hit one and watched him fall before Carven and Colt rushed each side of me and leaped, slamming into two more soldiers.

They were the most chilling killing machines I'd ever seen. Knifes, fists. Colt was an animal, driving his fists into one soldier's face before he charged another. But Carven...Carven was cold precision. He carved a dagger sideways, slicing the throat of one of them before he spun around, grabbed the head of another, and twisted so fast all I heard was a *snap.*

I stumbled backwards as Hunter, Kane, and Thomas joined in taking out soldier after soldier. But the soldiers weren't the only danger. I lifted my gaze to where Coulter's Sons stood watching the attack, only they weren't there...

What the hell?

I spun around, searching the room. But they weren't there. My pulse raced as I turned back, finding Carven rising from the floor and another body. Vivienne cried out. I stumbled backwards and turned, racing for her.

"Helene," she cried out, doubled over.

"The Doc is on his way." London looked fucking terrified. "We have to get you out of here."

I wrapped my arms around her, holding on. "Are you okay?" I pulled away as tears filled my eyes.

"She has to leave." London raked bloodied fingers through his hair and looked for the Sons.

I nodded, pushing her toward him. "Go...we'll be okay. Just go."

"Trouble."

I spun at the sound of my name to find Riven limping as he headed for me. Behind him the room was still...and filled with the dead. A sob ripped free from me as I stumbled forward. But Riven was tearing his bloodied shirt free, yanking it down his arms as he came to me.

"Here," he croaked, wrapping the shirt around me.

"Give me the gun, precious," Hunter murmured, holding out his hand.

But I looked down at my hand cramped around the weapon. "I...I don't think I can."

He slowly stepped forward, capturing my hand in his. "Let me help." He was so gentle, unfurling my fingers to take the gun.

"We're getting you out of here." Riven moved to my other side, tugged the shirt closed, and buttoned what he could.

Vivienne unleashed a low moan.

"Right." London bent and picked her up as he turned. "We're taking you out of here now."

He didn't even call for the Sons, but they were there, moving soundlessly around us until suddenly Carven stopped, then turned and fixed that icy stare on me. "The Sons...the other ones who were here. Where are they?"

I shook my head, looked over my shoulder to the last place I'd seen them, and opened my mouth to speak. Only when I did, the memory of that cold-blooded male lifting his foot to trip the bastard who'd hurt me reared in my mind. He'd known. Don't ask me how I knew that, but in the cold recesses of my mind there was no doubt whatsoever. The Son knew he'd hurt me and he'd made sure he didn't hurt me again.

"I don't know." I said and met Carven's stare.

There was a scowl before Vivienne moaned. "Carven, leave it... *please.*"

He looked at her, then slowly nodded. I doubt there was anyone else alive who could command that killer like my sister. Not even London or his twin had that much sway. But Vivienne did. He turned around as London made for the gaping double door and disappeared.

"We need to go, as well," Riven said.

I flinched as he lifted his hand. He stilled and pain flickered in those dark eyes before he moved more slowly this time, to brush my cheek.

"Let's get you to the Doc, then we'll make a plan, okay? After you see your sisters."

My sisters? Ryth's face filled my mind and a sickening wave of dread followed. "Ryth. Oh, *fuck.*"

I stumbled forward, clutching Riven's shirt closed around me, and hurried after them. But my knees trembled, causing me to buckle.

I was grabbed in an instant. "Easy, Trouble." Riven growled in my ear before he bent and lifted me into his arms.

"No...I—" I started, wriggling in his arms.

He jerked his gaze to mine, those dark eyes full of sorrow. "You fought hard enough. Let us take care of you now."

I searched for that aching need in his eyes before I glanced at the others. It was the same need in all of them. The same sadness, as well. A shiver of vulnerability cut through me. I didn't want to be weak, not like I had been. Never again. *Never. Again.*

But as I looked at them, that desperate need for walls around me eased. I didn't need to be like that. Not with them, or my sisters. I could still be strong. I could still protect those I loved. I just needed to allow them to protect me, as well.

They'd risked their lives to protect me and here they were, asking me to risk something to be with them. How could I push them away now?

I gave a slow nod, allowing Riven to lift me higher, curling his arms to press me against his chest.

"No one else will hurt you now." His voice echoed in my ear. "Not while we're alive."

The others followed as we headed out of that godforsaken library, leaving the dead behind. Still, I couldn't fight the need to scan every dark corner as we walked out of that house and into the night.

Coulter's Sons were still out there somewhere. Were they watching me like they had before? I didn't know why they hadn't attacked when Coulter's men rushed the library. They'd watched me instead, with that same intensity I'd felt earlier that night.

There was something electric between us and not in a desire kind of way, but more like it was the kind of connection I had with my sisters. A familial connection. One I shouldn't have had with someone like *them*.

"When we're finished with the doctor, promise me something."

"Anything."

"I want us to find the Sons, all of them." I lifted my gaze and watched a flicker of confusion and worry rise before he gave a nod.

"Whatever you want, Trouble."

I waited for the questions to start, the ones that I knew raged inside his head. But he kept his lips pursed, not saying a damn thing and instead, carried me away from that place and toward a black four-wheel drive.

That was love. The feeling of overwhelming desire and the need to be with them. Love reminded me to compromise. I'd had to learn that lesson hard when I'd found my sisters. I wanted them in my life. Just like I wanted these men. A new need filled me as Riven rounded the open back door of the Explorer.

"Easy now," he urged, sliding me along the seat as Hunter climbed in through the other side and reached for me.

He towered over me, curling his big frame to pull me onto his lap. "You scared the hell out of me back there," he murmured, his gaze fixed on the house as Thomas climbed in behind me and Riven and Kane slid into the front seats.

I lifted my gaze to the hard line of his jaw, remembering the last time I'd seen him, being attacked in that room in the underground tunnel. "You scared me too."

He lowered his focus to mine as the front doors closed and the four-wheel drive pulled away from that place. Thomas reached for my hand. I took his, curling my body on Hunter's lap so I could face him as well.

My pulse raced and my body trembled, but still, this felt like home. Right there. With them. We didn't need to defend ourselves, we defended each other. My head dropped to Hunter's chest and I closed my eyes.

We were free.

But we weren't safe.

Not yet.

Not until the rest of The Order was destroyed.

My thoughts turned to Melody. The sister these men had given up their lives to find. But she wasn't the woman they'd thought they knew.

You belong to the New Order now. The words spilled from my lips.

"What did you say?" Riven snarled.

I opened my eyes, finding his panicked stare in the rearview mirror. "That's what she said...your sister. That's what she called it, *The New Order.*"

The Explorer surged forward, making me bounce as we crested the rise. Hunter gripped me tighter.

"The New Order, huh?" Hunter murmured.

Only it was the kind of soft, spoken words that sent a chill along my spine. The four-wheel drive braked hard then turned. Tires squealed as we shot out of that fake government compound and headed for the city.

Vivienne, London, and the Sons were long gone, leaving us hurtling toward the sunrise as it peeked around the towering buildings in the distance.

My babies!

Vivienne's screams resounded my head. *"Please, be okay."* I whispered. *"Please."*

THIRTY-NINE

Riven

I PUSHED THE CAR HARDER, FORCING MY FOOT ALL THE way to the floor. In my head I was still hunting, still desperate to find Hale and that treacherous bitch we once called a sister. I lifted my gaze to Helene, curled up on Hunter's lap in the back seat, and that savage need for violence returned.

Melody wasn't our sister. Not anymore.

I focused on the suburban streets and turned onto St. James' street to find two cars parked sideways at the end of the cul-de-sac. The doors were thrown open, the interior lights on.

"Is this a good idea?" Hunter asked.

I braked hard, pulling up alongside the dark gray Audi and killed the engine.

The answer came from Helene as she pushed across Hunter's lap and shoved the door wide. She was a blur, lunging across the blinding beams of the headlights. My ruined, bloody shirt flapped wildly behind her.

"That's your damn answer," I muttered and pushed open my door, charging after her. *"Trouble! Trouble, wait!"*

But she didn't, racing for the open front door a heartbeat behind St. James himself. I flung the door closed and lunged after her, listening to the car doors slam shut behind me. I was through the open front door a second later, grabbing Helene as we passed through the foyer. A bodyguard waited, stepping forward the moment St. James strode through the front door. One glance at the broken fucking look on the male's face, and I swallowed hard.

He opened his mouth to speak, until London lifted his hand, silencing him without saying a word as he headed after Carven and Colt, who carried Vivienne toward the hallway on the left.

The wounded sound that came from the bodyguard was fucking brutal. I winced as a man and a woman stepped out of a room at the end of the hallway.

"In here," the male called, ushering the Sons forward into the room.

"Helene," I lunged, grabbing her arm gently, stopping her. "Let them work."

She shook her head, but she didn't fight when London stepped into that room and closed the door behind him. Instead, she spun around with tears streaming down her beautiful, blood-splattered face. "Tell me they're going to survive." She searched my eyes. "Tell me, Riven."

I'd sworn I'd never lie to her. Even though my version of the truth had been fucking weak at best. It'd only been for her own good. But this...this wasn't going to be good for anyone. "I don't know." I answered carefully. "I wish to God I did."

Her lower lip trembled, moving me to slide my hands up to her shoulders and pull her against me as my brothers filled the entrance of the hallway behind us. "But what I do know is that we will get through this together."

She lifted her head. "Promise?"

When I stared into her eyes, how could I do anything else?

"I promise," I answered, watching a look of relief wash through her stare.

A promise that made me feel cautious. What the hell was going on in that beautiful head of hers? I brushed her hair from her eyes, searching for a hint of what it was, until she looked away.

"Do we trust that doctor?" Kane asked.

That alone piqued my interest. That was a first coming from him. I glanced at the closed door at the end of the hallway. "I have no idea. But if London allows him to touch the woman he loves, then I'm guessing that's our answer."

Helene's teeth chattered, causing me to press her harder against my bare chest.

The bodyguard moved, stepping close. "I'll get some coffee on the way."

"And a change of clothes," Kane added. "For Helene."

The guy just gave a nod and turned, walking, heading deeper in the house.

"Hunter." I called my brother. "Keep Helene warm, will you?"

I didn't wait for a response, knowing damn well the male would be only too happy to share his body heat with her. I went after the bodyguard, following him back to the hallway near the entrance, then to the kitchen. The moment I stepped through, he started.

"Whatever you have to say to me, just go ahead and say it."

I scowled as I watched him pull cups from a cupboard overhead and fill the coffee machine.

"Whatever happened between you and St. James stays between you." My tone was colder than I wanted. I winced, watching the male work. "We all fucked up tonight. But that changes nothing."

He spun around, holding the coffee filter in his hand. "If she loses the babies, it changes everything."

Tell me. Helene's own desperation still lingered. *Tell me they're going to survive.*

I strode forward and gently placed my hand on the stranger's shoulder. "Then we'll pray that doesn't happen."

He met my stare and I had to wonder who the fuck he looked at. Because I sure as hell wasn't anyone I recognized, not anymore. One slow nod and I pulled away, leaving the bodyguard to turn around and operate the coffee machine.

"Guild," He said finally. "That's my name."

"Riven," I answered.

"I know who you are. You and your brothers."

My breath caught as I waited for the other name to spill from his lips. *Principal.* But he never said that. Instead, he gathered cream and sugar on the counter in the middle of the room and poured coffee into the mugs, handing them to me one by one as though I knew how my kin took their brew.

They all had cream and no sugar, tonight anyway. I grabbed three, leaving Guild to carry the other three before we headed back to where the others waited.

"Here." I handed Helene a mug. "Press your palms around the outside, it'll warm you up."

She did, closing her eyes in relief as I handed Thomas and Kane the other two, taking the last one from Guild. We drank and waited, our focus fixed on that closed door at the end of the hall. Then in an instant, it opened.

London walked out slowly, his shoulders hunched, his hands fisted by his sides. I searched the male's tortured expression as he lifted his head. "She's asking for you."

I glanced at Helene. Her eyes widened. "Me?"

One nod and she turned her head, glancing at me.

"I want to come with her." I said instantly.

Worry filled her as she glanced back at London. He scowled, not liking it one bit, still he gave a small nod. "Whatever."

Helene handled her coffee to Hunter and rushed forward. I handed Guild my own cup and followed. It wasn't that I wanted to see her sister. It was the pure simple fact that we were about to be in a room with three unhinged males who were pacing the floor, desperate to see if their children survived.

London headed back to the room, Helene barely a step behind, slipping inside the door for me to close it.

The moment I did, a guttural purr rose in the air, causing the hairs on my arms to stand on end. It didn't take long before I realized what it was. A savage gleam shone in Colt's eyes as he lifted his head from where it lay on her belly.

"I can't work like this, DeLuca," The woman muttered, trying to press the ultrasound wand over Vivienne's belly only for the Son to snarl and bare his teeth. "He needs to leave."

"No," Vivienne croaked.

She lifted a trembling hand to his head. "He stays. They *all* stay."

"Then he needs to stop that sound," she snapped before her voice softened. "So I can try to find out if your babies are still alive."

Vivienne lifted her gaze to the female doctor. "What do you think he's doing?"

The woman just scowled, then looked back at him as the Son lowered his head, pressed his ear against her belly, and unleashed a keening, purring sound.

Her belly moved instantly.

The female doctor looked dumbfounded. "What...what just happened?"

The rumbling, throaty sound intensified until it resounded off the walls so loud I felt it in my teeth.

"Hurt," Colt snarled. *"They hurt her. They hurt my daughter."*

Vivienne closed her eyes and fresh tears slipped from the corners.

"They took...they took from her," Colt growled.

"The needle," Vivienne answered, opening her eyes to find him. "They injected something into me, but they took something else. They took blood."

"Motherfuckers." London turned and paced. "It wasn't blood. They wouldn't just take that."

"No," Vivienne hissed. *"No. No..."*

"They took her DNA," London finished. "They took our daughter's goddamn DNA."

Colt lifted his head and closed his eyes. An unmerciful keening sound ripped from his throat to pierce the air. Helene jumped and slapped her hands over her ears, as did the doctors, and I followed, muffling the brutal sound.

But Vivienne didn't, nor did Carven or London.

They stood there, staring at the bloody mess on Vivienne's white shirt. Their breaths deepened as though they were about to destroy the world. I had no doubt they would.

"Get to Ryth." Vivienne's dull words filled my ears.

She looked at Helene. Her sister lowered her hands and stumbled forward.

"Whatever you do, get to Ryth."

Helene glanced at the doctors. "I'm not going anywhere. Not now. I'll be right here. We don't even know where they are."

"Sisters of Mercy Private Hospital," DeLuca said and glanced at London.

There was a murderous gleam in the bastard's eye as he nodded, encouraging the doctor to continue.

"Floor five. You'll see them immediately. They'll be the ones surrounded by armed guards."

Helene glanced his way. "Who?"

"The Rossis." DeLuca answered, glancing at his companion. "Who else do you think sent us."

The Rossis? They were a dangerous family. Not one to who align themselves to another. Not unless they were blood...or the closest thing to it.

"We're going to need to induce," the female doctor said carefully.

"No." Vivienne shook her head. "It's too early. Two more weeks, that's what you said, right, DeLuca? Two weeks."

"Only *if* it was safe," He answered.

Vivienne looked to Colt, who lowered himself back down, rubbing his face against her belly. Her fingers slid through his hair, pressing his head against her. "Then we'll make it so it is safe." She looked to London. "Make it safe, London. Make it safe for us."

I'd never seen a man more murderous as I did in that moment. Not even the Devil himself would want to stand in that male's way. If Hale wasn't the Devil, then he was the closest goddamn thing to it.

"Get to Ryth, make sure she's okay." Vivienne turned back to Helene. "Promise me."

Helene gave a slow nod. "I promise."

There were clothes waiting for us when we left the room. There was a shirt for me and what looked like Vivienne's clothes for Helene. She took them from Guild and gave him a soft smile before she hurried for her sister's room to change.

I tugged the clean shirt on, watching until Helene appeared a few minutes later. She hadn't showered, but she'd taken the time to wash the blood splatter from her face.

"Ready?" I asked.

She gave a nod, then strode toward Guild before wrapping her arms around him. I fought that cold, deadly hunger inside me. The one which had driven me to hunt down a complete stranger and murder him in cold blood just because she gave me his name.

His fucking name.

I still saw that look of pure terror as I lifted my gun and took aim.

"Thank you," Helene said quietly. "Thank you for taking care of my sister."

The bodyguard didn't move. He just stood there, his arms trapped by his sides, unable to hug her back, even if he'd wanted to. The wounded look on his face told me he didn't.

She didn't expect one, just pulled away and strode toward the door.

He didn't look at me, not even when my brothers headed after her, leaving me to walk behind.

I stopped alongside him. "You want to blame someone? Blame Hale. Blame my sister. But do not blame yourself. This had nothing to do with you, and everything to do with them."

I'd taken a step, heading for the door, when he quietly said, "I'll kill them. I just want you to know that."

"Not if I kill them first." I answered, and headed out the door.

"ARE you sure you're ready for this?" Kane asked as we pulled up outside the private hospital and parked.

"I don't know," she answered. "Is anyone ever ready for any of what happened to us tonight?"

The answer was no.

No one was.

Nor would they believe us if we told them. I inhaled a heavy breath as the door cracked open and Hunter climbed out. We had no idea what the hell we were walking into. Still, I climbed out, closed the door behind me, and waited for us to gather ourselves before we strode for the automatic double doors.

Two bodyguards waited in the foyer, standing against the far wall, eyeing everyone who walked in. Hunter glanced their way, those dark eyes taking in every inch before one gave a nod, allowing us to head to the elevators.

"Can I help you?" The receptionist rose from behind the desk.

"Not really, no," Helene answered and kept walking.

She stopped at the elevators, then stepped inside as the doors opened. I pressed the button as soon as we were inside and waited for the doors to close. There was no touching, no careful smile, nothing but silence as we rose.

The moment the doors opened, we were faced by bodyguards. Two waited, holding us back as we stepped out, until a deep rumble came from further down the hallway. "Let them through."

Helene pushed past, striding toward the room where Lazarus Rossi and his wife stood outside the door, waiting.

"Rossi," I said, no more than a step behind.

Those piercing blue eyes missed nothing as he looked from me to my brothers. "Cruz."

The Banks boys were inside the room, Tobias pacing around the foot of the bed. The backs of the other two pressed against the glass in front of us. I couldn't quite see the small figure on the bed, but I knew it wasn't good.

"Can I...can I go in?" Helene asked, but it wasn't the Stidda Mafia Prince she looked at. It was his wife, Ka, a stunning redhead.

"I think they've been waiting," Kat answered and stepped forward. "She's asked about you."

Helene gave a nod and headed for the door.

"Only her," Lazarus murmured quietly.

I knew an order when I heard one. The last person I was prepared to take one from was the goddamn Mafia. But tonight wasn't a night for a damn pissing contest. One careful nod and I met Helene's gaze. "We're right here. Take as long as you need."

She tried to swallow, those damn muscles of her throat working hard to force the lump down. Christ, the sight of it hurt as I watched her walk to the door, then still for a second before she pushed through.

The hallway was filled with silence, each of us riveted on the sight of Tobias turning to watch Helene move around the bed to her sister.

"If you need protection," Lazarus turned his gaze to mine. "Consider it yours."

"We don't," I answered as Hunter's cell went *beep*. "But thanks."

My brother glanced at the message, then shook his head. "Now, if you get any information on where Hale and my sister are hiding, that I'd be interested in."

"Don't worry." He stared into that room. "If I do, then I'll let you know where you can collect the bodies."

"Oh, don't worry. There's nothing left to collect. She can be buried by the state under Jane Doe for all we care. We just want them dead."

Movement came from inside the room. Helene collapsed, her arms wrapped around her sister. My chest tightened at the sight. There wasn't a goddamn thing I wouldn't do to protect that woman from the vile filth of this...

"The New Order." I glanced at Lazarus Rossi. "What do you know about it?"

He scowled, then shook his head. "What is it?"

"Not sure," I answered as Helene straightened, then headed for the door. "I'll let you know when I find out."

I took a step as Helene pushed through the door, hope glimmering in her eyes.

"She's going in for surgery in the next hour, but she's okay. The bullet nicked a vein. They're going in to fix it up, but she'll be here for a few days."

"That's good." I opened my arms, wrapping them around her. "That's really good, baby. How about we get out of here, get a shower and some rest."

"I'm sure the guys will call if there's any change," Kat said and gave us a smile. "Have a good rest. You look like hell."

Helene smiled. "I feel like it."

I gave Lazarus a nod, turning as Helene headed for the elevators. The moment we all stepped inside, she sagged against the wall. "She's going to be okay." Her eyes closed. "Thank God, she's going to be okay."

"Now you get to focus on you." I answered.

She opened her eyes. "You made me a promise."

I scowled. "I remember."

"Good," She said, glancing at my brothers as the elevator came to a stop and the doors opened. "That's what I want. All of us... together."

I strode forward in front of her. "We're one step ahead of you, Trouble. I just hope you know what you're in for."

FORTY

Helene

I'D ASSUMED WE WERE HEADING TO RIVEN'S HOUSE. AFTER all, it was the closest and right now, I just wanted to sleep like the dead. But Hunter was behind the wheel, turning the four-wheel drive to the highway that took us out of the city, not back into the suburbs of it, and I realized we weren't heading to Riven's at all...

We were heading for the mountains.

I eased in against the back seat. Thomas's arm was around me and Kane's was draped across my thighs. For the first time in what felt like forever, I let myself relax. My spine curled, sinking against the seat as the vehicle climbed. Before I knew it, we were braking and pulling into the driveway, and stopping at the camouflaged gate until it slowly rolled open.

The crunch of the tires filled the soundless interior. Hunter braked, pulled up alongside his Hummer, and killed the engine. I'd never felt so utterly tired in my entire life, as though I'd lived a lifetime in one single night. Hunter climbed out, then Riven from the passenger's seat, leaving both Kane and Thomas beside me to follow.

I moved slowly, inching forward to slide across the seat. Kane held my hand as I climbed out. My head dropped low and my boots scraped the stones as I ambled to the front door. But the moment I was there, Hunter grabbed me and heaved me up and into his arms.

I said nothing, just wrapped my arms around his shoulders and laid my head against his chest. The heavy thud of his boots resounded on the stairs as we climbed. I knew where we were heading and I was glad.

He didn't just carry me into the bedroom but straight into the adjoining bathroom instead. Steps sounded all around us as he eased me to my feet. I was suddenly surrounded by all four of them, crowding me in the bathroom.

"I'm okay," I started.

"Hush now, Trouble," Riven answered. "Let us take care of you."

I met his stare as Thomas sank to his knees, gently lifting one foot to slide my sister's shoes free. This was more than the act of showering. The other shoe was tugged free. Thomas rose, sliding his hand around the back of my neck, then leaned in to kiss me gently. I closed my eyes, letting them do whatever they needed.

My mind returned to Colt, or Beast, as my sister had called him. He'd been frantic when I'd stepped into that room, crowding over her, smelling her, rubbing his face against her belly protectively. Not once did she push him away. Instead, she slid her fingers through his hair and stared into his eyes. He'd needed her and she understood that.

My sister's t-shirt was tugged upwards and over my head, leaving me bare. I shivered, goosebumps racing, as Kane moved to switch the shower on and undress, kicked off his shoes, then yanked his shirt off and hurried to push his trousers and boxers down.

They needed this. The touching, the comforting. Just like Beast had. Thomas worked the button on mys jeans, sliding them all the way down.

Kane led me into the spray, turning me until my back was against the stream. Thomas followed, grabbing the soap to lather in his hands.

"There's not a thing you need to think of now," Kane murmured, that deep throaty sound like satin against my skin. I closed my eyes instantly. "Not a thing you need to think or worry about. There is no yesterday, no tomorrow. There's only now. The feel of the water at the back of your head and Thomas's hands."

Firm fingers slid along my arm and over my shoulders, gently digging in to find every knot in my muscles. I moaned at the sensations, my head rolling to the side as those deft fingers worked the aches in my neck.

Don't you touch my sister!

My screams slammed into me.

"Follow Thomas's fingers," Kane urged. "That's what's real."

His thumbs pressed either side at the base of my neck, massaging the points under my skull.

"Oh, God," I groaned.

His hands slid down my neck to my breasts, those thumbs dancing around my pebbled nipples. Still they slid lower, over my stomach, to the sting at my side. It took me a moment for my brain to work, connecting exactly what he was doing.

My eyes flew open, my hand lashing out to catch his wrist. "Don't."

Panic raced, tearing me from this moment of perfection and hurtling me back to that moment where Coulter's sick words had invaded.

I'm going to put a baby in your belly, Helene. I'm going to fuck you so hard you'll always be full of what's mine.

A sob wrenched free. I stumbled backwards, aware of everyone in the bathroom watching.

"Easy now." Kane lifted his hands, his gaze fixed on the cut on my side, the one covered with two neat stitches.

"You c-can't." I shook my head as my back slid down the cold tiles. "I won't allow it. I *won't allow it!*"

Riven pushed past Hunter and stepped into the shower, still dressed and wearing boots as he knelt in front of me. "Talk to me. Tell me what he did."

I shook my head, my tears blurring his face.

"He cut you." Riven looked down. "Did he...did he implant something in you?"

His voice was filled with rage.

"No." The word burst free. "He took something from me. He took...he took..."

My power.

My future.

My body.

"He wanted...he wanted to breed with me, so he opened my tubes. He made it that I could...that I could." *Have babies. One's he could take. One's he could use.*

The flicker of rage was instant. His lip curled. "That motherfucking bastard." He held my stare. Even without me saying the words he knew. "I wish he was alive so I could kill him all over again."

But he wasn't alive...because I'd killed him.

"I don't want children." I searched his eyes.

"Good," He answered, and pushed upwards, holding out his hand. "Neither do I."

"Me either," Kane added.

"Nor me," Thomas chimed in.

I took Riven's hand and slowly rose from the floor of the shower, my focus fixed on Hunter.

"I can't have children either," He said with a shrug. "Vasectomy."

I stilled. "You did?"

"The Order will do that to you."

An ache filled my chest, moving upwards into the back of my throat. I nodded. "Exactly."

"So that's it," Riven answered as if it was a matter of fact. "We'll take care of it."

He glanced at Kane and Thomas and both nodded.

"I'll have the doctor booked the day after this is all over," He said.

"Doctor?" I murmured.

"For the vasectomies," He answered. "Unless...unless you're not ready for that kind of commitment?"

I lunged, wrapping my arms around him as a cry ripped free. He hugged me back, standing in the middle of the shower, then gripped my chin and eased my gaze upwards. "I told you before, Trouble. Let us take care of you."

For the first time in my life, I realized this is what that meant.

This and more.

One nod, then he bent and swept his arm under my knees as he carried me from the bathroom.

"You're wet," I said.

"Who gives a shit." Was his answer.

He laid me gently down on the bed. Hunter headed toward me with two thick towels in his hands. The shower turned off, then they were all there, drying my body, then my hair.

"Stay here with them," Riven murmured. "I'll be back soon."

He rose, but I pushed up on my elbows. "Where are you going?"

"Not far. Don't worry."

But I did worry, even when Hunter tugged his t-shirt over my head and slid a pair of his boxers up my legs, lifting me enough to tug them into place. Kane dried himself, pulled on another pair of boxers, and slid into the bed next to me, letting me curl up in his arms.

"I think my brothers are in love with you," he said, smoothing down my wet hair as he stared into my eyes. "I think I am too."

Love was always meant to be out of reach.

My sisters and my father had taught me that.

But this love, this was different.

"You saw me kill a man tonight." I said carefully. "You've seen what I can do."

"If you think that's going to scare any of us away, then you're mistaken. We've all done things to protect those we love. We'd do them again in an instant. Love makes a monster of us all."

Those words hit hard as he lowered his head and kissed me softly. "Now close your eyes and sleep. God knows you need it."

The bed dipped hard behind me. Hunter climbed in, the warmth of his body pressed against my spine. I was still hurt, vulnerable, and afraid. But I wasn't afraid of them. I finally had what I'd always wanted. I closed my eyes and let that heavy wave carry me down. The bed dipped again later, rousing me enough to crack open my eyes.

"I'm here, Trouble," Riven said, pressing against me.

I looked for Hunter, but he was gone. The brush of Riven's curled fingers grazed my arm, lulling me back to sleep once more.

I didn't dream, not of darkness or death or even my sisters. Instead, I floated, carried by a murky gray river that lapped my arms and brushed down the back of my hands to my fingers.

"Let me love you." Riven's words filled my ears.

That brush came again, soft and tender, grazing the side of my neck.

"You're mine, Trouble, except now I get to share you."

My leg moved, making me crack open my eyes. Kane leaned down, running his hand along my thigh. "And we like to share," he added.

I turned my head, finding that dark, intense stare. "Are you okay with this?"

Kane lifted his gaze, watching as I slowly nodded.

"Good," Riven answered. "Kane, let's see how well you worship her with your tongue."

"My goddamn pleasure." Kane slipped his fingers into the waistband of the boxers, carefully pulling them over the wound in my side before easing them down my thighs and casting them aside.

"What?" Thomas groaned, his voice thick with sleep as he rolled over. "What are you doing?"

"Helene," Kane answered, leaning in to brush his lips against my skin, kissing my thighs. "That's what I'm doing."

My body shivered as he slid his hand between my thighs and gently spread them.

"That's my girl," He murmured, leaning down to lick my crease. "Oh, the beautiful, dark things I want to do to you."

I moaned and reached down, my fingers slipping through his hair as he licked once more. My body had battled, had raged, had only known violence and pain for so very long.

"Oh, God," I whimpered as his tongue pushed in deeper, sliding all the way up to circle my clit.

"Keep saying his name, baby, and I'm going to have to up my game." Kane lifted his gaze to mine, his lips glistening. "My name...*say it*."

"K-Kane," I stuttered as he gently slid his finger inside and curled it, finding that spot inside me that made me arch my back and fist the sheets.

"That's better."

"Christ, you look beautiful like this," Riven murmured. "With your legs spread and your hands clenched around the sheets, with my brother's face against your cunt." He slid his hand around my throat and gripped tighter. "Look at me."

I did, turning my head to stare into his eyes.

"And in the middle of our torment, there was you," He murmured, searching my stare as Kane licked deeper, making me open my legs wider.

Thomas watched.

Riven searched.

Kane tasted, making me writhe and moan.

The sensation kept building and building inside me.

"Oh," I cried out, my gaze fixed on the man who knew me better than anyone else alive.

"That's it, Trouble," he urged. "Come all over my brother's tongue."

My ass clenched and my knees pressed against the bedding as I drove his face harder against me and his tongue deeper into my core.

"Who the fuck needs air," Riven murmured as I dropped my head backwards and shuddered, releasing in a rush, "When you have this."

FORTY-ONE

Helene

I CRIED OUT, MY FINGERS FLUTTERING AGAINST KANE'S head as he rose from between my thighs. My body trembled, but still it ached, wanting more as though my hunger wasn't sated.

"More," I moaned, turning my head to Riven. "I want you."

There was a hint of a smile, nothing more than a twitch of those beautiful, cruel lips. I craved him, this man, his hands, his stare, His *intensity*. He turned, reaching behind him to something on the dresser.

"What are you..." I started as he fumbled with a box and leaned back.

There was a condom in his mouth, the foil packet pinned between his lips. That was why he'd left. The realization hit me. That was why...

He pulled it from his mouth, then used his teeth to tear the corner. "Told you before, we'd take care of you, Trouble."

A sob rose, thick and heartfelt. My tears blurred his face, but still he reached up and captured mine in his hands. "You belong to us. In every way. What you need, what you desire. What you don't want. That is all we care about."

I'd never had someone so consumed with my happiness before. It felt so...surreal. He lifted his body, grabbed the condom from his mouth, and looked down.

Latex glistened, stretched over the thick head of his cock. I reached down and slid my grip along the smoothness until he was sheathed.

"You ready for me, baby?" He lifted his gaze.

Movement came from the doorway. Hunter stood there, leaning on the frame, watching as I nodded to Riven and eased backwards.

Desperation and panic tried to push in. I kept them at bay, watching between us as Riven rolled on top, rising up on his strong forearms to guide himself between my legs. Slick warmth pushed in. My pulse raced, fluttering and a tiny bit panicked.

"Eyes on me, Trouble," Riven commanded.

I did, meeting not the hunger or the infernal rage he always seemed to carry, but love...and devotion. He pushed in deeper, slowly thrusting until I was stretched by the feel of him. My hands went to his back, his muscles tight and trembling.

"More," I moaned, rocking against him. "I need more."

He lowered his head and his lips crashed against mine. That was what I wanted, his mouth, his body. I could get lost in these men. Lost in their love. My soul yearned for that.

I tightened my body, clenching my core for Riven to break the kiss. "Jesus, Trouble. Can't you see I'm trying to pace myself here?"

A smile twitched the corner of my lips. "Don't hold yourself back on my account." I shifted my ass, thrusting my hips against his.

He unleashed a moan and dropped his head beside me, driving his cock deeper and harder. That was where we'd met, the angst and desperation, the need to consume each other in the most primal way. I reached up, fisted his hair, and yanked hard enough to pull his head backward. Electricity tore through me.

"Fuck me like you love me," I groaned.

In a blur of movement, he gripped me and rolled, holding me on top.

"This good enough for you, Trouble?" He moaned, driving his hips upwards.

Deeper, smoother. I rocked my hips, grinding against him as that howling need inside me grew. That was love for him, holding back that darkness, that need to wrap his hands around my throat and ride me until I lost sight of myself.

I grasped his hand and lifted, guiding his grip to where I needed it. The moment he clenched, pressing those perfect fingers against the veins on the sides of my neck, I slammed my hips down, coming hard against him.

He curled his lips, that bestial urgency unhinged for a second as he grunted. His cock twitched and warmth spread within me, until he slowly softened.

I sucked in hard breaths, cupped his hand, and looked down at him. "I love you." I whispered. "All of you. I want this all the time, you, me, and your brothers."

Riven looked to Hunter, who still leaned against the doorway of his own bedroom, watching us. "Can we do that?" He wasn't asking me.

"I can't see why not," Hunter answered. "I'll have to be away from time to time working, it makes sense she is protected."

Riven's thumb brushed my racing pulse, "And well sated," he added.

"We can stay here." Hunter stepped into the room, stopping at the side of the bed, his focus on me. "If you want that?"

I glanced at Riven, who waited. "Yeah, I think I do."

Riven rolled me over to my back, cradling me as he pulled out. "I guess that's settled."

"What's settled?" Kane asked as he stepped into the room, towel drying- his hair.

"We're living here from now on...until we find a place where we can all be together," Riven murmured.

"Oh, suits me." Kane moved to the side of the bed behind Hunter. "If that's what you want?"

I nodded as my belly unleashed a low snarl. "It is."

"Good, then we're going to need more food." Riven pulled the condom free as he climbed from the bed. "Because I'm goddamn starving. I'll have my housekeeper go to the market and bring it out here."

Hunter just shook his head with a smirk. "It's started already. First with the food, next it'll be a housekeeper and a goddamn chef."

"Now *that* sounds wonderful." Riven disappeared into the bathroom. "And we're going to need a lot of those." He nodded to the open box of condoms on the dresser, then glanced at me spread out on the bed. "A *lot* more."

I gave a chuckle, watching him pull on Hunter's boxers that were far too big for him. This wasn't happiness, not yet. But it could be, right? Riven gave Hunter a shoulder bump as he headed out of the room.

Yeah.

It could be.

We passed the day in playful surrender. All of us, including Thomas, laughed as we ate. Riven made a list for his housekeeper, paying her a nice extra sum to deliver it all the way out to where we had hidden ourselves away. Ten bags of groceries later and four bags of clothes and necessities, the refrigerator was full of vegetables, fruit, vegan cheeses, and freshly baked bread that smelled heavenly.

"The living arrangements are one thing, but vegan?" Hunter muttered as he watched me smear another slice of sourdough bread with vegan butter and a drizzle of syrup before biting down.

"Eat all the meat you want." I gave a shrug. "Seriously, nothing bothers me anymore. Just don't expect me to eat it."

"It's fine." Thomas reached over, grabbed a slice of bread, and helped himself to my butter. "I've been thinking of making a change myself."

Really?

I stared at him, watching him take a bite and give a shrug. "It's not too bad. I could get with this."

I grinned at him. We ate, we laughed. Even Thomas unleashed a deep chortle when Hunter tasted my vegan butter and chomped down on a carrot, finally shaking his head and muttering, "No goddamn way."

But then in an instant, mid-laughter, everything changed, like a bubble had burst somewhere. One that seemed to have insulated us from everything we'd endured. In the quiet, a dark ominous feeling rose over us like a heavy thunderous cloud, ready to unleash a storm.

I heard the rumble.

I smelled the ozone.

But I couldn't seem to outrun it, or wait for it to pass. It haunted us. "We have to stop them." I stared at the kitchen counter. "Whatever it takes."

"I agree," Riven answered. "But until we get more information as to where they are, our hands are tied."

"So we gnaw them off."

We all looked at Kane.

"We gnaw them off and we survive." He added. "Any way we can."

"How do you suggest we do that?" I shook my head. "We know what they want, they want me and my sisters. Are you saying we give up on one or all of us?"

I hoped to God he wasn't, because there was no way in hell I was letting them anywhere near Hale or his *New Order*. We were back to square one. I closed my eyes, remembering the sound of Coulter's face breaking under the force of my blows. Maybe not all the way back to square one. But we were missing a key piece of information. One that'd lead us to the end of this hell once and for all.

"That doesn't necessarily mean your sisters," Kane began.

I jerked my gaze to his. "It could be another of your bloodline," he explained.

I knew who he meant.

My former father.

I shook my head.

"He has a lot to answer for," Riven snarled. "But I'll say this, there is *nothing* he could say that'd stop me putting a bullet in his head. Not now. Not ever."

I flinched at the ruthless tone.

But he was right.

In my head, I saw that look on his face when they'd pulled me into that auction. It was almost as though he'd *expected* it.

"He's not my father." The moment I said the words, I knew they were true.

"Just as Melody is not our sister," Hunter added. "Not anymore."

"The map," Thomas said suddenly.

We all looked at him.

"What map?" Riven asked.

"The one from the study." Thomas looked at Kane. "The one we threw out the window."

"You mean the one you risked our damn necks to grab?" He sounded pissed.

I realized there was so much more to last night than I knew. Maybe one day they'd tell me...but not anytime soon. Right now, I wanted this to be over, and to forget The Order or The New Order, or whatever they called themselves ever existed.

"The map is important. I know it is. There was a symbol on it. One I'm sure I've seen before."

I looked at Riven, watching as his scowl deepened. "Then we go and find it."

My breath caught in my chest. The last thing I wanted was to go back there. But it looked like we didn't have a choice. "It could lead us to Hale."

"It could," Riven answered.

A shiver of determination tore through me. "It could be the end of everything."

He turned, his eyes sparkling. "Yes."

"Then I'll get dressed and let's get this over with."

I left them behind and made my way up the stairs back to Hunter's room, finding the bags of clothes Riven had his housekeeper bring us. Jeans, a black t-shirt, boots, and a jacket later, I walked back down, to find them ready.

"We go together." Hunter grabbed the keys to his Hummer.

That pang in my chest grew bolder. "Always together."

We headed out and climbed into the four-wheel drive with Hunter behind the wheel. My thoughts returned to Ryth and Vivienne. I hadn't heard from Tobias or London. I was guessing that meant there was no news. At least not bad news.

The closer we came to the city and the shrouded streets where billionaires like Coulter lived, the tighter my grip became on the door handle.

We passed a police car, no doubt patrolling the neighbourhood.

"We hide in the forest. Thomas, you scout ahead and find out if we can get through."

"If I'm found, I'll say I'm part of his church. Sick motherfuckers like Coulter like to hide behind religion."

Hunter pulled the vehicle onto a dirt track that headed deeper into the forest that surrounded the estate. The moment we were in deep enough, he killed the engine, and we all climbed out.

Memories assaulted me. This was the last place I wanted to be.

"Trouble." Riven called quietly. "Next to me, baby."

This time, I never argued, just made for his side. Hunter and Thomas moved up front. Kane walked behind. My feet refused to cooperate, scuffing the dirt and the leaves as though my body physically repelled this place and all it stood for.

But I forced myself to keep going, to push through the last line of trees to what was left of the mansion. In the light of day, it looked so much worse. There were cracks in the earth, massive, gaping holes you could almost drive a car through.

My gaze went to the entrance of that tunnel where Coulter had forced me to stand and watch while he detonated the bombs which had almost killed the men I loved. My fists clenched and that shell-shocked, violent part of my nature rose to the surface. "Let's just find that thing and get out of here."

"Sounds fucking perfect to me," Riven snapped.

I knew he felt that murderous hunger too.

We made our way along the side of the destruction, stepping over hunks of walls and onto shattered glass until we rounded the corner. Thomas looked up, found the open windows high above us, and tracked forward.

"It has to be around here." He said. "It's a large map, there's no way you could miss it."

A sound came from inside. We stiffened, and stopped. Both Hunter and Riven lifted their guns, ready to take out anyone who tried to stop us.

"Hurry," Riven muttered. "Find the damn thing and let's get out of here."

We moved, bending low to move debris aside. It took us too long. Inch after inch, we scoured the ground until Kane heaved a hunk of wood aside and stopped. "Here," He called, "I have it."

Thomas rushed forward and the rest of us crowded in.

It was a map, like a lot of others I'd seen before, only this one was torn and sodden in one corner. Kane picked it up carefully as a heavy *thud* came from inside the house once more.

"We need to leave." Hunter watched for movement. *"Now."*

I stepped backwards with the others, then turned and hurried for the covering of the trees once more. We didn't stop until we got back to the Hummer. By the time we got to the vehicle, I was out of breath.

"Show us." Riven turned, reaching for the map.

Kane handed it over. They opened the back door of the four-wheel drive and spread the map out.

"Trouble," Riven called, moving aside. "Is there anything here you recognize?"

My pulse boomed at the sight of the thing. At first, I couldn't make anything of the hard lines and structure marks, until I lifted my gaze to the elegant scrawl and the name at the top.

King's New Order.

"No." I shook my head and stumbled backwards, swiveling to run.

I barely took a step before my knees buckled.

"Easy." Hands gripped me, holding me upright.

I lifted my gaze to Hunter's tortured stare. "No...*no.* It can't be."

No one said a thing.

All that time.

My entire GODDAMN LIFE! He had played with us.

He had played with me...

"We have to figure this out." Hunter urged. "We have to put a stop to this."

I tried to swallow the scream trapped in my throat and forced myself to nod instead. My steps were achingly slow as I made my way back to them. Riven couldn't even look at me. He just stood there, his hands fisted against his sides.

I forced myself to look at the map once more. My gaze skimmed over the name again. It was that puncturing agony in my chest all over again...until my gaze moved to the symbol drawn in the corner.

A swirling pyramid I'd seen before. "I know that symbol." I said, my memories flooding back to me. "I saw it on the guard's shirt...and I remember it from a new compound my father oversaw years ago. They had this exact same symbol printed on the gates of the compound.

"Do you think you could remember where this was?" Riven lifted those unflinching eyes to mine.

I gave a nod. "I think so...yeah."

As I stared at the symbol, I knew without a doubt that was where Hale had hidden from the rest of the world...

Him and the Sons of The Order.

"Then we make the calls so London, the Banks' and we go after the fucker." Riven answered. "We blow him and his compound off the face of this earth."

Hope rose inside me.

This time there was no bait.

This time we stayed together.

And ended this once and for all.

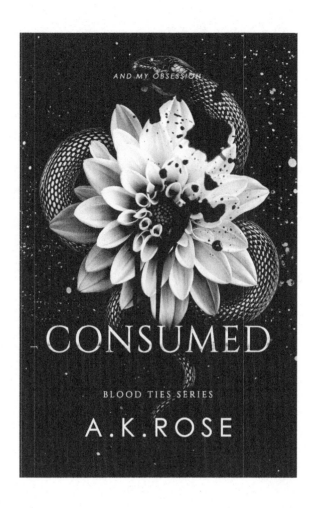

AND MY OBSESSION

CONSUMED

BLOOD TIES SERIES

A.K.ROSE

The final book in the Blood Ties Series coming March 30th

Made in the USA
Coppell, TX
05 December 2024

41730159R00233